A DYING WISH—A LIVING PROMISE

"So you figure it, Pettis. How do I ride out there with twenty or so Sioux blocking the trail? I don't imagine One Ear could manage it, and he's ten times the horseman I am. I'd probably die of this wound anyhow. All I really wanted to do was see my kid."

"You've got children?"

"Had children. Oldest one died at Shiloh. You learned that a while back, remember?"

"I do," Pettis said . . .

"I've got another boy, Corporal. Hector's his name, but he likes to be called Tory. He wore a uniform, too, once, but he carried it off better than I did. Won himself promotion and a Medal of Honor. He's twenty-five years old now, and I haven't seen him since he was a pup of a boy. He has his ma's eyes and disposition, and none of his pa's faults that I've noted other than a reluctance to write. I haven't given him much, but I would like him to have my watch. It might take him back to a time when I was a better man. You'd do me a service to get it to him. Tell him I didn't run this time. Tell him I stood my ground. You can do that, can't you?"

Berkley Books by G. Clifton Wisler

MASSACRE AT POWDER RIVER
UNDER THE BLACK HILLS

UNDER THE BLACK HILLS

G. Clifton Wisler

B

BERKLEY BOOKS, NEW YORK

UNDER THE BLACK HILLS

A Berkley Book / published by arrangement with the author

PRINTING HISTORY
Berkley edition / February 1999

The Penguin Putnam Inc. World Wide Web site address is
http://www.penguinputnam.com

ISBN: 0-425-16740-2

BERKLEY®
Berkley Books are published by The Berkley Publishing Group, a member of Penguin Putnam Inc., 375 Hudson Street, New York, New York 10014.
BERKLEY and the "B" logo
are trademarks belonging to Berkley Publishing Corporation.

PRINTED IN THE UNITED STATES OF AMERICA

10 9 8 7 6 5 4 3 2 1

I

THE DESERTER

ONE

It was like a holiday, a Sunday afternoon church social with music and dancing and fine parades. The band had come along, and the buglers were in fine form, blowing up a fanfare to bring on the general's favor. He was a fine one for music, Custer. He'd even had the band playing when the regiment rode down old Black Kettle and his people at the Washita River back in 1868.

This time there were no Cheyennes to fight.

Just as well, Lucius Bratton thought. Bobbing up and down on the back of a stumble-footed mare, he felt each and every day of his forty-eight years. He was too old for soldiering. Too old for the long hours, the pesky mosquitoes, the vicious horseflies. His eyes were cold with disdain for the little German privates who clicked their heels in obedience to command. As for that Italian bugler, well, best Martini keep to his own mess.

"Ain't a half of 'em fit to ride with the Seventh," Corporal Isaac Pettis had observed the week before. "And here we're takin' 'em into the Black Hills, where ol' Sittin' Bull hisself's sure eager to make mischief for us."

"Little chance of that," Bratton had argued. "Red

Cloud's eager for his summer annuity. He'll sit on the young bucks' tail feathers till he has his coffee and tobacco.''

"You just hope he does, old friend," Pettis had grumbled. "Was that Indian chewed up Fetterman in the Big Horn country."

But that was years before. Old Red Cloud did his fighting the white man's way now—with speeches and complaints to Washington. He might be a headache and a hindrance, but he'd make no war on the Seventh Cavalry.

In truth, that was why Bratton stuck to the Seventh. It was George Custer's personal escort. Except for a few holdovers from the late war like sour-lipped Major Marcus Reno, the officers were mostly young and prone to general-worship. Custer's glee club, Pettis dubbed them. Where another command would spend its evenings planning the next day's march, Custer's lieutenants would sing old camp songs or listen to the band.

"Wish the general'd pay a hair more attention to his horses and his soldiers," the post surgeon once remarked. "Won't either of 'em hold up on a long campaign."

But then the Seventh hadn't come to the Dakotas to fight. It was there to escort railroad surveyors and look pretty for the Eastern correspondents. And just now, in that summer of '74, ten of its companies, together with some foot soldiers and three Gatling guns, were laying out a road through the heart of the Black Hills.

"Ain't just road buildin' and mapmakin' we're about, though," Boyd Higgs had said that morning when they'd saddled up. "Got miners along. And an assay man. Custer's come to find Sioux gold, Bratton. And to hear the talk, it's here. Nuggets the size of your fist cloggin' up the streams. Man could get rich easy hereabouts."

"Then how come nobody's done it already?" young Joe Rodman asked.

" 'Cause this is sacred country to the Sioux, boy,'' Higgs explained. "And them that's tried lost their hair real quick. Only now here's General Custer and the Seventh ridin' along. I expect any Indians hereabouts got bigger game to stew than a poor ol' miner."

"Could be you're right," Bratton had admitted.

"They shoot deserters," Rodman had warned. "Or hang 'em."

"Got to catch us first," Higgs had added. "I'll bet a fourth o' this regiment has skedaddled since I signed the muster book, and ain't many been caught. Who'd go lookin' for us in these hills? We stay clear o' Sioux, we got nothin' to worry over."

Bratton had chewed on the notion some, but it was too risky for his taste. He didn't like soldiering, resented the youth wasted on his messmates, and ached from the rigors of the march. But he'd tried his hand at other pursuits, failing each and every time. The Seventh fed its men sparingly, but a private's pay bought whiskey and women at Fort Abraham Lincoln, and beans and bacon kept a gullet full.

He changed his mind that afternoon.

The morning had been rather ordinary. Custer and his court had ridden off to shoot eagles, and the regiment, free of its commander's harsh eye, straggled out through the piney hills. The surveyors continued their work, and woodcutters felled timber for the cook fires. Bratton and the rest of Company C were splashing across a shallow river, laughing at the antics of Charley Reynolds and a pair of Ree scouts.

That was when Bratton saw the gold. Maybe the nuggets weren't boulders, but they blazed up from the muddy riverbed—everything but danced in the crystal water before clouds of sediment swallowed them.

"Bratton, hold your pace!" Corporal Pettis barked.

"Can't, Corporal," Bratton answered. "I believe this poor nag's gone lame on me."

"Check her!" Pettis shouted.

Bratton pulled out of line and dismounted. To all the

world he appeared to be inspecting hooves and checking tendons. But the old man's fingers probed the mud and plucked small pebbles. His trousers and boots were speckled with glitter, and his pockets soon filled with golden nuggets.

"Bratton, you finished down there?" Pettis called from the hillside beyond.

Not by half, Bratton thought. But he kept his thoughts to himself. He remounted his horse and nudged it into a trot.

"Just picked herself up a stone, Corporal," Bratton explained. "Be good as new tomorrow. I'll watch her close the rest of today."

"Be makin' camp in another mile or so," Pettis explained. "You ride along as you can or walk her if you must. I'll keep a weather eye out for Sioux."

"You do that, Corporal," Bratton said, pretending fear. "I wouldn't want my hair endin' up a war trophy."

"You ain't got but a little hair left, old man," Pettis replied. "Never will understand the army takin' on grandpas and children."

"Ain't many normal people stupid enough to soldier," Bratton countered, laughing as his pockets jingled.

"You ain't got a jug, have you, old man?"

"If I did, I'd be considerable less bothered by this rock-beset road the general's put us on. That's the Lord's truth, too, Corporal."

"Maybe it is, Bratton, but you'd do well to keep your opinions in your pocket. General Custer don't take to swearin', and he's powerful touchy, what with havin' to leave his lady and all them correspondents back at the fort."

Bratton came close to smiling. The regiment wasn't due back before August, if the mess talk could be believed. A man clever enough to steal away and work that stream would be rich in a matter of weeks, long before any Eastern newspaper could herald news of a gold strike in the Black Hills.

Best to leave tomorrow night, Bratton thought. *Put some distance between the regiment and the river.* Besides, he was assigned picket duty then, along with Higgs and Rodman. The three of them would go together.

Bratton kept his plans to himself. While the rest of the regiment roasted eagles and stewed strips of venison, Lucius Bratton brushed gold flakes from his trousers and sewed nuggets into folds in his blankets. It might have seemed peculiar to some, the old man off in the cottonwoods, sewing. But Bratton had always been a loner, and the soldiers were accustomed to his brooding.

"He's been in the army a long time," Pettis told the others. "Makes a man melancholy, such long service."

Bratton ended his silence the next night when Isaac Pettis posted Higgs, Rodman, and himself as night guard for the company's horses.

"There's a strange feel to these hills," Higgs noted as he stirred the embers of a small fire.

"Indian spirits," Rodman observed. "I heard the Rees babblin' with Charley Reynolds. Sioux hold it a spirit place, and the Rees are spooked."

"Just stories meant to keep out visitors," Bratton declared.

"Why?" Higgs asked.

" 'Cause your stories about gold are true," Bratton said, taking three large nuggets from his pocket and holding them toward the light of the fire.

"Lord A'mighty, where'd you come by them?" Higgs cried.

"Not far from here," Bratton explained. "Filled both pockets in the blink of an eye. I judge a small fortune's to be scooped up there."

"Why you tellin' us?" Rodman asked. His large green eyes filled with suspicion, and he hugged his trapdoor Springfield to his chest.

" 'Cause one man'd be hard-pressed if Sioux happened by,'' Bratton answered. "There's enough gold for ten, too. And it ain't so easy for a single man to slip off in the night.'

"You mean to go tonight, then?" Higgs asked.

"Soon as things quiet down," Bratton explained. "Pettis is a restless sort, and he'll be by to check on us before takin' to his bed. We'll each take a spare horse along, and we'll hide our trail in the river yonder.''

"You've thought it out proper," Higgs said, nodding.

"All but me goin' along," Rodman argued. "I ain't keen on desertin'. My daddy fell chargin' the Rebs at Shiloh. I got to think o' family honor.''

"You can buy a new family once we've dug out that stream," Bratton argued. "I've got a boy myself, Joe. Not much shy o' your age, as it happens. He's back east scratchin' out his livin'. Sack o' gold nuggets'd buy him a first-rate chance. Now, what sort of family do you have, son? Anybody whose high thoughts can't be bought for a few thousand dollars?''

"Only got a brother left, and he's not yet shavin',''" Rodman said, scratching his ear. "They put him in an orphans' home. He'd be happy enough to be out o' there, and rich to boot.''

"Then that much is settled," Bratton announced. "We wait for Pettis. Then we leave.''

The others nodded, and Bratton returned the nuggets to his pocket. Shortly thereafter Pettis appeared. After walking the picket line and seeing all precautions had been taken, he drew Bratton aside.

"Rees smell Sioux," the corporal announced. "Keep your eyes open. And watch that Higgs. He's the sort to take his leave given half a chance.''

"Trust me to see it's done, Corporal," Bratton replied. "I know the routine.''

"See it's followed.''

Pettis returned to the camp then. Bratton remained on

watch until he was satisfied the corporal was abed. Then Bratton stole back to the camp, collected his gear, and returned to the picket line.

"You boys do the same, one at a time," Bratton instructed. "Keep out of sight, too. Anybody stops you, say you've come to fetch your blankets. There's a chill in the air."

In truth, there was. It wasn't just the night air, though. Fear was creeping into Lucius Bratton's being. And its icy touch was worse than any December blizzard.

Even so, Bratton felt the eyes of his companions on him. Higgs was spooked already. Under his breath he alternately babbled prayers and curses. Young Rodman was fast losing heart.

"You two go along without me," Rodman whispered as Bratton began freeing horses from their picket pins. "Just give me a wallop over the head. I won't tell 'em nothin'. Just say you clubbed me and lit out."

"It'll take three," Bratton argued as he turned a broadbacked gelding over to the young soldier. "Don't you have the appetite for gettin' rich, Joe? What about your brother?"

"I'm scared," Rodman confessed.

"Well, you got a right," Higgs said, taking a horse. " 'Tween Custer and the Sioux, we got our share o' peril."

"Custer's too busy with his road," Bratton declared. "The company's sure to be half a day roundin' up their horses. And if we do this up right, they won't know whether we were taken by Sioux or deserted till we've collected our gold and started south. The river'll hide our trail, after all."

"Charley Reynolds'll know," Higgs said, shaking his head. "Him and his Rees. They'll read the signs true. They'll pick out our tracks."

"Sure, but what'll that matter? The general won't believe us desertin'. Won't admit it anyhow. And he won't spare many men to look for us. Pettis, maybe, and a corporal's guard. Pettis couldn't track a grizzly bear through a snowbank.''

Bratton paused long enough to give young Rodman a slap to the shoulder.

''And in three days we'll have our gold and be on our way to Kansas,'' the old man added, holding up the three nuggets in the faint moonlight. ''Rich!''

The gold captivated Higgs and Rodman. Fear floated away, and they collected two horses apiece, saddled mounts, and tied on their equipment. Bratton had collected spades, spare cartridge boxes, and rations from a supply wagon. He saw to it everything was securely tied.

''Don't aim to leave Pettis no clues,'' he explained. ''Now, let's lead these horses to better grazin'.''

With a grin on his face, Bratton nudged the company's mounts along past the camp and beyond into a grassy valley. At first the three deserters kept their movements and voices quiet. Later, though, they shouted and waved wildly, driving the horses into frenzied flight.

''Somebody's sure to hear all this ruckus!'' Rodman objected.

''Our relief'll be risin' soon anyhow,'' Bratton explained. ''Can't even Charley Reynolds and his Rees chase very fast afoot.''

Rodman managed a grudging smile, and Higgs laughed at the notion.

''Shame we couldn't leave Custer to walk a bit, too,'' Higgs added.

''No, you wouldn't want to give him cause to chase you,'' Bratton insisted. ''He ain't much of a general in some ways, but you'd find him a bearcat if he took onto your trail. And he ain't one for forgivin'.''

No, sir, ain't any of those army fellows long on that suit, Bratton reminded himself. But money put a man past their power. A new name, a new future, a chance to redeem himself—yes, gold could buy it all. Maybe it would even make up for—

"Which way, Bratton?" Higgs called as the moon dipped into a cloud, leaving the hillside draped in darkness.

"Into yon river and on ten miles or so," Bratton explained as he nudged his horse into the stream. "I know the spot, Higgs. Trust me to get you two there. Just keep in mind without me you two go south with empty pockets. Wouldn't be smart to get no notions of breakin' up our partnership."

"Not me," Higgs cried. "Given the choice, I would've invited half the company along. I've got no urge to break ranks in Sioux country."

"Thirty'd be too few to help in a fight," Bratton said, laughing. "And they'd be sure to bring on attention. No, any Indian prowlin' these hills'll be off chasing cavalry mounts. And we'll have our fortune dug 'fore they know we're there."

"You sure, Bratton?" Rodman asked.

"Well, I don't figure it to matter either way," the old man answered. "If they come, we're dead. Ain't no goin' back, son. We made our charge, so to speak. Now best thing's to ride quiet and slow, find the spot, and set to diggin' Pray, too, if you ain't lost the habit."

Who knows? he thought. *Maybe God's got a favor held by for Lucius Bratton.*

"Call it retribution," he muttered. Just maybe a better fate lay ahead for him after all.

TWO

They splashed their way through the river for hours. In the murky darkness, Bratton felt a thousand eyes peering out at him. Every shadow threatened to send an arrow his way.

"We close?" Rodman called again and again.

"Closer all the time," Bratton answered each time. "Can't be much longer."

But it was. And every foot of the way sharp splinters of fear pierced Lucius Bratton's heart. His hands perspired so that he had difficulty holding his horse in rein. He was wet through. It hurt to breathe.

I'm too old for this foolishness, he told himself. But there was no going back now.

Dawn's first yellow streaks found them approaching the very crossing where Bratton had chanced upon those nuggets shining in the muddy stream bed. He halted his horse and motioned his companions toward the bank.

"This is the place," he announced. "Time to be rich."

"First I aim to get myself out o' this saddle," Higgs grumbled. "Time to dig gold after I get me some sleep."

"Don't suppose the Sioux'd begrudge us that, eh, Bratton?" Rodman asked.

"Not so long as we hide the horses good and don't go buildin' fires," Bratton answered.

And so they dismounted, led the horses into a stand of cottonwoods, and drove their picket pins into the rocky earth. The animals shuddered from weariness, and young Rodman began freeing them from their burdensome packs and saddles.

"Been a long night for them, too," the youngster observed.

"Well, don't go wastin' pity on them," Bratton muttered. "They got some time to rest up. We'll be slavin' away proper by midday."

Never were truer words spoken. It seemed to Lucius Bratton that he had barely touched his head to his blanket when the morning sun was rousing him. His belly rumbled, and he managed to drag himself to where he'd piled the tins of beans. Cooked with a slab of bacon, those caked beans were barely digestible. Only a hungry man could get them down his gullet cold.

Or a greedy one, Bratton thought as he opened the lid with his knife. A river full of gold was waiting, after all. And if things went well, there would be time to snag some trout by and by. That afternoon they might risk a cook fire.

He chewed the crusty beans with contempt and dreamed of how different things would be when he arrived in Chicago in tailored clothes, with a valise full of crisp new greenbacks. There would be a fine new house, servants, a carriage with matched ebony mares. He would summon young Hector from St. Louis.

Yes, Hector. The boy would be . . . well, a boy no longer. Twenty-five now. Older than Achilles had been when the Rebs had struck at Shiloh. Curse those devils. If not for them—

Bratton flung the empty bean tin at a nearby cottonwood and cursed loudly the foul luck that had plagued his life.

The sound stirred Higgs to life, and his thrashing around roused Joe Rodman.

"What's happened?" Rodman cried.

"Nothin'," Bratton muttered. "Time you got your-selves up and had somethin' to eat. Ain't any gold gettin' dug out of that river by itself."

"Yeah, gold," Rodman said, blinking away his weari-ness. "Close to forgot where I was."

"Ain't a day you ever saw Custer leave a man to sleep past daybreak," Higgs said as he pulled on his pants. "That's a fair advantage of civilian life, eh, Bratton?"

"What is there to eat?" Rodman asked, yawning.

"Cold beans," Bratton explained, pointing toward the tins. "Best hurry 'em down, too. Then drag your hide along to the river and join in the work."

"Cold beans?" Rodman growled.

"You're apt to eat worse 'fore we sit down to buffalo steaks in Kansas," Higgs said, laughing. "Might want to pull your trousers on, too, boy. Them bare legs's sure to draw Sioux. White as the colonel's sheets!"

"We'll leather him up, though, won't we, Higgs?" Bratton called. "Nothin' like a Dakota summer to harden a boy."

Bratton paused a moment to stare at the fuzz-cheeked youngster. It was Hector filled his thoughts, though. Twenty-five? The boy'd been scarcely thirteen the day Bratton had left Peoria back in '61. And since then there'd just been letters. Not even a photograph!

Bratton followed the bend of the river to where the cur-rent slowed. There, where the spring flood fed by melting snows slowed enough to deposit its golden treasure, Lucius Bratton scooped his plate into the sandy bottom. As he sloshed the sand around, water carried away the lighter particles and left only a few pebbles besides the glittering specks of gold. Bratton collected the yellow sparkles in his cavalry kerchief. The nuggets that he dug from the bottom he placed in his pockets.

"Any luck?" Higgs asked as he splashed into the shallows.

"Not more'n a thousand dollars' worth so far," Bratton said, laughing. "Bet we can dig ourselves rich inside a week."

"Sioux'll find us by then," Higgs declared. "Or Custer's Rees. We'll have three days if we're lucky."

"Won't manage but a million dollars by then," Bratton said as he grabbed a thumb-sized chunk of twisted yellow.

"Guess it'll have to do," Higgs said as he scooped a plateful of bottom mud. "But then that'll buy a lot of good times in Kansas City."

"Or even New York," Bratton added.

"New York?" Rodman cried as he trotted over. "I favor San Francisco. They got a mile of fancy houses, I hear."

"Best to get the gold gathered first, boy," Bratton advised. "As for spendin' it, well, there's plenty of time for that."

But even as they worked, Bratton dreamed. The kerchief filled. Then a flour sack swelled with gold flakes. As for the nuggets, he dropped them one by one into wool stockings.

"Won't take three days to dig all we can carry, Bratton," Higgs declared an hour later. "By nightfall tomorrow we'll be ready to leave."

"Not likely," Rodman argued. "There's enough here to keep us busy till Christmas."

"No point to diggin' more'n we can haul out," Bratton explained, dipping his sweat-streaked forehead into the cool stream. "Greed's lost many a miner his hair in this country, Joe. Higgs is right. We take our share and head south."

"It's best," Higgs echoed. "You spend it all, Rodman, come along back with that pup brother of yours and dig some more. You're young enough for reckless ways. Me and ol' Bratton here got simpler tastes."

"Scared?" Rodman asked, grinning.

"Reason to be," Higgs replied, gazing at the nearby hills. "Good reasons, and every single one of 'em's wearin' buckskins and eagle feathers."

As it happened, though, the three men worked the river unmolested that afternoon and most of the following day. When the heat of the unrelenting sun overcame them, they shed their sweat-soaked clothes and swam off the weariness. As their fears abated, they fished a half-dozen trout from the river, fried them up for a midday supper, and resumed the work.

"Strange thing the way the sun bakes a man red at the same time the river nigh freezes his toes," Higgs observed in the middle of the afternoon. "Rodman, ain't much left o' you that's pale now. Burned red as a tomato."

"Take some explainin' in those Frisco bawdy houses, Joe," Bratton added with a laugh. "Ain't easy burnin' them parts."

"Guess not," Rodman said, laughing at the notion.

"Won't be feelin' too easy 'bout it when you put that end o' you in the saddle," Higgs pointed out. "Guess we can scare up some berry juice. The Rees dabbed ol' Bart Henry with it once when he got himself scorched down on the Platte. Remember that, Bratton?"

"He was ridin' escort for some emigrants bound for Fort Laramie," Bratton explained. "Lost the wagon train. Made his bed by the river, thinkin' that safe. Woke up next mornin' stark naked. Band o' Crows rode down and picked him clean."

"Lucky it was Crows," Higgs said, laughing loudly. "And that Rees come across him afterwards. Sioux or Cheyenne, well, they wouldn't't've left him with all his parts. Saw two fellows the Kiowas caught in Kansas. 'Sides the arms and legs, wasn't much you could recognize. Kiowas and buzzards did a fine job on 'em."

"And the Kiowas don't hold a candle to the Sioux," Bratton grumbled as he climbed out of the river. "They got a powerful dislike of soldiers. I heard how Red Cloud's batch cut up Fetterman's command.''

"Whittled on some o' them while they was still alive," Higgs noted, grinning at young Rodman.

Bratton only half heard him. A movement near their camp drew his attention. At first he thought it only imagination. Fear. Then two riders emerged from the cottonwoods.

"Quiet," Bratton warned, motioning toward the visitors.

He could barely see them. They weren't much more than brownish blurs outlined against their pale horses. They spoke harsh, foreign-sounding words before dismounting. Then they began picking up discarded bean tins, a torn wool sock, and several fish bones.

"Scouts," Higgs whispered. "They'll tell the rest of their band."

"No, they won't," Bratton insisted as he dug a knife from his boot. Higgs drew his as well, and the two veterans crawled on to where the Indians were exploring the camp.

"I got the one on the left there," Higgs whispered.

Bratton nodded and crept toward the other Indian. With a sudden ferocity that surprised himself, Bratton flung himself on the Sioux.

"Ayyyy!" the startled Indian cried. He managed to block Bratton's first blow with his wrist and stagger backward onto the grassy slope. *"Wasicum!"* he shouted as Bratton's knife slashed into his thigh. The knife struck again, higher, and again. The young man's shirt reddened as his belly and chest were opened.

Bratton felt the moist flesh beneath his hands, and he saw the terror in the young Sioux's face. It was Shiloh again, the bloody bundle that had been one soldier after another.

"Lord, no," Bratton mumbled as he threw the knife aside and buried his face in his bloody hands.

The second Sioux sat a few feet away, staring at the knife Higgs had planted in his belly. One arm was gashed, too, and there was an ugly tear across his forehead.

Bratton made a move toward the youngster, but Higgs waved him away.

"He's finished," Higgs declared.

The Sioux gazed weakly at his companion. Then he muttered a brief chant before rolling onto one side and coughing out his life.

"You killed 'em both?" a wide-eyed Joe Rodman gasped as he stumbled out of the river.

"Grab a foot," Bratton ordered as he fought to keep his stomach down. "We got to get 'em covered."

"Sure," Rodman answered, bending down and grabbing an ankle. Bratton did likewise, and they pulled the two corpses behind a tangle of briars. Then Bratton dug them a shallow grave while Higgs and Rodman did their best to erase all signs of the brief battle.

"They were just boys," Rodman said when it was finished. "Not much older'n my bitty brother."

"Old as they'll get," Higgs said, producing a small pocket flask and taking a long draw on it.

"Once a Sioux's that age, he's a warrior," Bratton declared. "They would've joined the scalp dance if they'd killed you, Joe. Just bad luck brought 'em past here tonight instead o' two days hence."

"How much you figure we got dug up, Bratton?" Higgs asked. "Twenty, thirty thousand?"

"That much at least," Bratton answered. "Likely more."

"Them boys most likely followed their brothers on a hunt. Come along to hold the horses. Others won't be far off, you know. Somebody's bound to happen by lookin' for 'em. Best we were on our way 'fore they get here."

"Better we hide and wait for them to pass by," Bratton argued. "We'd stand a fairer chance holed up here than caught in the open."

"They catch us here, they'll know we kilt their boys," Higgs argued. "Elsewhere they might even let us pass."

"Not a prayer of that," Bratton said, shuddering. "We need another day's diggings. Then we go."

"Not me," Higgs complained. "I got money enough already."

"Then you go alone," Bratton said, staring at the faint trace of Boyd Higgs reflected in the dim moonlight. "What chance is that?"

"He's right, Higgs," Rodman added. "We don't stand any chance split up. We got two more horses, too. They can carry gold."

"Now, there's a thing we _won't_ do," Bratton insisted. "We ride with those two horses, won't a Sioux in Creation give us leave to pass south."

"I ain't stayin' here two more days, waitin' to get scalped!" Higgs cried.

"I'll split the difference with you," Bratton offered. "We can pan the river awhile yet. Then leave toward nightfall."

"And if the Indians come lookin' for their friends before that?" Higgs asked.

"We've got good rifles and lots of cartridges," Bratton pointed out. "We'll give an accountin' of ourselves."

"And get scalped," Higgs grumbled. "Best come up with a better plan than that one."

"Nothin' else to do," Bratton insisted. "We take off now, we'll raise dust a half-blind prairie chicken's bound to spot. Come on. Let's get back to the river. Dig while we can and lay low afterward. Make our break at dusk."

"That's hours you're talkin' about," Higgs complained.

"Liable to be hours long in comin', too," Bratton declared. "Work might hurry 'em along."

"Maybe," Higgs said, clearly unconvinced.

Bratton couldn't blame him. He wasn't convinced himself.

THREE

Lucius Bratton had never worked as hard in his whole life as he did in the hours after burying the Sioux boys. He could see his future reflected in every glimmer of gold he panned or scooped from the river. A lifetime of disappointment could be erased that single afternoon. He could build a fine house, buy a shop or even a small factory. His father had manufactured rifle barrels.

I've had enough of war, he thought as he plucked a thumb-sized nugget from the pan and admired the way it glinted in the dying sunlight. Perhaps it would be better to make furniture for the new settlers that would flood into the Dakotas after word got out that there was gold in the Black Hills. *Might make out better crafting coffins for the Sioux,* he told himself. Strong as they seemed, no tribe had ever stood between Americans and gold!

"You see that?" Higgs called from upstream. "There, past those pines!"

Bratton glanced over to where his companion was pointing. A bull moose scratched his back against a branch.

"Guess you don't see many of those critters back in

Jersey, eh, Higgs?'' Bratton said, enjoying the humor of
the moment.

"Could've been scouts," Higgs grumbled.

"You won't have to look hard to see the Sioux that
come next time," Bratton argued. "Like as not there'll be
plenty of them, and they won't bother scouting us. No,
they'll come riding like hellfire out of the trees, screaming
and waving those coup sticks."

"Coup sticks?" Rodman asked, trembling so that he
dropped his pan in the river and had to scramble after it.
Bratton couldn't help laughing at the floundering youngster.

"That how you figure it?" Higgs asked, making his way
downstream to where Bratton was working. "They'll take
their time about it. Count coup. Take us alive?"

"That's how they'd do it, all right," Bratton remarked,
setting his pan aside long enough to retrieve Rodman's as
it floated toward him. The younger man splashed over to
take it, cursed the current, and walked up onto the bank.
He was soaked now, and the wind was up. Stripping his
clothes, he appeared both pitiful and comical at the same
instant. Burned red by the sun, he was shivering from the
effects of the afternoon wind. It carried an eerie chill that
bit like a dagger into every inch of exposed flesh.

Bratton saw that much in Rodman's eyes. He felt the
wind himself. Maybe it really was time to leave.

"Not yet," Higgs said, sensing his elder's thoughts.
"This is a good stretch of river here. Look," he added,
producing three large nuggets. "We can still get off by
sundown. If there's Sioux through here before that, we've
had it. Here or farther south, we got no chance in day-
light."

"Little enough by night," Bratton noted.

"What about him?" Higgs asked, nodding toward the
freezing wretch that had been Joe Rodman.

"He'll need the time," Bratton observed. "Hang those

clothes up in the trees," he called to Rodman. "Wind can dry them."

"What about a fire?" the younger man replied.

"Don't want things to get that hot, do you?" Higgs asked.

Rodman recognized the alarmed gazes of his fellow deserters. He began draping his garments over limbs of nearby trees.

"Ever seen a man burned, Bratton?" Higgs then asked.

"In a fire, you mean?" Bratton asked. "Once, in Tennessee. During the war."

"No, I mean Indian burned," Higgs explained. "Set afire on purpose. Sioux do that?"

"I've heard about Comanches doing that sort of thing," Bratton said as he went back to work. "Set some fellows on wagon wheels down in Texas. Roasted them."

"I don't know that I like to hear such talk," Rodman muttered as he started back toward the stream. "You figure you could just keep quiet for a time? Let my nerves settle a hair."

"Or let the hair settle, eh?" Higgs asked, grinning at the way Rodman's short, fair hair seemed to stick out from his head. "Reminds me of a frazzled cat."

Rodman smoothed down his hair and glared at Higgs. Bratton frowned. Sometimes young Joe looked so much like Achilles—like Tory, too, maybe. Only Tory had several years on Joe Rodman now. Achilles, well, he would never know what it was like to be eighteen. Not now. Not after Shiloh.

"You all right, old man?" Higgs asked.

"Fine," Bratton answered, waving Higgs back upstream. "I'm no pup of a boy needing help."

"Just appeared strange's all," Higgs said, shaking his head. "Guess you saw some things in the war, eh?"

"Enough," Bratton said, grinding his teeth.

"Odd you'd want back in the army. What happened? Your woman run off?"

"She's been dead more'n ten years now," Bratton said, surprised that he'd allowed that much of his past to leak out. He turned away and scooped his pan in the river. It wouldn't do for them to know the truth. And Lucius Bratton didn't want to admit to himself that the memories could still hurt him. He didn't fear Sioux arrows half as much.

It's your doing, Tory had written him last winter. *You got my brother killed. Ma died of that more than from any fever. I've been alone since then. You didn't offer me much comfort when I was fourteen and homeless. I learned to survive on my own then. What reason would I have for seeing you now?*

"This reason," Bratton said as he filled another sock with nuggets. "Millions of them. I'll make it all up to you, son. They won't remember Bratton, the coward. Bratton, the ruin. They'll only know Bratton, the millionaire. And Tory, you won't half mind being at my side when all that happens!"

"You say something, old man?" Higgs called.

"No," Bratton replied. "Must have been the wind."

Bratton shook his head in disbelief. Was he talking to himself again? The truth of it was that he couldn't be sure anymore what he was thinking or what he was saying. Sometimes he found himself standing guard with young Achilles, dead twelve years now. Other days he would dream of dancing with Eliza, introducing her to his old friend Sam Grant.

"Now there are two paths that have sure taken turns." he said as he picked sparkling particles from the pan. Sam's president. And I'm—

Bratton bit down on his hip until it bled. Enough! There was work to do. Wouldn't the ghosts leave him alone long enough to do it?

I'll show them all, Bratton vowed. *Even Tory will forgive me.*

It had been the hardest thing in his life, leaving his

young son behind in Peoria. But Lucius Bratton was a pariah in Illinois, and who could have guessed Eliza had only months left to her.

"He puts you too much in mind of Achilles," she had scolded him. "He's not his brother. He wouldn't follow you into the army if you asked him. Well, your military days are behind you now, aren't they, Luc? What have you to show for it? A broken sword? Disgrace? A dead son?"

The terrible irony was that Hector Elliot Bratton *had* enlisted. Not long after burying his mother, the boy had ridden a train to Chicago and signed on with the infantry. He had probably forged his grandfather's signature, granting him permission. Tory sure wasn't eighteen! Short of soldiers, the recruiters didn't examine anyone very carefully. Worst of all, the boy called himself Tory Elliot, turning his back on the father and family that had brought only grief and shame. He'd owned up to his name only when a captain from back home recognized him.

Tory had made a good soldier. The boy had never written his father that, of course. Bratton had learned it from a cousin. Twice the youngster had discarded a drum and taken up a discarded rifle. Once he'd helped hold George Thomas's lines in Tennessee. Later he'd killed two rebel soldiers in Georgia. For that last deed and the capture of the Alabamans' flag Tory had won a Medal of Honor. George Custer didn't have one of those, although his brother Tom had two. Bratton had written his first letter to the boy afterward, but it had been months before a reply came.

When a boy's on his own, he sometimes acts foolishly, Tory had written. *I wasn't brave. Just stupid. I wanted to bury the medal with Achilles, who, according to all accounts, earned such a thing. I gave it to Em. I hear it's hanging on the wall in Peoria now, so I won't be staying there. I'm not any good at playacting. I can't pretend to be a hero, and I'm tired of being a coward's son. I'm off*

*to St. Louis to work for my old lieutenant. He's as close
to family as I have now.*

Yes there were things that hurt worse than arrows.
Stung more than Comanche torture. Lucius Bratton was
sure of few things, but he was absolutely certain of that.
And as he slaved away that afternoon under the fading
Dakota summer sun, he was more determined than ever to
make amends, to give his surviving son more than a legacy
of cowardice and desertion. Gold would make the difference. That and the years. Twenty-five was old enough to
understand that a man can make mistakes. The boy had
seen war. The man would understand a colonel's sudden
panic.

As the minutes passed far too slowly, Lucius Bratton
fervently wanted to believe in his new dream. He wanted
to welcome an admiring son, see again the pride and ad-
miration that had filled Tory's eyes when his father had
ridden off to battle at the head of a regiment of blue-clad
recruits. Mostly, though, he concentrated on the tiresome
task of panning the stream bed, emptying specks of gold
into his kerchief and dropping nuggets in stockings. The
chill water had numbed his legs, and he had lost all feeling
in his fingers hours before. Higgs and Rodman had stopped
long enough to shake off the fatigue and eat. Bratton la-
bored on.

"Sun's nearly set," Rodman finally announced as he
splashed his way out of the river. "Guess it's time we
finished."

"Just a little while longer," Higgs pleaded. "I found
me a real rich streak here. There's a couple of nuggets the
size of eyeballs I got to pry loose."

"Thought you were the one in a hurry to leave, Higgs?"
Bratton asked. "Sioux seem a little less frightening with
a world of gold in your pockets, eh?"

"Seems so," Higgs confessed. "It's either that or
knowin' I can outride the both of you. Won't be my hair
a Sioux's wearin' to the scalp dance."

"I don't want it to be mine, either," young Rodman insisted as he collected his clothes from the tree branches. "I'm half-frozen, and my clothes are still wet. The sooner I'm clear of this country and sitting by a warm fire, the happier I'll be. To blazes with your nuggets! I'm quittin'."

"Suit yourself, boy," Higgs answered. "I'm not leaving without these."

"We said sunset," Rodman declared, hands on his hips. "Bratton, didn't we say sunset?"

"We did," Bratton admitted. "Tell you what, Joe. There's plenty to be done before we leave. You go and ready the horses. Saddle three. I'll start packing up the gold."

"We each pack our own!" Higgs shouted. "I'm not sharin' these nuggets with anybody."

"Fine," Bratton agreed. "I'm satisfied with what I've got. Joe?"

"Probably best we do it this way," the younger man replied. "Avoids arguing over shares. When we clear Sioux country, we can go our own ways."

"It's agreed, then," Higgs said, grinning as he pried the first nugget from its muddy lair. "I won't be much longer, either," he added. "You can ready my horse."

Joe Rodman busied himself saddling the mounts. Bratton began securing his treasure in a rubber blanket. He paused only long enough to draw a brief sketch of the river and surrounding country. To his left stood an imposing cottonwood split in two by lightning. On the right was a raw sandstone cliff that resembled the profile of a battered old man. He drew out his compass and recorded the bearings. Perhaps, once the Sioux were attended to, he and Tory could come back.

Higgs was still trying to pry loose his second big nugget when Bratton heard them. Four, maybe five, horses. His instinct was to glance up at Rodman and growl at the boy for letting the horses wander. Rodman had the mounts under firm control, though. A look downstream brought worse news. Four young men, their bare chests painted for war, stood staring sourly at the miners. Each had a bow strung and ready, but they seemed in no great hurry to attack.

"Rifles!" Bratton shouted as he pulled his Colt pistol from its holster. "Get the rifles, Joe!"

One of the young Sioux understood enough English to realize that their prey would soon be armed and alert. He shouted, and the horsemen vanished past the scorched cottonwood.

"Whew," Rodman said, collapsing against a boulder. "I thought they were going to attack."

"Pity they didn't," Bratton said as he worked feverishly to shape the rubber blanket into a pack.

"We might have stood 'em off, but you can't be certain," Rodman argued as he began packing his gold onto the back of a strong-backed gray.

"No, but it's for certain they won't come back alone," Bratton explained. "Those fellows weren't even old enough to be buffalo scouts. Most likely the rest of the horse holders, off searching for their two friends."

"They were painted—"

"I know," Bratton said, shuddering as he realized the meaning of the paint. Those youngsters had taken the time to prepare themselves for a fight. They hadn't happened along the three miners. No, they had come with fighting in mind. Whether they were after the deserters or perhaps some of Custer's Rees sent after them, it didn't matter. The Sioux would not send four boys to do a man's work. Others would arrive shortly.

"Time to leave, Higgs," Bratton announced.

"Just another minute or two," Higgs pleaded.

"Your hair," Bratton replied. "I'm packing up and getting clear of here, though. Joe?"

"I'm with you," Rodman said, tying bags of nuggets behind his saddle.

"Better to pack the gold," Bratton growled, waving

Rodman over. "Use your rubber blanket. I'll show you how to tie a diamond hitch. That will secure the whole load on your pack animal."

"We're taking everything?" Rodman asked. "I thought we might be better off to grab a little and make a run for it."

"Dead or alive, I'm bringing my gold," Bratton insisted. Rodman reluctantly nodded.

As the two of them managed to maneuver Bratton's weighty load onto the first extra horse, Higgs continued to struggle in the river. Bratton took a deep breath to calm himself. Then he showed young Rodman how to intertwine the lines of a rope and secure the load on the packhorse's back. He then helped Rodman pack his own takings onto a second animal.

"You did fine for yourself," Bratton noted. By the feel of things, Rodman might well have the best haul of the three of them.

"Come on, boys!" Higgs called from the river. "I can't get this one loose. It's a giant, I tell you. I'll share it. Please, won't you help?"

"I'm cold enough without goin' back into the river," Rodman replied. "We're leavin'."

"It's no use, Higgs," Bratton added. "Time to clear out."

Higgs reluctantly abandoned the nugget and started packing up his gold. Rodman wanted to leave, but Bratton knew the three of them stood a better chance together. He helped Higgs arrange the load and pack the third spare horse. Once they were finally mounted and ready to leave, Higgs hesitated.

"I've got to have a final try at her," Higgs said, turning back to the river.

It proved a fatal mistake. As Higgs resumed digging out the streambed, the unmistakable sound of ponies splashing in the water returned. Bratton couldn't tell how many Sioux were coming this time, but he knew there would be more than four. This time they wouldn't be fighting pony boys, either.

They reached Higgs first. Alone, with only a pistol for protection, he had no chance. Even so, he managed to fire off five shots before a tall warrior wearing a single feather tied in his hair drove a lance into the former cavalryman's gut. Higgs, stunned, stumbled toward the bank, screaming for help. A second Sioux shot an arrow through his right forearm. Three other arrows found their marks in his left hip and thigh.

"They've kilt me!" Higgs hollered as he turned his revolver toward his head and pulled the trigger. Nothing happened. All the chambers were empty. Higgs seemed puzzled. He had forgotten the sergeant's instructions to leave the first chamber free while on the march.

"I've seen many a man shot by his own pistol," the grizzled veteran had explained.

"Shouldn't we do something?" Rodman asked.

"We will," Bratton answered. "Leave them to their sport and ride clear of here."

Bratton whipped his pony into motion. He had previously tied his own packhorse behind him. He quickly grabbed the lines of Higgs's horses and brought them along as well.

"He won't need gold where he's going," Bratton explained. "Come on, Joe!"

Behind them they heard their dying companion cursing and screaming. The Sioux were taking their time finishing him off. That suited Lucius Bratton. He needed every spare moment he could manage to make good his escape. He wove his way into a thick stand of pines and then on past a small spring into a fertile valley.

"They don't seem to be following," Rodman said as they paused to secure Higgs's horse and readjust the packs.

"Don't need to," Bratton said, staring at the gathering darkness. "They know the country. We don't."

"But—"

"Joe, we don't have a whole lot of chance left to us. We don't stand a prayer unless we get some distance between us and the river. I figure we've got maybe five or six miles of open country here. On the other side, we'd best find a place to hide. We can cache our gold and come back later, when the Sioux have other concerns."

"We can take some with us, though?"

"Not too much, Joe." *Not enough to make the start I'd hoped.* "But if we ride the horses in relays, we can cover some territory."

"I'm taking my gold with me. My share of Higgs's, too."

"You didn't do anything to merit a share," Bratton growled. "As for the other, you'll do as I say or find your own way out of these hills. I've done what I can for you, Joe, and if you're willing to keep up, I'll get you south. I won't let gold fever get us killed, though. I won't do that."

"You think we have a chance to get clear of those Sioux?"

"I think we've got a poor chance at best. Thing is, Joe, it's not just those Sioux we have to worry about. It's the thousands we haven't even seen yet. Best hope we've got is that they enjoy Higgs long enough that Custer's Rees come along and square things."

"You're certain the Rees are looking for us?"

"You signed on with the Seventh, what, three months ago? If you'd gotten to know anything about George Custer, it would have been that he's got about as bad a record for deserters as anybody in the army. Back at Fort Riley, they'd leave the barracks and get on a train. They could get to Chicago and disappear. Here, though, a man only has his horse, and he doesn't know the country. You count on those Rees, boy. For once I'm halfway glad of them."

"We won't be better off if they catch us, though. I've heard deserters are hung."

"Hanging's nothing to what the Sioux do," Bratton remarked. "You see Boyd Higgs's ghost, you ask him about it. Now, you ready to ride hard?"

"I'll keep up."

"Then follow me!"

Having said that, Lucius Bratton eased his pony into a trot and started first west, then south. In his mind he continued to mark each landmark. Once they crossed the open ground, he wound his way through thick stands of pines until he grew too weary to continue. Joe Rodman was nearly asleep in the saddle.

"Look there," Rodman said, pointing to his right. "There's a gap of sorts. Down there's a cave."

"Appears so," Bratton said, trying to make out the shadows in the faint light cast by a midsummer's moon. "Good a place as any to rest."

The two deserters made their way inside the cave's mouth. They were quickly disappointed to discover the ceiling dropped dramatically ten feet from the entrance.

"We'll unburden the horses and eat something," Bratton declared.

"Make a fire?" Rodman asked.

"Quicker to dig a grave. I plan to be alive in the morning. That cave back there narrows. Be a fine place to hide the gold."

"Most of it, anyway."

"You hide it on you, Joe, make sure no Sioux or Ree could come by it without looking hard. They know why we were here, we haven't got a prayer."

"We might be able to offer them some."

"If they were soldiers, it might even work," Bratton explained. "But a Ree would only take it and slit your throat. Sioux, well, this is sacred land for them. They know what a gold strike hereabouts means. That's why their eyes are on Custer."

"And us?"

"It's why they'll kill us, Joe. If they can find us."

FOUR

Cold beans and stale bread did little to drive away the hunger pangs brought on by exertion and fear. Worse, the cave was wet and cold. Lucius Bratton couldn't help wondering if it was worth the discomfort and risk. They were still days from safe territory. Higgs was already dead, and what use was a youngster like Rodman if it came down to a real fight? For that matter, what use was Lucius Bratton?

"How long we goin' to stay in this hole?" Rodman grumbled from his sentry post at the mouth of the cave. "We got better treatment from Custer. On a bad day."

"You weren't with the Seventh long enough to know what a bad day was," Bratton replied. "Old Snake Eyes used to send out parties of us looking for trouble or cutting wood. One batch didn't come back. Kiowas caught them in the open and killed every last one. Some of the old-timers remember the Washita, too."

"When Custer took the Cheyennes to task?" Rodman asked. "I recall my uncle talkin' about that."

"Did your uncle tell you how the colonel sent his major

and a few dozen men out to check the flank?'' Bratton
asked.

"No," Rodman confessed. "Would seem a wise thing
to do, though.''

"Only Custer didn't wait for them to come back. Didn't
send anyone to see what happened to them. Later scouts
came back with a tale of how they ran across another band.
Outnumbered ten to one, they held 'em off till their cartridges gave out. Then they died, one at a time, and some
of them real slow. By then some Cheyenne women came
along. They remembered Washita and Sand Creek when
the Colorado Cavalry cut up their kin. Don't guess it was
a pretty sight by the time it was over.''

"But they didn't burn 'em, did they?'' Rodman asked.
"I've got a powerful dread of fire.''

"A Cheyenne woman starts to cutting on you, you'd
likely welcome fire,'' Bratton argued. "Anyway, you keep
your eyes open. I'm going to bury my gold.''

"And mine?''

"Yours, too, if you like.''

"I'll do it myself. I remember how you grabbed Higgs's
takings when the Sioux got him.''

"Joe, I wouldn't've objected to you doing it. You didn't
think of it first, though. Couldn't leave it behind for them
to find. We've got to keep them from knowing we struck
it rich.''

"You don't think they know? We worked a whole day.
Somebody probably saw us.''

"Only the scouts, and we tended to them. That other
batch may have seen us working the river, but they can't
be sure we came away with anything. I plan to keep it that
way.''

"Just the same, I'll tend to my own gold.''

"Suit yourself,'' Bratton said, shaking his head. "Be an
extra hole to dig is all. You keep watch for now, though.
I'll be along when I've finished.''

As it turned out, the ground was far too hard for digging.

The limestone floor withstood every effort by Lucius Bratton to scratch more than an inch or two. Instead Bratton went deeper into the slimy interior. He wished he had thought to bring a torch, but there was the danger of light carrying. Overhead, the squeaking of bats betrayed their presence. He recalled exploring caves in Missouri one summer with his brother. A hundred of the flying rats came pouring out of the cave flapping their wings and diving at their campfire. No, darkness wasn't so bad by comparison.

Eventually Bratton reached a natural spring. He sampled the water, but it had an odd taste. Just past the spring he located a rift in the wall of the cave. It was only by accident that his fingers located it, and even a man carrying a torch would have difficulty spying it. He lifted the heavy stockings and flour sacks filled with nuggets one at a time and stashed them in the fissure. Then he covered them with bits of debris and two shattered bits of limestone. He made a mental picture of the spot.

It was only later, after relieving Rodman of lookout duties that Bratton took out a small lead pencil and began to draw a map on the side of an envelope. Then, angry with himself, he ripped the paper into shreds.

"Won't do to hide the gold and give them a map to it," he rebuked himself. Instead he tore a smaller bit of envelope and began making a series of dots and dashes. Tory's old code. No Indian would make sense of it. As for the words he coded, well, they were biblical passages. Eliza's folks were high on Bible reading, and he was certain young Tory would be able to decode it. If anyone else had a try, he would be only a hair holier for his trouble.

Once he finished, he stared at the yellow glow spreading across the eastern horizon. He saw no sign of trouble on the hillside below or beyond, in the meadow. A plume of smoke marked a camp five or so miles to the north. Sioux, most likely. That, or others had deserted the ranks with like intentions.

Bratton grinned for the first time in hours. Perhaps they

would make it out. He would be rich after all. But what of the map? Where could he hide it? He considered his coat or even a boot. He wished he had brought one of those heels with the hollow spot like some of the Reb spies liked to use during the war.

"Old fool," Bratton told himself. "You've thought of almost everything."

Then it came to him. The watch. The one prized possession he'd kept from his earlier stint as a soldier. It kept good time, but that was only part of it. That watch had once stopped a rebel musket ball. The insides had needed replacing afterward, and Bratton had done that himself. His German grandfather was a craftsman, and timepieces were a specialty. That watch lost less than a minute a month. Of course, he wasn't certain it was *his* watch that was off.

"No matter what happens," he promised himself, "I'll see to it that Tory gets the watch. And the gold."

But as the morning sun illuminated the landscape outside the cave, Lucius Bratton believed he might just escape southward after all. The smoke he'd spied earlier had vanished. Perhaps there had been others. The Sioux might be busy elsewhere. Maybe the Rees had blundered into them. Or perhaps their blood lust had been satisfied with the killing of Higgs. Bratton didn't know. He didn't really care. He stepped into the cave, roused the slumbering Joe Rodman, and pointed to the horses.

"We'll make better time today," Rodman observed. "Without the gold to carry, we can ride the horses in relays. Make a lot of time."

"You can't outrun Sioux," Bratton replied. "Sure, the extra ponies will help, but we'll be slow, cautious. Look at that sky! Clear all the way to Canada! Atop one of these ridges, a man can see halfway to tomorrow. We won't raise any dust today, Joe. We'll stay to cover when it's possible. And if we're lucky, we'll make it out of these hills alive."

"And then?"

"Bide our time. The Sioux won't stand still for Custer riding through the heart of their sacred country. And once fighting starts up, the cavalry will be back up to strength. Sam Grant's president, you know. A real soldier, that fellow. He won't let the Sioux off this time. No, he'll send the whole army down on them."

"And we'll just ride back to the cave and collect our gold?"

"And more besides. That river's got plenty more to give. Once word gets out there's gold in the Black Hills, people will come pouring into this territory. Be plenty of help even if the Sioux decide to try and do something. I don't figure it that way, though."

"Hope you're right, Bratton," Rodman said as he prepared to saddle his horse. "All the gold in China won't do a fellow with a Sioux arrow through his head much good."

Bratton found himself laughing. He then prepared his own pony for the trek south. They left the packs and everything but rations in the cave. Then, after silently bidding his future fortune adieu, Bratton led the way southwest.

It was an odd, eerily quiet morning. There was something haunting about that country. It wasn't hard to see how Indians could imagine spirits inhabiting the place. The wind whined mournfully through the tops of giant pine and spruce. The streams cut through rock as a knife might slice through one of Eliza's lemon cakes. Hawks screamed out overhead, and ground squirrels chattered from treetops. It was only the odd call of a mourning dove that attracted Bratton's attention.

"You see something?" Rodman asked.

"No, just my ears playing tricks, Joe," Bratton declared. Still, he kept a wary eye out. There was something a little too human about the sound of that dove. And when it continued past noon, Bratton swung his way sharply south, away from the little trading towns that had sprung up near Red Cloud's agency.

"What's wrong?" Rodman wanted to know.

"Queer sounds," Bratton explained.

"Sioux?"

"Well, they're not coyotes, Joe. That's for sure."

They crossed a narrow river and took the time to devour tins of beans before changing mounts.

"Don't," Bratton warned as Joe started to toss his empty tin into the stream. "We can't leave anything behind."

"Well, if I don't leave *something* behind, there's goin' to be an awful stink," Rodman said, starting into the trees.

"Feel the call myself," Bratton confessed. It was the beans, no doubt. He hoped that fool boy would have the sense to cover up his waste. Bratton sprinkled pine needles over his own, taking care not to denude any stretch of ground enough to leave proper sign. To his dismay, he heard the sound of a twig snap.

"Lord, Joe, don't go leaving a marked trail," he grumbled.

"What?" Rodman called.

The sounds hadn't come from the same direction. Immediately alarmed, Bratton pulled his pistol and hurried toward the waiting horses. They weren't there. Twenty feet away a couple of half-naked boys led them back toward the river. Laughing and boasting, they had no notion of the danger posed by two desperate men.

"Pony boys," Bratton muttered as Rodman appeared. "We lost our horses to a handful of boys!"

"Lost more than horses," Rodman said, growing pale. "I kept one of my gold pouches."

Bratton's eyes widened. He wanted to grab Rodman and choke the life out of the young fool. But silence was their only shield at that moment. The young Sioux were more intent on splashing around in the stream than watching the horses, so Bratton decided to make a try at them. If older men were nearby, they would come only after the horses' owners anyway.

"Go around to the left and get the horses," Bratton said, biting his lip. "I'll cover the Sioux."

"A shot's sure to alert the whole valley," Rodman pointed out.

"That's why I'm giving you leave to get the horses," Bratton explained. "I'm less apt to start a battle."

Rodman dropped his chin onto his chest and sheepishly snaked his way toward the purloined animals. Bratton wove his way through the boulder-strewn bank until he had a good position high above the swimmers. He kept his pistol ready, hoping all the while that the horse stealers would remain distracted. One of the horses gave out a cry, though, and the boys immediately started for the bank.

"Keep back!" Bratton warned, waving his pistol at the nearest one, a youngster of twelve or so. The sight of the pistol had an effect, as did Rodman, who had retrieved his rifle. Near naked and unarmed, the Sioux could do nothing but stare hatefully at the two former bluecoats. An older boy of fourteen or so shouted something, but Bratton knew nothing of their language. The nervous deserter waved at the surrounding hills and pointed to his uniform. The boys frowned. Bratton knew there weren't any cavalry coming to the rescue. The Sioux didn't.

"What'll we do?" Rodman asked. "You know they're goin' to run to their papas as soon as we leave!"

"Might be they're a ways off," Bratton said, taking a deep breath. "Joe, you head on out with the extra horses. I'll watch these boys a bit. Then I'll follow."

"I don't know the way," Rodman objected.

"There's a clear trail heading toward that ridge," Bratton pointed out. "Stay on it until you see a good place to turn south. Keep the sun on your left shoulder. I'll catch up."

Rodman nodded, collected the spare horses, and started down the trail. The Sioux, now watched by a solitary white man, grew bolder. When Bratton rammed back the ham-

mer of his pistol and pointed the pistol at the youngest
boy, the others shrank back.

I m the last man on earth to cause harm to a boy,''
Bratton told them. He tried to let the truth of those words
come through. "I'll kill you all, though, if you try and
follow."

The Sioux boys didn't understand many English words,
but their ears certainly knew the meaning of *kill*. They
huddled together, shivering. Bratton wanted to let them
come out and collect their clothes, escape the chill grasp
of the stream, but that would have been foolish. Soon he
would need time, and the boys, their feet and legs numb
with cold, were less apt to follow.

Lucius Bratton waited twenty minutes. At least that's
what his watch told him. It seemed longer. The old timepiece wasn't working quite like it had been. Sounded peculiar, too.

"No helping that," Bratton muttered to himself.

It wasn't a minute later that the air was torn by the
sound of an awful cry. The Sioux boys backed away. They
recognized the sound of a white man in pain. So did Bratton.

"Ran afoul of 'em, eh, Joe?" Bratton spoke to the wind.
"Well, it's your own doin' for bringin' that gold along!"

The tough part was that Bratton needed the youngster's
help. A solitary man had no chance in Sioux country. The
spare horses were with Joe, too. A second cry more hid-
eous than the first brought a shiver of cold fear down Bratton's spine. He hadn't heard such agony since Shiloh.
Then it had been his own son, Achilles, struck hard and
sudden by three Reb musket balls in his upper thighs.

Bratton's horse grew skittish, but he managed to grab
the reins and keep the animal from bolting. In that wink
of an eye, the oldest of the pony boys leaped from the
river.

"Easy, boy," Bratton pleaded as he aimed his pistol at
the fourteen-year-old. The Sioux strung his bow and nim-

bly notched an arrow. As he raised the bow, Bratton fired
his pistol. The bullet struck the youngster in the temple
and threw him back into the shallows, dead. His four companions then raced toward his side, and Bratton barely had
time to get mounted before they were chasing on foot. One
managed to fire an arrow past Bratton's left ear. A second
had better luck. His arrow found its mark.

At first Bratton didn't realize he had actually been hit.
His canteen was rubbing against his left hip, and he attrib-
uted the sting he felt to the sharp edge of the tin canteen.
When he later felt moisture on his side and hip, he thought
it was only water leaking. After he lost the pursuing pony
boys, though, he realized the left leg of his trousers was
stained red.

"Not now," he muttered as he grasped the arrow. A
quick tug informed him that the flint point had found only
flesh. "Good, no bone to get mended," he reassured himself. Then he saw the blood. It was murky and black, nothing like the bright red he was accustomed to seeing from
arrow wounds.

"Kidney, most likely," he remarked. "Too low for the
liver."

It was bad enough, though. It meant stopping, bandag-
ing, probably surviving a fever as well. He could already
sense the weakness spreading throughout his body. He
searched the landscape for a refuge, but there was no ap-
parent haven for a wounded man. Worse, Joe had all the
food and most of the water!

Joe. Turning toward the direction of the younger man's
screams, Bratton heard a third and a fourth outcry. There
was nothing else to do. He had to hope it was only fear,
that Joe was still in one piece. Bratton needed help. He
nudged his horse on, but once he topped a low hill, he
saw what he was hoping and praying he would not. Three
Sioux warriors had Joe Rodman pinned between two boulders. They had already cut away his clothing, and the
youngster's arms and legs were horribly slashed.

"No, these aren't Sioux," Bratton observed. "Cheyenne. Lord, we've gone and blundered into worse trouble."

He hadn't thought that possible a moment earlier, but now he saw his future painted in the agony-streaked canvas of Joe Rodman's face. As the Cheyennes carved on Joe, a half-dozen Sioux argued over the horses. When one located the gold pouch, he angrily grabbed his own knife. Bratton couldn't understand what was said, and he couldn't tell what the Sioux was doing with the knife. Joe Rodman screamed out guttural answers, though, until the Sioux finally made a slashing movement with the knife. Joe's scream rent the heavens. The Sioux held something up in his hand, and the others laughed hideously.

"Poor soul," was all Bratton could say as the Cheyennes went back to work. Below the neck Rodman was little more than a mass of blood and exposed organs. He lived another ten minutes. By then his eyes and tongue were gone. One of the Cheyennes was compassionate enough to end it by slicing through the living corpse's heart.

Bratton had heard all of it and seen a fair portion. His own pain was growing worse, and he'd fallen off his horse. He lacked the strength to remove the arrow, and the bleeding went on unabated.

"So, this is death," he said, staring at the sun blazing overhead.

He closed his eyes, but he didn't find the solace of death waiting. Instead he saw himself standing atop an ebony mare, proudly wearing his new uniform with the polished brass buttons. His father-in-law had paid for both the horse and the uniform. The people of Peoria had given him a sword and a handsome gold watch after nominating him as colonel of their new regiment.

Sam Grant, the bankrupt, the failed farmer, the old friend who had passed his most recent years clerking in a relative's Galena store, had asked for Lucius Bratton.

Grant, a hero since Belmont and soon to win glory in Tennessee by capturing a whole rebel army, had wired the governor. *Lucius Bratton knows soldiering. Trust him with one of the new regiments.*

There was young Achilles, dressed in similar uniform and beating a fine new drum procured from a New York music shop. But Bratton found himself remembering his other son, the one that was still breathing. Hector Bratton was only a sliver of a thirteen-year-old, barely five feet tall. He had hugged his mother's skirts when the drill company fired off a salute. Now, though, he gazed out proudly at the father that was to lead his neighbors south to vanquish the accursed rebels.

"Mind your ma," Bratton had told the boy. "Do your chores, and don't neglect your studies."

"Get some growing done, too," Achilles had added, squeezing his brother's scrawny shoulder with a hand that hadn't yet held a razor. "If this thing lasts long enough, maybe Mr. Lincoln'll need three Brattons to win it."

"You'll do no winning of wars, young man!" Eliza had scolded. "Father, you promised me the boy would only be going along as company and to entertain his elders. He's not to be put in danger, is he?"

"I'm a soldier, Ma!" Achilles had argued.

"You're not yet sixteen," Eliza had reminded him. "You do as I say or I'll come down to the camp and haul you back home by the ear. Hear?"

"Yes, ma'am," Achilles had whimpered.

There wasn't a Bratton present who didn't believe it possible.

"Oh, Eliza," Bratton mumbled. "You were right. About Achilles. You said he'd rush into trouble, and it got him killed. You were right about me, too. I never had the disposition for command."

He'd shown it again, too. Two men had followed him south, and both were dead. They would have company when the Sioux found him. Maybe even if they didn't.

It was Tory's eyes he saw most of all. Those bright blue stars that flashed with pride when his father gave them a final glance, then saluted. Tory returned the honor smartly Achilles was oldest, bravest, a natural leader. And Tory? The boy was clever, kind, forgiving. Yes, he'd been all those things. But when they'd last met, there had been no warmth in those eyes.

"Where's my brother?" the youngster had asked, knowing full well the answer.

"He's gone on to a better place," Lucius Bratton had answered.

"Maybe he can look out for Ma," Tory had said. "You never did."

The youngster then turned and walked through the open door of his grandfather's house. It was the last time they'd met face-to-face. Tory had given no hint of forgiveness in the rare letters he had sent from the battlefields of Georgia or afterward. And now there would be no fortune to share.

"Still, there's a chance, son," Bratton said, clasping his side as pain racked his being. "A chance for you."

But it was a poor chance, even by an optimist's standards. Lucius Bratton had never numbered himself among that ilk. Not since Shiloh.

FIVE

Lucius Bratton should have died that afternoon. Blood loss alone should have finished him. Instead the wound clotted, and he was still alive when nightfall arrived. Perhaps even more amazing to the weary man, the Sioux and Cheyennes had finished with Joe Rodman and ridden back to their camps. He could see the pinpricks of light cast by the dancing flames of their campfires sprinkled across the rugged hills all around him. He counted six separate sites. Only one was to the south, though. That knowledge gave rise to the slightest hint of hope, and he began dragging himself toward the remains of young Rodman.

The smell alone was enough to drive away a less desperate man. Bratton was thankful the darkness hid the worst from his view. The Indians had taken away the ponies, but they had no use for the tins of beans. A small pile of them marked the trail, and Bratton used his knife to open first one and then another. He knew he needed the strength food would give him, but he wasn't really hungry. It was the probably the wound.

An hour earlier he had managed to draw the arrow out

of his back. The point had been mercifully small. It was only, after all, a boy's hunting arrow. A grown man might have used a larger stone point, or even one made of white man's iron. Few soldiers walked away from an encounter with one of those, especially if it touched a vital spot.

Bad as Bratton's wound was, removing the arrow seemed to have helped. He knew he had a fever, but the blood leaking from the puncture had changed. The dark, foul fluid had changed to a brighter red. Perhaps the kidney had only been nicked. He tore his shirt into strips and did his best to bind the wound tightly. His vision began to clear, and he considered for the first time that he might survive. That was when he had started toward Rodman's corpse.

He now forced himself to eat. Even with a bit of food in him, he lacked the strength to crawl more than a hundred yards that night. To escape the Sioux camped in those hills, he needed a horse. His own mount had strayed that first night. An alert Sioux probably had it by now. He would have to wait until he got stronger before considering how to get one.

Another day came and went before Bratton ventured out of the shelter of the pines. Then it was only to refill his canteen and collect the last tins of beans. He tried not to look at poor Rodman, but it was hard to ignore the buzzards circling overhead. Two of the ugly creatures picked at the bones, and Bratton had a strong urge to unload his pistol at them. Caution overruled impulse, though. A gunshot would bring unwelcome company, and the buzzards would make their next meal on Lucius Bratton!

He contented himself with muttering a curse at the birds as he stumbled back to his makeshift camp in a nest of boulders. It was a proper hiding spot, and he took care to cover his trail. Except for the pony boys who returned each afternoon to swim in the river, he spied no sign of human life. It was a puzzle. Surely the boys had told their fathers that there had been two men. The one who planted his arrow in Bratton's side would have boasted of the feat. Why wasn't anyone hunting him? What could be more important? They'd seen the gold in Rodman's pouch. They had to know a white man knew of the treasure waiting in that sacred place.

They're out there, all right, Bratton told himself. Maybe they had some other deserters to carve up, and maybe they had fought the Rees a bit. Unless George Custer turned his whole outfit around, though, there would be Sioux left to attend a wounded old man afoot and on his own.

That night the wind brought an unusually hard chill to the Dakota air. For summer, it was especially odd. Bratton hugged himself, hoping somehow that what little warmth remained inside himself might somehow flow from limb to torso and back to limb again. It didn't. He slept fitfully, dreaming of past battles and future dangers. He awoke to find a heavy dew on the ground. The sun was already well above the distant hills, and he scolded himself for wasting the morning. Shouts from the river warned that the boys from the nearby camp had come earlier than usual. He recognized the one who had shot him. The youngster wore an eagle's feather tied in his long braided hair.

"You told it, all right," Bratton said, spitting a bitter taste from his mouth. "But maybe you added a touch, eh? Said you saw me fall, maybe into the river. They think I'm dead, don't they?"

His words were little more than thoughts flowing off his tongue. He neither wanted nor needed an answer. What he did need was a horse, and he saw four of them peacefully grazing beside the river.

"You owe me a mount, boys," Bratton whispered to the swimmers. But could he creep to the river and climb atop a pony without alerting anyone? In his present condition, he stood a poor chance of getting away from even a handful of children. Bratton knew, though, that he stood no chance at all of reaching their camp undetected, of stealing a pony from the guarded herd, or of challenging full-grown men in a fight.

There's nothing else you can do, Bratton thought. *Won't get easier. Best do it now.*

And so Lucius Bratton, still dizzy with fever and weak from loss of blood, started to make his way slowly, carefully, toward the river, toward the ponies, toward the only chance of escape and survival he could imagine.

He got halfway before snagging his bandages on a cottonwood limb. When he freed himself, a twig snapped, and the horses grew nervous. He held his breath and waited for his heart to slow before continuing. The boys chased each other through the shallows on the far bank, unaware of the enemy that was closing on their ponies. Bratton approached the closest one, a spotted mare with a cavalry carbine tied behind an elkhorn saddle.

Somehow the sight of the weapon kindled an anger in his heart. It was Rodman's gun, and the hair tied to its barrel was Rodman's hair. Bratton didn't fault the boys for taking trophies. Lord knew the Seventh had its share of souvenirs. Ears and hair and worse. Once a corporal had tossed two leathery ears onto a poker table, claiming they were worth ten gold dollars in Denver. Bratton had become sick.

"Wasn't any loss to the boy," the corporal had insisted. "He was long dead by then. I might as well've had the ears as some wolf or buzzard."

Afterward the others had laughed about it.

"Don't trouble Bratton with your stories, boys," Ike Pettis had announced. "He's got sensibilities. Don't you know he's an educated sort of a man. Look to his boots. Those are officer's boots, aren't they? Likely he was a reb during the war."

Bratton had rarely struck out at a man, but he did at that moment.

"I buried my oldest son at Shiloh," he said as held a

knife to Pettis's throat. "He was no reb! You watch what you say about me, hear?"

For that moment of passion Bratton had straddled a howitzer for twelve hours. Afterward he hadn't been able to ride for more than a week.

"You're too old for a soldier, Bratton," Pettis had told him later. "You don't know when a man's jestin'. I didn't mean to get your dander up, fellow. But to tell you the truth, I'm glad to see you've got a spark of life left in you. We've too many young fools and petty thieves in the Seventh for an honest man's likin'."

"Nobody sensible would join this army," Bratton had answered. "We're all of us runnin' from somethin' and chasin' adventure. That's why the desertion list continues to grow."

"Well, to hear tell, we'll soon have plenty of adventure to chase."

Pettis was a prophet, all right. If he'd been a little less inclined to drink and a little less inspired toward three stripes, Bratton might have invited him along. He would have been a better man in a fight, but he likely would have reported the offer to some lieutenant. He'd never have agreed to leave the gold behind, either.

Sounds of laughter from the far bank brought Bratton back to the present. He gazed from behind a boulder in time to spy two tall Sioux warriors ride past. Between them ran a naked Ree scout. The men of the Seventh had dubbed him Hollow Leg because of his thirst for corn liquor. He was good at his job, though, and he'd twice kept wood-cutters from riding into traps. Now his eyes were filled with terror, and Bratton knew why the men had vanished from the river.

"Guess you might as well do it now as later," Bratton said, taking a deep breath. Maybe the Ree would use the diversion to make a break for it. With him as a guide, it would be easier to get clear of Sioux country. It was a waste of time, imagining such things, though. As the scout passed closer, Bratton could see the Ree was already bleeding from two dozen tears in his flesh. Someone had cut away his forelock, and his eyes were gone. A blind scout wasn't much good. Still—

Bratton stepped out and grabbed the spotted mare. As he climbed into the smallish saddle, he tore the rifle loose from its rawhide straps. Years of military service had taught him to load and fire almost without thinking, and he had plenty of cartridges for the Springfield. He raised the trap and slipped one into place. He then aimed and dropped the nearest Sioux horseman.

The boys shrieked in alarm, and the other horseman turned toward Bratton. The Ree, screaming like an enraged eagle, leaped at his remaining tormentor and tore him from his horse. The two struggled a moment in the river before the Ree drove the Sioux's own knife through his heart. Blind but victorious, he managed to cut away his enemy's hair before the pony boys fell upon him. Using stones from the river, they beat the pitiful Ree to death. Bratton wasn't watching, but he knew that was what they were doing. Hollow Leg had already sung his death chant, though. The end was a respite from tortures awaiting his arrival in the Sioux camp.

Bratton, meanwhile, drove the other horses ahead of him as he turned southward. For a time he rode like the wind, dodging branches that slapped at his shoulders and leaping over obstructions in the trail. He made a good five miles before his head began to grow cloudy. He saw a rocky hillside just ahead and directed his horse toward it. It was a natural corral with a solitary opening, and Bratton rode through, then blocked the opening with what remained of the ill-fitting elkhorn saddle.

"We'll be all right here," Bratton told the weary pony. "For now anyway."

"Less well than you imagine," a somewhat familiar voice answered. "Set that rifle down, Bratton, and keep your hands clear of the pistol."

"Pettis, that you?" Bratton asked, staring with disbelief as a muddy and tattered Isaac Pettis emerged from his hiding place on the far side of the rock enclosure. Two Rees, Yellow Horse and One Ear, followed.

"You put us to a fair amount of bother," Pettis said as he snatched the rifle from Bratton's hands. The corporal then took Bratton's pistol.

"Come after me, did you?" Bratton said, scowling. "Where are your horses? Don't tell me there's a place back there to hide them, too."

"Lost 'em in a fight," Pettis explained. "All but one. Sent Hollow Leg out to bring us some fresh ponies. He'll be along with them."

"No, he won't," Bratton said, shaking his head and feigning sorrow as he related the sad tale. The Rees took note of the exaggerated way Bratton described their comrade's gallant death. He left out the pitiful wretch's mutilation.

"Was a good thing you did, giving Hollow Leg a chance," Pettis observed afterward. "Doesn't change anything, though. The general sent us to bring you boys back. Now, we come across Higgs. What was left of him anyway. Where's Rodman?"

"Not too far from Hollow Leg," Bratton explained. When he told of the young man's torment, the Rees nodded knowingly. Bratton suspected they now considered themselves in his debt for sparing their friend a similar end.

"You three must be the biggest fools in God's creation," Pettis grumbled. "Of all places to take French leave. The heart of Sioux country? Don't you know they were already worked up about us being there? If you had in mind to take off, why not do it before, when you could catch a train? You're from Illinois, ain't you? Half the deserters in tarnation must be hiding out in Chicago."

Bratton considered telling Pettis about the gold, but something deep inside warned it would be a mistake. Pettis would tell others, and word would spread like lightning. Before he could get the news to Tory, the Black Hills would be crawling with miners. One might find the cave, and—

"What is it?" Pettis asked when Yellow Horse motioned for silence.

Bratton didn't need to ask. He could already hear the horses. Five or six at first. Then more. One of the boys led the way. Bratton hurriedly led the mare from view, but it didn't matter. The young Sioux stopped two hundred feet from the enclosure and pointed to the discarded saddle. A slightly older youngish man smiled and nudged his horse toward the enclosure. He spoke only a few words, and they were to the Rees. One Ear stepped out and waved his bow at the Sioux.

"Stay put, you fool!" Pettis barked, but it was too late. One Ear marched out toward the Sioux, and the two hurled insults at each other. Bratton wasn't sure either knew what the other was saying. Both understood the gist of it, though. The Sioux dismounted and took out a knife. One Ear threw his bow aside and likewise took a knife from a scabbard on his hip. The two men circled each other for a few moments. Then they lurched forward.

A single slash directed at a vital spot will tear the life from a man, but the dueling Indians were well versed in the art of knife fighting. Each blow was parried. Each counterstroke thwarted. It appeared for a time as if the two would continue all morning. Then one of the pony boys tossed a stone that struck One Ear on the jaw. It brought only an instant's distraction, but that was enough. The Sioux's blade sliced through the Ree's belly and opened him up like a tin of peaches. With his insides spilling out, One Ear dropped to his knees and uttered his death chant. The Sioux could have ended his life with a second blow, but instead he turned disdainfully upon his brother. Harsh words flew back and forth. An older man tore the eagle feather from the boy's hair.

"They know you lied, boy," Bratton said, grinning for the first time in what seemed like ages.

They weren't the only ones who were angered by the boy's interference. Yellow Horse notched an arrow and leaped out from the rocks. Before the Sioux could react, the Ree fired his first arrow through the throat of the younger Sioux. He then slew the older brother in like fashion. Before he could fire a third time, the Sioux were upon him. He fought them with his dying breath, killing a third Sioux after Bratton was certain he must be dead himself. The surviving Sioux counted coup on the Rees and dragged their bodies off, shouting to high heaven. For an instant Bratton thought he and Pettis were left alone. Then the first arrow flew into the enclosure. It was followed by an entire volley.

"Our turn now," Pettis observed.

"I'd judge it so," Bratton agreed, reaching for his pistol. Pettis yielded the rifle instead.

"I don't see a pack," the corporal said, frowning. "How many shots do you have?"

"Got a pocket full of cartridges, and a box of pistol bullets for my Remington. You find me something to shoot at, and I'll give an account of myself."

"What'd you do to your back?"

"That little fool with the rock did it," Bratton explained as he cowered beside Pettis under a rocky outcropping. "If he'd had anything but hunting arrows, it would have done the job. Seemed like I might make it out alive after all. Then I happened onto you three."

"You're the one that put us here, friend," Pettis growled. "Fine mess it is, too. They can stand off there firing their arrows until the whole Sioux nation arrives to watch us die."

"Don't believe that's the way I'd choose to end my life," Bratton announced, gazing at his watch as the sunlight glinted off its golden shell. "How do you figure they'll go about it?"

"Keep our heads down till sundown. Then creep up and finish us. I don't know. Maybe they'll wear us down a bit, come later when we're tired so they can get us alive. Have some sport of it."

"They're not mounted, those Sioux," Bratton said, studying the flight of the arrows. "Mostly they're firing at us from east and south. Nobody at all's north of us."

"They think they're chasing a deserter," Pettis realized. "If we make a run up north—"

"I don't see a lot of future for a deserter in Custer's camp," Bratton noted. "When he hears he's lost three Rees, he won't have much trouble ordering me hanged."

"Requires a court-martial to—"

"You figure anybody's going to speak for me, Corporal? I've got no friends in that outfit. Less now than ever. They might not know there are two men in here, though. They saw me ride in, but they can't know for certain you're here."

"What's on your mind, Bratton?"

"I stay. We let my horse go to distract 'em. Then you make your way north out of these rocks."

"Alone? Afoot? A poor chance at best."

"Got a better notion?"

"Can't say I do. Only thing is, how do I know you won't use me as a diversion and make a run for it yourself?"

"You don't. Look, Corporal, I expected to be dead two days ago. I've done more things wrong in my life than right, and I don't see it's exactly fitting not to try to close the book with something halfway decent."

"You're going to bring those Sioux down on you so I can get away? Sorry, old man, but I've seen you play cards. You've got lying eyes. They're forever hiding at least half the truth. More often than not, they're hiding all of it."

"So you figure it, Pettis. How do I ride out there with twenty or so Sioux blocking the trail? I don't imagine One

Ear could manage it, and he's ten times the horseman I am. I'd probably die of this wound anyhow. All I really wanted to do was see my kid.''

"You've got children?"

"Had children. Oldest one died at Shiloh. You learned that a while back, remember?'

"I do," Pettis said, laughing. "Surprised me then, too. Never knew you to have that sort of passion about anything.''

"I've got another boy, Corporal. Hector's his name, but he likes to be called Tory. He wore a uniform, too, once, but he carried it off better than I did. Won himself promotion and a Medal of Honor. He's twenty-five years old now, and I haven't seen him since he was a pup of a boy. He has his ma's eyes and disposition, and none of his pa's faults that I've noted other than a reluctance to write. I haven't given him much, but I would like him to have my watch. It might take him back to a time when I was a better man. You'd do me a service to get it to him. Tell him I didn't run this time. Tell him I stood my ground. You can do that, can't you?''

"I won't lie about this, Bratton.''

"I'm not asking you to. You tell Custer I ran away. Tell him I was always the worst sort of slacker. I never was a decent soldier, but I'm a fair enough shot, and I'll be a time dying. You can tell my boy I deserted. It wouldn't be the first time I ran from a fight, you see. He knows what I am. I just want him to know that at the end, when it mattered to somebody, anybody, I kept my word and stood my ground.''

"So I can get away?"

"That's the bargain, Corporal. I stay and die. You take the watch to Tory. He's in St. Louis. Works in a store on River Street. McNamara's. They sell general merchandise. It's just next to—''

"I know the place," Pettis interrupted. "Got a sister in

St. Louis. She buys piece goods at McNamara's. I once got a pistol repaired there.''

"Likely that was my Tory did it. He's a gunsmith by trade, so he says.''

"Shouldn't be a hard thing to do then,'' Pettis said, offering his hand. Bratton took a final glance at the watch and placed it in the corporal's rough hand. Pettis then returned Bratton's revolver.

"I swear that if you fail to do this, Pettis, I'll send all the devils in hell after you.''

"You save such venom for those Sioux,'' Pettis advised. "You'll need it when they come after you.''

"Could be,'' Bratton agreed. "Now, you start north. I'll give you a count of, say, twenty. Then I let the pony go.''

"I'd wish you good luck and a quick end, but that's not what I need of you, Bratton.''

"I'll keep my word, Corporal. You keep yours. And don't trouble yourself about what they do to me. Isn't anything I haven't earned thrice over.''

"You're a hard man to figure, Bratton.''

"Well, you'll need not worry yourself over me much longer. Now go. I've got to coax this mare into motion.''

Pettis lingered only a moment longer. It seemed as if he still wasn't entirely sure what was going to happen. Bratton only laughed at the man's consternation. If only Pettis knew what he was holding!

"Ayyyy!'' Bratton shouted, rushing out and flinging the Sioux saddle away. He then raced back and slapped the pony on its rump. The horse darted forward, only to fall, writhing, as a shower of arrows met its escape. Two Sioux rushed out to examine the horse, and Bratton opened up on them with the rifle. He then switched to his pistol.

One of the Sioux dragged the other to cover, and soon a dozen of them encircled the stone wall. They hurled insults and taunted Bratton to come out and face them. Bratton returned each shout, each curse. Glancing backward, he saw Pettis snatch an idle horse and climb atop. The cavalryman then made his way through the trees to the north.

"Good luck," Bratton bid him.

The Sioux made their first rush then, and Bratton emptied his pistol. As he hurriedly reloaded, the first arrow struck his left elbow. Bratton swallowed the pain and tried to get his fingers to work. Another arrow scraped his neck, and a third carried away the ring finger of his right hand.

"Well, come on, boys!" Bratton screamed as he readied himself for a final charge. "Come on, won't you?"

A shower of arrows followed, but they were aimed at the back of the enclosure. Bratton was no longer cowering there. A fierce-eyed warrior then appeared on horseback, followed by another twenty or so men. They wasted little time in mounting a charge. Bratton leaped out past the rocks and aimed at each rider in turn. With calm, clear eyes he fixed his target and pulled the trigger. The leader fell first. Then a man with buffalo horns protruding from each end of a warbonnet. A pistol ball tore through the fleshy part of Bratton's right thigh, but he still managed to drop a third Sioux before the multitude rode him down. A shield knocked him to the ground, and a lance plunged through his belly and lit his insides afire.

"Not yet," he said, firing his pistol into the face of barechested assailant. "Just a bit longer."

A hand grasped the pistol and tried to tear it from the dying man's grip, but Bratton was steel that day. He shook the gun free and pointed it at his latest enemy. The face before him was young, too young. He couldn't have marked his fourteenth birthday, and he wore no bonnet of eagle feathers. His eyes were clear and fearless, but he held his lance still a moment, recognizing the death a loaded pistol could bring.

"Well, Achilles, you took your time coming for me, boy," the delirious Bratton called. "What are you waiting for, boy? Come on! Finish it!"

The puzzled young man started to drive the lance home,

but an older man interceded. He pulled the boy back and stared hard into Bratton's eyes.

"Well, it's only death after all, isn't it?" Bratton asked, fighting to keep his vision clear. He had eluded it long enough. It was time.

He took a deep breath and coughed blood in spasms. His heart skipped a beat, resumed, and then stopped. The darkness then swept over him like a velvet shroud, and he felt himself grasping for help in the sudden darkness. He longed to feel Eliza's soft touch. He called to Achilles. But Lucius Bratton found neither. Only darkness.

II

THE TIMEPIECE

SIX

Corporal Isaac Pettis rode like wildfire northward through the rocky valleys and across the pine-covered ridges of the Black Hills. It required no strong imagination to envision the fate awaiting him should some party of prowling Sioux catch him in that sacred country of theirs. He had seen for himself the treatment accorded Rodman and the Rees. He knew by now they would have finished with Bratton. Whether or not those others considered a pitiful corporal worth their time wasn't worth thinking about. There were plenty of Sioux shadowing Custer, and it wouldn't take that many to kill a lone rider.

Custer! That parade-ground colonel, with his high-toned airs and peculiar ways, had gotten enough cavalrymen killed. Why bother chasing three men in the first place?

"Leave the Sioux to tend to them," Charley Reynolds had advised.

Instead three Rees were dead, and Isaac Pettis was worried out of ten years' life already.

General Custer. So he'd been a hero fighting stray rebs at Hanover when the rest of the army was saving the Union at Gettysburg! Marcus Reno had a brevet star, too, and he

could barely find a latrine without a Ree to guide him
there. Custer! Sheridan's pet monkey, some called him
even down in Texas. On the merits of things, there were
plenty better men to lead the Seventh Cavalry. Merit had
little to due with promotions, though.

It's time you were finished with the army, Pettis, he
scolded himself. A corporal's pay was hardly enough to
satisfy a man's thirst. The handful of dollars left after the
quartermaster took out what was owed for clothing and
lost equipment would hardly offset the hazards of another
campaign. Isaac Pettis had seen enough of the Sioux. He'd
ridden the West from the Dakotas to the Yellowstone ba-
sin. When those fool correspondents wrote about beautiful
vistas and sparkling streams, Pettis recalled only hasty burials and the blistering heat of an unrelenting summer sun.
And the winters? Weren't they even worse?

"I don't blame you for runnin', Bratton," Pettis called
to the wind. "Sure picked a poor time and place for it,
though."

As much as Pettis yearned for the safety of his regimental camp, he was first and foremost a cavalryman.
Once the Sioux pony began to tire, he slowed the pace and
then found a sheltered place with good grass and a flowing
stream nearby. He had no intention of walking into camp,
dragging himself like the wretch he was fast becoming.
Worse, he knew the chance a lone man stood fighting
Sioux on foot.

"There you go, boy," Pettis said, stroking the flank of
the pony. "You drink all you want. I've got a thirst myself."

Pettis drew out a pocket flask and took a quick swig.
The whiskey warmed his insides, and he licked the taste
from his lips. He then drew Bratton's watch from his
pocket and turned it over in his fingers.

It was odd what a man was willing to die for. What
folly! To make a lone stand against a couple of dozen
Sioux just so your boy can have a watch. There was writ-

ing scribbled on the outside, and Pettis found himself wondering who might have presented the timepiece to a fellow like Lucius Bratton. Had Bratton come of a good family? Was there a reward waiting for a tired old corporal in St. Louis?

"Shame you never learned to read," Pettis told himself as he watched the pony chew on the soft leaves of the water plants that lined the streambed. He would have to get somebody to look at the watch and tell him about the words etched there. He hoped one of the laundry gals that haunted the river outside Fort Lincoln might help him. The engraving was poor, though, and there were long words there. If he had to go to one of the officers, he stood a poor chance of keeping the watch. If there was opportunity for profit, leave it to an officer to trample an enlisted man's rights. That was the natural order of things in the cavalry!

Pettis tried to measure the passage of time with Bratton's watch, but something wasn't quite right about it. Bratton had once boasted that watch lost less than a minute a month, but it was clearly slow. Isaac Pettis might not be able to read letters, but he knew the sun well enough. It was later than the hands on the watch showed.

Maybe he forgot to wind it, Pettis thought. *Lord knows his mind was on other things.*

Pettis took it upon himself to turn the winding wheel until it resisted further movement. The watch gave little indication of neglect. It wasn't damaged.

"Well, might just be time's caught up to it," Pettis said, laughing as he rubbed the gray that now streaked his thinning dark hair. "Does to most things, don't you know?"

He waited a bit longer before remounting the Sioux pony. Then he continued northward.

In all, he was three days catching up to the rear of the column. Custer had brought along all ten companies, together with wagons for supplies and surveyors to record landmarks. There were reporters along, naturally, although they were supposed to be left behind. The yellow-haired wonder was anxious to see his profile splashed across Eastern newspapers. Custer had brought along miners to pan the streams and relatives to share the adventure.

"It's a grand picnic," his sergeant, Otis Turner, had declared. "With ourselves, the fightin' part of the Seventh, brought along as bodyguard."

It had been a jest, but there was more truth in the statement than either wished to admit. The Seventh Cavalry had done its share of fighting on the frontier. It had broken the Kiowas and killed the Cheyenne. It had cleared out settlers reluctant to give up their plowed fields for the pennies the railroad offered. Now it was time for the army's favorite regiment and its pet colonel to convince the Sioux of the folly of holding on to the Black Hills.

Pettis's arrival brought two receptions. Enlisted men noticed the Sioux pony and nodded knowingly. The Rees not scouting ahead stared searchingly into the corporal's eyes. He gave them a respectful nod, and they immediately shouted angrily at the surrounding hills.

It was only later, when he reported to Major Reno the details of his search, that he heard the only response that truly mattered.

"Well, it was a fool's errand, Corporal," Reno grumbled. "Lost three men to find three corpses. We won't hold it against you, the loss of your horse. Get something to eat and rejoin your company. I'll see to it a report's made."

"I was hoping to tell the general myself," Pettis declared.

"He's off scouting ahead again," Reno explained. "Unless you brought the deserters back, he likely won't care. Better for you, too. He prizes those Rees, and you've gone and lost some of them."

"I'm lucky to have my hair, Major," Pettis argued. "As for the Rees, they chose to take on those Sioux."

"Well, *they* paid for their mistake, didn't they?" Reno asked. "A wise corporal would do his best to avoid a similar fate."

"Yes, sir," Pettis said, stiffening. He saluted and left. Only when out of hearing did he mutter, "Officers!"

In the days that followed, Pettis had reason to regret his failure to pay closer attention to the final resting places of his fellow cavalrymen. He learned to his dismay that the miners brought along at Custer's insistence had, indeed, found traces of gold in some of the streams. The Rees had said something about Bratton's trousers, but Pettis had been worried about the Sioux. He hadn't listened closely. Now, as he examined the watch more closely, he saw flakes of yellow dust clinging to the chain.

"You weren't half the fool I imagined," Pettis said, staring southward. "You found it, didn't you, old man? Gold!"

It explained why the Sioux were so stirred up elsewhere while they seemed unconcerned with Custer's column. He saw plenty of young scouts peering out from nearby hillsides or studying the column from the far bank of one stream or another. Except for a party that rode in to accuse the whites of violating treaties, no Indians appeared willing to challenge an entire regiment of well-armed cavalry.

"Autie's even got the Sioux buffaloed," Custer's younger brother Tom insisted, using the commander's pet name as a brother might. Pettis noted the young captain was less apt to do so with the elder Custer nearby.

Maybe they are buffaloed, Pettis thought, *and maybe they're not.* After all, the Sioux had plenty of time left to organize an ambush. Old Red Cloud had bided his time before cutting Fetterman's command to pieces. During the Yellowstone expedition, the Seventh had learned the folly of underestimating Sioux cunning. They'd lost the regimental surgeon a quarter mile from where Custer, in customary fashion, had ridden ahead with the scouts to study the country.

The trip through the Black Hills held no similar peril, though. George Armstrong Custer, with the Seventh Cavalry seemingly along for the exercise, filled a wagon with

personal trophies. He shot eagles and owls and even a
grizzly.

"He's skinned the bear, all right," Pettis observed,
thinking about the Sioux.

The Rees, naturally, did the skinning of the bear. They
considered that a brave heart deed and celebrated it with
a dance. As for killing eagles, and especially owls, they
held no similar celebration.

"Pure bad luck, according to them," Otis Turner told
Pettis. "They say nothing good can come of it."

While Custer and his brothers went exploring sacred
hills and crawled through daunting caves, Pettis chose to
take his woodcutting details down narrow streams. Whenever possible, he stirred up the beds and used a tin cup to
search for gold. He had no luck at all. The miners, who
had better tools and more experience, claimed there was
little enough to be found by casual labor.

"There's gold here, sure enough," one of them boasted.
"We've not panned a hundred dollars' worth anywhere
we've tried, but upstream, we'd do better."

"I was in Colorado," another added. "You might not
find much one place, but along the same stream, a mile or
so away, a man made himself a millionaire. All the signs
are right. There's paying color here."

Before the column turned homeward, half the men in
the regiment tried their hand at panning those streams. Few
found more than a flake or two. Nevertheless the newsmen
wrote wild dispatches about giant nuggets, and what little
the miners had scratched from the hills found itself exaggerated into nuggets the size of eyeballs.

"Custer's got what he wanted, I guess," Turner told
Pettis when the regiment finally returned to Fort Lincoln.

"And what's that, Otis?" Pettis asked.

"An excuse for Phil Sheridan to snatch the Black Hills,
of course," Turner explained. "A chance for one more
campaign. A showdown with the Sioux that can make him
as famous as U.S. Grant."

"I served with Grant," Pettis said, frowning. "He near got my whole brigade killed in two hours' time at Cold Harbor."

"Aye, I heard of that," Turner said, spitting a mouthful of tobacco juice into the straw of the stable where they were tending to their mounts. "Custer won't have a brigade of men to lose."

"No, just the Seventh," Pettis noted.

"That's a truth, my old friend. Only us."

Pettis considered that notion and groaned. As stories of a Black Hills gold strike circulated across telegraph wires and appeared in one newspaper after another, swarms of greedy miners found their way into the Dakotas. Desertions worsened, and the Black Hills filled with white men eager to find their fortune.

"You knew the place, didn't you?" Pettis asked the watch that continued to abide in his pocket. "Pity you couldn't have told me where."

It was while he was in a particularly thirsty state that Isaac Pettis finally showed the watch to Kate Shaw, a hostess of sorts for Ted O'Hare, the post sutler.

"It's a pretty thing," she said, touching the golden casing. "Time's wrong, though," she added, glancing at the clock over the makeshift bar.

"It's been that way since I had it," Pettis complained. "Old Lucius Bratton, who used to own it, boasted it kept fine time, but you couldn't prove it by me."

"I remember him," Kate said, examining the watch more closely. "Look here. He's got his name on it, too."

"You can read that?" Pettis asked. "Tell me what it says."

"Why, darling, it's a presentation watch," she replied. "From his men, I suppose. Reads 'Lucius Bratton, Colonel.' "

"Colonel?" Pettis asked, laughing. "An officer? That fellow?"

"He told me once he fought in the war. The big one,"

Kate added. "Led his hometown boys at Shiloh. Knew the president, too, from fighting before, down in Mexico."

"Had all imagination that man," Pettis grumbled. "An officer! I'm hanged if I'll take that blamed watch to St. Louis now!"

"St. Louis?" O'Hare asked, stepping over to have a glance at the watch. "What would you want to go to St. Louis for?"

"Promised old Bratton I'd take the watch to his boy," Pettis explained. "Didn't know it was an officer's watch, though."

"You might make some money off it," Kate suggested.

"Probably a Reb," O'Hare argued. "Lost all his money when Sherman burned his farm."

"No, honey, it says it clear enough," Kate said. "He was with the Illinois troops."

"It says that? On the watch?" Pettis asked.

"Let me have a look," O'Hare said, easing his way closer. "It's as Kate says, Corporal. Reads '8th Illinois Volunteers.' He must've been a big man once, old Bratton."

"What's he doing in a private's uniform, riding with Custer?" Kate asked. "A friend of President Grant, he claimed, too."

"Must not have been much of a friend," O'Hare observed. "Could've got himself a postmaster's job at least. My brother-in-law fought at Vicksburg and got a post office just asking for it. He voted Democrat before the war, too."

"You might make a friend or two, returning that watch," Kate advised.

"Whose watch?" Turner asked from the far side of store. "You're not still carrying that fool watch you got off old Bratton, are you, Pettis?"

"I am," Pettis said, stiffening. "Turns out he was a colonel, old Bratton. From Illinois."

"He *that* Bratton?" a stranger asked. "Lucius Bratton of Peoria?"

"Could be," Pettis answered.

"I was with the 8th, and he was our colonel, all right," the man said, reddening. "He did a fair enough job against the rebs at Fort Donelson, but at Shiloh! Why, the first time the rebs let loose a volley, our old colonel, a hero of the war with Mexico, according to him, turned tail and ran for cover. Took the better part of the regiment along, too. His boy, now, there was a soldier. Took the regimental flag and planted it on the hillside, wouldn't budge. Got killed for his trouble, too."

"Must be somebody else," Pettis insisted. "I'm to take the watch to his boy. Lives in St. Louis."

"That'd be the younger boy," the Illinoian went on. "Hector. Don't know what was wrong with the father, but that younger boy proved he was up to the job, too. Fought well enough in Georgia to earn a Medal of Honor, as I recall it."

"Sure, that's likely him," Pettis said, taking the watch from Kate and staring hard at it.

"Do the boy a favor," O'Hare said, placing a full bottle of Green River whiskey on the table in front of Bratton. "Swap me the watch. As for Bratton, a man who'd run from the enemy's not due any consideration from a man like you, Corporal."

"An officer, too," Pettis said, staring at the bottle. "He never told me he was any officer."

"He wasn't one for long," the stranger added.

"Why not share your good fortune?" Turner asked. "We were Bratton's family, weren't we? We boys of the Seventh?"

"Bratton didn't likely know if that boy was even alive," Pettis said, working on the cork. "What am I to gain from a trip to St. Louis?"

"Boy'd likely toss that watch at your face," O'Hare suggested. "You might have to explain to him how his father died, too. How would that be, Corporal? Could you tell a boy, a hero with a Medal of Honor to show for it, that his father died of Sioux arrows running from his duty?"

"Be a hard thing to do," Turner added, making his way to his friend's side. "We could put that bottle to good use, Pettis. Only thing is, two bottles would be a fairer deal."

"Two it is," O'Hare readily agreed, placing a second bottle beside the first. "So, Corporal, what's it to be?"

"I fought my share of rebels and Indians, both," Pettis said, studying the reflection of his face shining in the copper-colored liquid before him. He watched Kate's face, too. O'Hare nodded to her, and she gave Pettis a knowing wink. With her thrown into the bargain, it was an easier choice.

Except for one thing. Bratton's words.

Promise me, they rang through his memory.

"Watch doesn't keep good time, Ted," Pettis confessed, handing it to the sutler. "You certain you want to make the deal?"

"I've got a knack for fixing things," O'Hare explained. "And I can scratch out the inscription easily enough. It's gold, don't you think?"

"Looks to be," Pettis agreed.

"I'll stand by my offer, then."

"What do you say, Pettis?" Turner asked. "Give the boys a taste, why don't you? Bratton's past knowing, and it don't seem he'd care anyway. I watched him drink away his pay many a time."

"Most of the time," O'Hare added. "You won't win the son's gratitude anyway, Corporal. It's a kindness, sparing him his father's shame."

"Kate, you think so?" Pettis asked.

"I wouldn't want my past chasing me down if I was in a better place," she told him. "Besides, we haven't passed a night together in a long time."

"Paymaster's not due for another three weeks," Turner pointed out. "Well?"

"Your watch, Ted," Pettis said, passing the timepiece to the sutler. "Sergeant, I expect us to have a night of it. Two bottles."

"Don't drink it all," Kate warned. "Why not invite some of the others over? You and me, well, we've got other business to conduct."

"Well, I'm bound to get it started, though," Pettis said, prying the cork out of the first bottle and taking the first sip. "For Bratton and the Garry Owen! Long may the Seventh ride!"

"To the Seventh!" Turner shouted, opening the second bottle.

As others of the regiment wandered in to join the celebration, Pettis poured a quarter of the first bottle into his flask and followed Kate to the storeroom. It wasn't what Bratton had asked, but when had an officer honored his word to a corporal? Isaac Pettis had lost two brothers at Cold Harbor while their own colonel cowered behind a pine tree. There were worse things than breaking promises, and being thirsty was one of them. He took a sip from the flask and nodded a final tribute to the founder of the night's entertainment, wherever his soul might have taken him.

"I won't wait forever, dear," Kate called.

"You won't have to," Pettis assured her. "I'll be there directly."

SEVEN

For weeks Lucius Bratton's watch sat on Ted O'Hare's store counter, largely ignored. What had seemed like a bargain, a gold watch had for the price of two bottles of second-rate whiskey, was turning into a nuisance. The original asking price of fifty dollars had fallen to fifteen, and still there were no takers.

"Pay's been slow," Otis Turner explained when O'Hare complained of the lack of business.

"Well, I've extended all the credit I can afford," O'Hare barked. "I've got my costs, too, don't you know? And look at that watch sitting there, a gem if ever you saw one. Can't even find a buyer. Everyone's bought my pans and hammers, but that watch—"

"Gold fever," Turner observed. "Half the regiment's talking of nothing else. Every day some new batch of miners heads into the hills. We're supposed to keep 'em out, you know. Treaty says so anyway."

"Truth be known, the army couldn't draw more of them if it tried. Sending Custer into that country with his newspaper friends! Did anyone expect the secret to stay a secret?"

"What secret?" Turner asked, grinning. "Gold? We didn't find enough to fill a man's pockets."

"Then this whole rumor's—"

"Well, I'd wager there's gold in there somewhere, Ted. After old Pettis came back, the Rees rode out to have a look for their friends. Found our boys, too. Bratton was just dead. That young fellow Joe Rodman, well, they cut him up awful. Rees found some nuggets in a pack close by."

"Nuggets?"

"Solid yellow they were, Ted. Wherever they came from, the man that gets there first is sure to be rich."

"The man that got there first is dead," O'Hare said, glancing at the watch. "Wish he'd given Pettis a letter with a map in it instead of that fool watch. Doesn't even keep proper time now, either."

"Maybe there's a map stuck in there."

"Thought on that some. Looked hard. My grandpa made watches, and I had a fair look at its workings. There's nothing in there. I'd stake my soul on that. It's just a watch's all. A good trinket, though, even if it doesn't keep time quite the way Bratton boasted."

"Looks like it's got a dent or two now," Turner said, examining it with caution. "Fifteen dollars, though. You'd have to find an officer to buy it at that price."

"Maybe one of these miners will have some luck," O'Hare said, scratching his chin.

"In Sioux country?" Turner said, laughing. "They'll have to have the Lord's own luck. Most of the saints'll need to be close by, too."

"You're probably right," the sutler admitted. "Tomorrow I drop it to ten. Wish I'd never seen the accursed thing. I'm the loser on this deal."

Of course he wouldn't be if he could find a buyer. That was at least what was on O'Hare's mind when he spread the word among the officers that he was practically giving the watch away. Officers' dollars arrived no more frequently than enlisted men's pennies, though. The watch remained on the counter.

It was still there a week later when Tom Custer spotted it. The younger brother of the most famous colonel in the U.S. Army wore the twin bars of a cavalry captain. Unlike his West Point–trained brother, Tom had learned to fight on the battlefields of Tennessee and Georgia. Although only sixteen at the start of the Civil War, he had nevertheless enlisted in an Ohio infantry regiment. When his brother achieved a star, young Tom had earned his superiors' praises by leading reckless charges with an invincibility that threatened to become legendary. Having fulfilled his three-year enlistment, Tom transferred his allegiance to the Sixth Michigan Cavalry and passed the war's final year in his brother's cavalry brigade.

Once he had tempted fate by charging ahead of his men in order to snatch the rebel banner of an antagonist. His unbridled gallantry won him the newly authorized Medal of Honor. When he subsequently jumped his horse over an enemy earthwork to break the heart of rebel resistance at Sayler's Creek, he was awarded a second Medal of Honor and a lieutenant colonel's brevet. Although temporarily trapped beneath a dead horse, Tom had gotten to his feet and grabbed the regimental and national colors of his enemy. No other soldier had won the medal twice, much less a young man of twenty-one years.

When his own brother accused him of stealing the family thunder, Tom had merely grinned. That same boyish charm was still there ten years later. He had been a favorite with the ladies at every post he'd occupied, and Fort Lincoln was no different.

The "dashing devil," his brother called him.

"He's a horse killer," Otis Turner had once said, "but he's a soldier. May get you killed, but you'll have fun in the meanwhile."

His exploits among the Cheyenne captives taken after the Washita River attack had won him the enmity of the

plains peoples. If his brother George's bizarre costumes
and exaggerated mannerisms attracted the attention of his
enemies, Tom Custer's liberties with female tribe members
bought him ill-concealed hatred.

That particular day Tom Custer wasn't thinking of
charging Sioux or Cheyenne. His eyes were set on the
charming daughter of a Pennsylvania railroad surveyor,
Miss Amanda Beale. The red-haired Amanda had an in-
nocent glow to her that attracted more men than the ru-
mored gold strike had done. She had entertained the
officers in Libbie Custer's parlor only two days before.

"I'm in need of a trinket to strike a lady's fancy," the
captain announced upon entering O'Hare's store. "What
have you got that can do the trick?"

"A trinket, you say?" O'Hare had asked. With sleight
of hand a Mississippi riverboat gambler would have admired, O'Hare managed to palm the price card he'd set
beside Bratton's watch. "A locket maybe. A ring?'

"Now, Ted, don't go connecting me up with rings,"
Tom cried, backing away. "I'm not so much looking for
a present as for something like, well, something like that
watch there."

"This?" O'Hare asked, feigning surprise. "A pocket
watch?"

"It appears to be gold, though."

" 'Tis gold, Tom, my boy. A fine piece, too. You'd pay
fifty dollars easy for it in Chicago."

"Well, nobody has fifty dollars for such a thing out
here," Tom countered. "One of the miners leave it here?
How'd you come by it."

"Was old Bratton's. You know, the fellow run off and
got himself killed by the Sioux."

"How'd he have such a watch?" Tom asked. Without
waiting for an answer, he picked up the timepiece and
examined it. When he saw the inscription, he paled.

"You see it there, eh?" O'Hare asked. "He was a colonel, too, like you were in the Rebellion."

"He was nothing like me," Tom said, scowling. "I remember hearing of it. He was with John McClernand at Shiloh. Took to his heels. You know, his boy died a hero on that field, Ted. I'm surprised he'd keep the watch long as he did. Traded it for whiskey, did he?"

"Well, no," O'Hare said, nervously shifting his weight. "I bartered it off Corporal Pettis."

"Isaac Pettis? From my company?"

"As I heard it, Bratton gave him the watch."

"I never knew old Bratton to give anything away," Tom said, frowning. "You sure Pettis didn't steal it?"

"Was a gift, I believe, Tom. The old man was dying, and he wanted it—"

"Wanted it taken to somebody, eh?"

"His boy, I think."

"I believe this falls under the category of ill-gotten gain, Ted," Tom said, dropping the watch into his pocket. "Until I talk to Pettis, I believe I'd best take charge of the watch."

"But I'm out the fifty dollars!" O'Hare complained.

"Ted, you never paid Pettis any fifty dollars for this watch. What was it, a bottle or two? Ten dollars maybe. Here," Tom said, setting a ten-dollar note on the counter. "For your trouble."

"It's worth more, son. Twice that."

"Ted, you know how Autie feels about post traders and sutlers. He's apt to want an investigation. Be a shame to rob poor Pettis of his stripes and bring your books into question. Don't tell me you want that?"

"You know I don't," O'Hare said, accepting the token payment.

"Likely I can keep you out of it this way," Tom added, winking at the sutler. "Wise decision."

O'Hare muttered a curse at the captain's departing feet. Pettis was right to feel as he did about officers in general. As for the way the Seventh viewed Custers, he counted himself no different.

Tom Custer located Isaac Pettis in the stables. The corporal was overseeing a handful of men tending to the company's mounts.

"Corporal, I need a moment of your time," the captain called from the back door.

"Sir, is it urgent?" Pettis asked.

"It is to you," Tom said, grinning as he produced the watch.

Pettis, slightly confused, sauntered to the door and stepped outside with the captain.

"I understand you got this watch off Private Bratton," the captain began. "Odd, but I don't recall anything about a watch in your report. He was dead, I believe you said, when you and the Rees came upon him."

"That was Rodman sir," Pettis answered.

"You make your reports to me, remember?" Tom asked. "I don't believe you have much education, do you, Pettis? You don't read or write?"

"I don't, sir," Pettis said, wiping sweat from his brow. "As I remember it, you and the colonel were out with the scouts. I told it all to Major Reno. By the time it come to you, well, I don't put things in a way to make myself understood sometimes. I'm a man of pitiful little learning, Captain. If I gave you to believe we come on Bratton dead, I didn't mean to. I was worn out from the ride, and I suppose I confused myself."

"He *was* alive then?"

"Still breathing, yes, sir. Had an arrow through his back and a pistol ball in him, as I recall. Wouldn't last long."

"Why did he give you the watch, Pettis?"

"Well, you see, sir, he meant it to go to his boy, but I had no way to write down where he said the boy lived. I just forgot it."

"You know what's written on this watch Corporal? Colonel Bratton was a hero of the Rebellion."

"Not as I heard it, sir," Pettis said, taking a long and deep breath. "I didn't even know Bratton was an officer till Kate, over at O'Hare's, read what the watch said. I had in mind to track down the boy no matter what. The son of an officer deserves no less, and I heard the boy himself was a hero, like you yourself, Captain. Won a Medal of Honor, and he just a child at the time.''

"You know quite a bit about this, Corporal," Tom noted. "Much more than you put in your report. I don't believe you forgot about the watch."

"Sir, you have to understand. I've seen what happens to a dead man's things. They don't make it home too often."

"They didn't this time."

"And that's my fault, sir, and I admit it to you now. Wasn't on account of my wanting the watch for myself, though. I'm due discharge soon, and I've got a sister in St. Louis. That's where Bratton thought his boy might be."

"I thought you forgot?"

"I lied about that, sir, and I'll stand company punishment for it if you like. Just let me explain, if you will. I heard from Sergeant Turner and some of the others that Bratton ran away from his men, disgraced himself."

"That's true."

"Then of all the people in the world, sir, you ought to understand why I didn't want to give his boy that watch. How would you take it, Captain, if a stranger come up and reminded you your pa was a coward? Then, to make matters worse, you told him he was running from the Seventh when you found him."

"Some sons would forgive a father's shortcomings, Corporal."

"What if this one did, sir?" Pettis asked. "What if he asked where his pa's buried? How could I look him in the face and say we left him to be carved up by Indians? How do you tell a youngster a thing that's bound to give him nightmares."

"*That* Bratton was up to it, Pettis. I heard about his regiment's charge at Chattanooga, the place the soldiers call Mission Ridge so it isn't confused with Gettysburg. You know how he won his Medal of Honor?''

"No, sir.''

"I do. He ran through enemy fire to bring off three wounded men at New Hope Church, out in Georgia. Shot two rebels to keep them safe. Then, when an Alabama regiment broke the line, he helped his company drive them back. Captured the enemy colors, too. I suspect the man who did that could have stood up to anything you had to tell him.''

"You want me to return the watch, then, sir?''

"No, I believe not, Corporal. I believe you're right in thinking the boy wouldn't want to be reminded of his father's disgrace. You were wrong to sell it to O'Hare, though.''

"I took nothing myself, sir. O'Hare put two bottles of whiskey on the table, and I left Sergeant Turner to see that the men all had a drink off old Bratton. Way I figured it, we were about the only real family he's had since the war. We sang an air or two for him, had a wake, so to speak. The sergeant said it's what a soldier would want, and I don't argue with sergeants.''

"Just captains?''

"No, sir. I wouldn't presume to tell you what to do or think. It just seems to me that, well, you don't have a proper watch your own self, and the Bratton boy wouldn't want it. You can likely find somebody to grind off the writing and maybe even scribble something about yourself on there. It's from a town, you see. I think they'd be honored if a hero like you was to have it.''

"You believe that?''

"I do, sir. With all my heart.''

"Then I suppose I have myself a new watch,'' the captain said, nodding as he examined the timepiece again. "You feel we're doing the right thing?''

"Yes, sir.''

"Well, I feel in a generous mood, Corporal Pettis. I

don't like amending reports, and since no one's really suffered a loss, let's just leave the matter as it lays. Get along with your duties. Consider the entire matter forgotten.''

Tom Custer turned and walked away. Pettis imagined he heard the captain whistling.

''Officers,'' the corporal said, adding a particularly vicious curse. ''May they all rot.''

The watch's latest owner put it to good use that evening, attaching it to a borrowed chain and using every opportunity to display it to Amanda Beale.

''You know, Captain, I read about your exploits in the newspapers,'' she told him as they walked alone around the parade ground. ''Of course, I was just a girl then.''

''You're a girl no longer, my dear,'' Tom replied.

''It must be difficult, living out here so far from civilized people. Don't you get lonely?''

''Often,'' he confessed, clasping her hand.

''I'm surprised that you haven't taken a wife. Surely you must have had your chances.''

Tom merely grinned. There had been the Cheyenne women and plenty of camp followers, but in truth there was too much of the boy hero left to consider sedentary life. He would never drag a woman around from camp to camp the way his brother dragged Libbie.

''I don't often find myself in such distinguished company,'' the young captain explained. ''I'm partial to red hair, too.''

''And if I was a blonde or a brunette?''

''I might be partial to them, at least for an hour or two.''

''You flatter me, Captain Custer,'' Amanda said, blushing. ''I must tell you that my father disapproves of you. Despite the efforts of your brother, we don't seem to be expanding the railroads quickly enough through the Dakota country. He thinks a more determined officer might settle these plains tribes on a good deal less land.''

''Tell your father to be patient,'' Tom said. ''We'll set-

tle with the Indians soon enough. The old men are happy
enough to make camp at their agencies, and the younger
ones will have their fill of fighting soon enough. There
aren't but a few places left to them, and those won't with-
stand the rush of settlers.''

"I thought the army was going to protect the claims of
the Indians."

"When have they ever done that?" Tom asked. "The
plains people are finished. The Cheyenne are all but dead
already, and the Sioux, well, they fought their war in the
Powder River country. Once this regiment is up to full
strength, we'll have a thousand riders ready to strike hard.
The Second Cavalry's up on the Yellowstone, and we expect help from the new forts down south. The Indian's day
is done, Amanda."

"And what will you and the general do without Indians
to kill?"

"Oh, we'll think of something," he said, laughing.
"There are Apaches and Comanches down south to con-
quer. And there are pretty redheads."

"How will you win me, Captain? Will you bring my
father five ponies?"

"I usually start with flowers. When that doesn't work,
I try a buffalo hide."

"A buffalo hide?"

"You'd be surprised what can go on under the cover of
a bull's hide."

She tried to act shocked, but his grin was contagious.
Perhaps once the Sioux were dealt with, Thomas Ward
Custer might go to work building railroads. Hadn't Autie
advised him to try that very thing?

"The evening's grown chill," Amanda announced. "I
think it's time I returned to the colonel's house."

"Probably," Tom agreed. "So, which shall I bring you?
Flowers or the buffalo hide."

"The hide," she said, blushing again. "But only if you
kill the beast yourself."

"I'll set out at first light," he vowed.

Tom Custer was as good as his word. Accompanied by a handful of Ree scouts and a corporal's guard from Company C, he set off downriver. The Rees had located a herd the week before, and it wasn't long before the hunters found thirty or so of the big woollies grazing peacefully beside the river. The Rees marked the herd and split up so to turn the animals once the shooting began. Tom waited for them to reach their spots. Then, giving a loud whoop, he charged the largest bull.

It was no different with Tom Custer, hunting buffalo or charging rebels. He picked the meanest and nastiest and went hard at it. With his eyes blazing as blue as the summer sky and his yellow hair flying behind him, he was half hunter, half demon. The bull, on the other hand, turned to face this reckless enemy with its head lowered and horns dangerously waiting to gore horse and rider. Tom slowed his horse and raised his carbine. As the mount came to a halt, the captain fired. It took two shots from his Springfield to bring the big bull down.

The captain waved to Isaac Pettis, and the corporal led a handful of privates to the spot. They were there to do the skinning while Tom Custer and the Rees did the hunting. It was quite a task, for Tom killed three bulls himself that day. The Rees dropped two others.

By then the surviving members of the herd had scattered eastward. Tom left Pettis and his men to tend to the odious job of skinning and butchering the buffalo. He turned his attention to Three Combs, a Ree girl of fifteen summers who had come along to cook for her brothers.

"We did well," Tom called to the scouts. "I killed three."

"This was a small herd," Many Horses, the oldest of Three Combs's brothers, answered. "It's not so hard to kill buffalo anymore. Soon there will be hunger here."

"I only want the hides," Tom explained. "You're welcome to all the meat."

"What do you want for this?" Red Rock, the other brother, asked.

"Your friendship," Tom answered. "Maybe your sister's friendship, too."

"We will carry the meat to the fort for you, Captain," Many Horses declared. "You should eat what you kill. We aren't Cheyenne. You can't take our women to your lodge."

"We know about you," Red Rock added. "You have no heart to understand our world. You only live to kill things, to take what fills your belly, what satisfies your needs. We ride with you today, but tomorrow you may hunt us. We won't give our sister to you."

"Maybe she wouldn't mind," Pettis suggested, eyeing the girl. She seemed to be flirting with the captain.

"*I* would mind," Red Rock said, stringing his bow.

"You threatening us?" Pettis asked.

"Just being careful," Red Rock explained. "The buffalo could come back."

"Let it go, Pettis," Tom said, shrugging his shoulders. "Worry about the hides. There's a little red-haired gal waiting for one of them tonight."

"Oh?" Pettis asked, grinning. "It's buffalo hides now, is it? I thought maybe that's why you took Bratton's watch."

"No, that's just for show. Hides have other uses."

Tom noticed that the girl laughed at that remark, and he wondered if the Rees were really set against him. Maybe he could have a talk with Charley Reynolds, convince him to speak to Many Horses.

That would wait, though. The problem at hand was skinning, drying, and tanning the buffalo hide. He spent most of that afternoon and some of the next waiting first for the skinners to finish and then for a couple of Ree women to treat the skin properly. When it was finally ready, he asked Libbie to organize a dance.

Captain Tom Custer wore his best blue tunic and white

trousers. Autie had recently paid for an expensive buckskin jacket, but Tom never felt the same need for putting on a show that his brother did. Besides, Tom Custer had a gold watch. More importantly he had the two small strips of cloth with the brass ornaments attached. The medals. For all his West Point training and newspaper clippings, George Armstrong Custer had no such medal.

"Don't worry, big brother," Tom had joked more than once. "If you don't get one, you can have one of mine."

Autie rarely showed his feelings, but Tom saw that those words tore at his brother's soul. It was why they both knew there would be another campaign, another battle. Autie had to have his chance to win that medal.

No one has three, either, do they? Tom thought. *Now, wouldn't that be something to help a man win a wife! Or at least an evening wrapped in a buffalo hide. Yes, at least that.*

EIGHT

Ted O'Hare, who had witnessed the Colorado gold rush in the 1850s, described the influx of miners as an avalanche. To Tom Custer they appeared more like a swarm of locusts. A man would have to look far and wide to find a worse, more desperate assemblage of the human race than the one that flocked to the Black Hills those next two years. Despite Sioux protests, the government did little to stop it. The wealth of the nation had been sapped by civil war, and the gold of the West promised to revive a depressed economy. For many ex-soldiers, the dream of a fortune dug from the mountains and streams of the Dakotas was a final chance to achieve a long-delayed dream.

There was something magical in the air that centennial year, 1876. Despite a two-year-old depression, the first true republic on earth proudly proclaimed one hundred years of existence. A great celebration was planned for July 4 in Philadelphia. Merchants and inventors planned to display their wondrous innovations. Meanwhile, hopeful farm boys and unemployed factory workers journeyed west as they always did when times were hard elsewhere.

Gold had overpowered human will from the beginning

of history. It overcame more cautious men than Lucius
Bratton. In the Seventh Cavalry, desertion became a
greater problem than ever. The hardships of the Dakotas
kindled a genuine hatred for the regimentation and bore-
dom that accompanied garrison life. The promise of a new
campaign against the Sioux led to talk of sudden and brutal
death at the hands of the desperate Indians.

"It's time we dealt with the Sioux," Otis Turner declared the first week of February. "If they won't sell those
hills, we'll just have to take 'em."

"With that bunch?" Isaac Pettis asked, gazing into the
eyes of the twenty-five recruits assigned to Company C.
"Germans and Irishmen, most of 'em. Half wouldn't know
the front end of a horse from the rump."

"They'll learn," Turner argued.

"Not from me," Pettis growled. "I've seen enough of
army life. I plan to be rich."

"On Sioux gold?" Turner asked. "Why, you're as big
a fool as old Bratton."

"His only mistake was picking his partners poorly,"
Pettis replied. "And choosing a time when the whole
Sioux nation was up and angry. I'll wait for you boys to
march out and distract 'em. That'll be my time. And I
won't have any Rees chasing me, either. My hitch is up
next week. Then I'm free to do as I please."

Tom Custer didn't hear that conversation, but he knew
his men well enough to sense their feelings. Rumors of a
new campaign spread faster than lice through the Fort Lincoln barracks. Almost daily some hapless fool of a recruit
was caught sneaking off toward the hills. With his brother
off in the East, sipping tea with politicians and lobbying
for independent command of the inevitable campaign,
command fell to Major Reno, a man who had proved himself capable enough fighting the remnants of rebel armies.
The major was no favorite of the Custers, though, and he
vented his resentment of one brother on another. Worse,
Reno was overly fond of the bottle, and he no longer pos-

sessed the drive that had once made him an effective leader of men.

So the Seventh daily grew more stagnant. The veterans left as fast as their terms of service expired. Some joined the mining camps. Others went to work supplying whiskey and powder. The wise ones, those able to save a bit of their pay and maintain some of their senses, went south to find happiness on a Nebraska homestead.

The same week that Isaac Pettis received his discharge papers, word reached Fort Lincoln that Autie and Libbie were returning at long last. The Northern Pacific Railroad was furnishing a special train, and they were expected to arrive sometime in March. Heavy snows fell that spring, though, and Tom grew concerned.

"Seems like even George Armstrong Custer can't talk the clouds into doing what he says," Reno remarked.

When a telegraph message arrived explaining that the train was hopelessly trapped in snowdrifts, Tom provided an answer.

"Shall I come out for you?" he wired back. Autie, in a message displaying his accustomed bravado, claimed aid wasn't necessary.

Tom knew it was. Moreover, he was bored to tears. Ever since Amanda Beale had returned eastward with her father, he had migrated from miner's daughter to post laundress to camp harlot. While most men required air to breathe, Tom Custer needed scented hair and nocturnal conquest. Winter had provided little of either. Weeks plunging through blizzards were small matters by comparison.

It wasn't a simple matter, rescuing Autie and Libbie. Tom first had to convince Reno of the merits of such a scheme. That actually proved simple.

"Consider this your chance to get rid of both Custers at once," Tom suggested, and the notion brought a rare smile to the stoic Reno's face.

"Have your try at it then," Reno urged. "Don't get too many of the men killed, though. We'll need *them*."

In the end, Tom rigged up mule-drawn sleighs to carry supplies and ordered a pair of trusted Rees to lead the way eastward. He brought along a dozen soldiers to help clear obstacles from the narrow trails and to cut firewood, cook, and care for the animals. A big Bavarian who was accustomed to traversing the Alps proved particularly useful. He was adept at judging the depth of the snow and had an uncanny ability to predict the next storm. Even the Rees were impressed.

"A man just has to have enough misfortune in order to recognize when more's coming," the man, who was currently using the name Brewer, explained. "When I was just a boy, I was befriended by a baron's eldest son. We would go swimming in the summer and hunting in the fall. When we were fourteen, he drowned when a bridge collapsed. The current was strong, and I was unable to get to him. I only am alive because a farmer hid me. My father then said I should leave the land of my birth.

"Later I discovered the baron threw my father in prison and hanged the poor farmer. My mother and two sisters starved. So I come here to find a better life."

"Found it yet, Brewer?" an Irishman named McNally asked.

"Well, I've not yet been hung," the big German answered. "I finish with the army in August. Then maybe I find myself some gold and a good woman."

The others laughed, but Tom wondered if most of them weren't wishing for the same thing.

The little expedition crawled its way almost seventy miles through the bleakest, coldest weather imaginable before burrowing through snowdrifts to find the trapped Northern Pacific train. Autie himself came out to embrace his brother, and Libbie offered "little brother" an even warmer welcome. She also rewarded the soldiers with a warming cup of brandy that lifted spirits and warmed insides.

The rescuers paused only long enough to load the Custers' baggage and three hounds into one of the sleighs. The commander of the Seventh Cavalry and his half-frozen bride climbed in as well. The Rees then led the way back to Fort Lincoln.

A week after the rescue party staggered into Fort Lincoln, the Northern Pacific train chugged past the fort and stopped at the depot in Bismarck.

"A week's a week," Tom told his weary Rees.

Libbie put it another way. "There's not a Custer born who has an ounce of patience."

The story might have added luster to Tom's name had not Autie been ordered back east almost immediately. Disdaining the train, the brevet general instead chose Tom's sleigh for what was to prove the greatest test of his life. Caught up in a whirlwind of congressional investigation and bad feelings, he was saved only by General Phil Sheridan from the wrath of President Grant and removal from command.

Tom ignored the newspaper headlines detailing his brother's troubles. As the weather improved, he devoted his time to drilling the misbegotten wretches assigned to fill the ranks of Company C. With all of the regiment's senior officers except for Reno detached for special duties elsewhere, Tom found many of his fellow officers looking to him as an example. The younger ones, eager to earn promotion and glory, welcomed news that the long-delayed confrontation with the Sioux was in the offing. They were less pleased to learn that George Crook had already left to confront hostiles camped along the Powder River.

"Don't worry over it too much," Tom told his younger brother Boston, who had arrived to pass the summer months under the clear Dakota skies. Young Boston was chronically weak-lunged, and their mother hoped for a Western cure.

"Autie won't survive the disappointment," Boston insisted. "He's been calling this 'his war' for two years now."

"Crook got himself captured in his nightshirt during the war," Tom reminded his brother. "He won't bring the Sioux to bay. No, that'll be our job."

"And Autie?"

"One thing you should know about our big brother is that he does his best fighting in tight quarters. Washington's a pit of snakes, and they don't always bite who you expect. When it's all over, they'll still talk about Custer and his luck. Autie will be back in time to lead the Seventh. Trust me to know."

On May 14, George Armstrong Custer arrived at Fort Lincoln with Brigadier General Alfred H. Terry, the nominal commander of what was to be the northern arm of a three-pronged strike against the Sioux and Cheyenne hostiles hunting buffalo on the plains beyond the Black Hills. Word of Crook's failure had previously arrived.

"Crook's to have another try from the south," Autie explained that evening at a reunion supper with his brothers. "John Gibbon's to come down from the Yellowstone, and we're to march from the east."

Tom could feel the energy in his brother's words. Here, at last, was the chance Autie had longed for. Tom was sure to share in the glory. Even their eighteen-year-old nephew, Autie Reed, was coming along. Already their sister Maggie's husband, James Calhoun, was serving as a lieutenant in the Seventh.

"It's important to have your friends around you when going after dangerous game," Tom told Boston, who was employed as a civilian scout despite the fact that he'd never been through the territory before. "Autie's heard the Democrats are looking for somebody to occupy old Grant's chair in the White House. Why not replace one general with another?"

Hopes of a successful campaign grew those next two days. The Seventh Cavalry was back at full strength after the return of four companies assigned occupation duties in the South. An infantry contingent had arrived as well, bringing with them a battery of rapid-firing Gatling guns. When the miracle weapons were demonstrated for the officers of the Seventh, the Ree observers were unable to conceal their terror.

"Won't any Sioux charge survive those guns," Tom remarked.

"Maybe not, but they're not coming with me," Autie grumbled. "They're worse than dragging cannons around. I remember that country south of the Yellowstone. You won't get a wagon through there. No, this is going to be a cavalry fight. Terry can bring the new toys with him."

Alfred Terry remained the great uncertainty. When Tom asked his elder brother about the general assigned command of what was becoming known as the Dakota column, Autie merely grinned.

"I've had long talks with Terry," the colonel explained. "He's not excited about fighting Indians. He's talked to Sheridan, too, and he understands I'm to have a free rein with the cavalry. He's along to placate Grant and little more."

"Won't he receive credit for the campaign's success?" Tom asked.

"In the end Sheridan will take the bows himself. What do we care? We'll be the ones to claim the glory. We'll be the ones with Sioux blood on our boots. We'll have the stories to tell, won't we? I'll be wearing a general's star again, this time confirmed by Congress. As for you, Tom, the Seventh will need a new commander. You can't imagine that will be Marcus Reno?"

The brothers laughed and enjoyed a rare evening of recollection and boasting. The following morning, while Terry wrote orders and reports, George Armstrong Custer put his command through its hardest day of training ever. At first it was laughable. Recruits fell off their horses. During shooting drills, half the new trapdoor Springfields jammed.

"They're fine weapons for firing at distant targets, but it's our revolvers that will do the best work," Tom boasted when the men complained.

"Sir, those rifles are life and death to the men," Otis Turner argued.

"No, the trick with fighting Indians is to catch 'em," Tom replied. "We'll ride out of the mists just like we did on the Washita. You'll get a shot or two away before the chase begins. Leave the infantry to cut down the runners. Our job's striking the first blow."

"Yes, sir," Turner agreed. "But none of us's been into that country. I hear the Rees talking. They're none too sure about this, sir. At full strength, we're just a thousand men. That's little comfort against a whole nation of Sioux."

"You worry too much, Sergeant," Tom said, shaking his head. "If the Sioux wanted to fight, why haven't they struck us here? Why not ambush us two years ago when we crossed into the Black Hills? It's having their women and children along that make them weak. We'll fight a few men and maybe some of the boys eager to win a name for themselves. Mostly we'll be rounding up women and children to haul back to the agencies."

"Maybe, but I still don't like the Rees acting so peculiar."

"When's my brother ever led us to defeat?"

"Not ever as I recall."

"Trust him to know his trade, Sergeant. You just concentrate on having the men ready."

There was little time to correct the men's shortcomings, though. Orders were sent out the night of May 16, ordering the regiment to assemble early the next morning. On a fog-shrouded morning, with the regimental band playing its hallmark tune, "Garry Owen," the Seventh Cavalry prepared to depart. Behind them came the infantry, Gatling guns, supply wagons, and a herd of beef cattle. Autie and

Libbie Custer led the way, and sister Maggie rode with her husband as well. After riding a dozen or so miles, the two-mile-long column camped on the banks of the Heart River. To a chorus of curses, the paymaster began handing out pay to the men.

"A fine time," Turner told his captain. "Nothing here to spend it on."

"Exactly," Tom said, laughing. The army had learned that paying its soldiers before departing on a long campaign meant that a third of them would be too drunk to sit in a saddle. Worse, dozens would soon be appearing at sick call with signs of the pox.

"It's nevertheless bad luck to have money in your pockets when you're chancing your life," Turner continued. "Casket money, my old dad used to call it. But the man that finds you doesn't spend it on you. No, not in Sioux country."

"Don't concern yourself too much over it, Sergeant. My sister's going back to the fort. She can take the money to your wife, if you like."

"When did I ever have a wife?" Turner asked, noticing the sparkle in his captain's eyes. "Ah, sir, you're having a laugh at a good soldier's expense. Does you no credit. Tell you what. You have your sister send the money to my ma in Philadelphia. She'll think it's Christmas in May!"

"We'll do it, Sergeant," Tom said, clasping the burly man's hand. "And if your thirst gets too powerful, I have a flask set aside."

"Ah, Captain, you've got the soul of a saint," Turner told him. They managed to catch Libbie and Maggie at the last possible moment. The women promised to send the money.

"Don't you want us to hold some of it for you?" Maggie asked.

"No, I'll be due more when we get back," the sergeant

explained. There was a darkness to his eyes, though, that even Tom noticed.

"Brother," Libbie said, motioning Tom aside. "Don't let him get himself killed. Not now, when we're so close to achieving everything."

"I won't outlive him, Libbie," Tom vowed.

"There's little comfort in that notion," Libbie added. "You'd swat a hornet's nest just to count the stings on your nose!"

"It's the Indians who should fret," Tom assured the women. "They're the ones facing the hard road." He failed to convince them, though.

Over the next three weeks, any misgivings Tom might have had faded into memory. The column wound its way westward without a hint of trouble. With Charley Reynolds leading the way, they put miles behind them as they passed a country so devoid of human life that it appeared to be at the edge of the world. Except for a freak summer blizzard that struck the first day of June, nothing slowed the march. The snows themselves passed after two days, and the march resumed.

"It's well-watered country," Otis Turner observed as the regiment rode along the Yellowstone. "Be fair land for raising horses. Once the hostiles are dealt with, I may come back here and build myself a little place, maybe run some cattle."

"A man could do worse," Tom said, glad that his sergeant had recovered his wits.

A few days later scouts sent out from Gibbon's column arrived with word of the northern prong's movements. Terry met with his commanders to make plans, but Tom merely grinned.

Still thinks he's in command, does he? Tom couldn't help thinking.

In truth, Terry *was* in command, and his actions that next week and a half perplexed Tom considerably. The general met with Gibbon to plan strategy, but he also dispatched four companies of the Seventh under Reno to scour the Tongue River for signs of Sioux camps.

"There's generalship for you," Tom remarked. "Split off a quarter of your command under the least able officer in the field and send them chasing shadows."

Indeed, others were saying far less kind things about the plan.

"If they run across Sioux, they're too few to do much good and too many to avoid being seen," Captain Frederick Benteen observed.

Autie seemed oddly distracted. He busied himself writing articles for the *New York Herald* and scribbling letters of reassurance to Libbie. Even when Reno failed to reappear as scheduled, the Seventh's colonel expressed no concern.

"The Rees don't expect any Sioux down there," Autie explained. "Terry's just being careful. He doesn't want us trapped between two bands. Crook did well enough in his fight, but he lost his supplies. We won't make the same mistake this time."

Later, when Reno finally reappeared, the major explained the delay was caused by his decision to turn west and scout the Rosebud.

"We found five camps, each of them large. Maybe four hundred lodges," the major exclaimed. "That's a lot of Indians!"

While Custer winced at the thought that Reno had risked half the regiment for little purpose, Terry exploded.

"Gibbon's already scouted that stretch!" the general shouted. "All you've done is lose precious time and maybe alert the enemy!"

Autie also had unkind words for the major. Everyone in the command heard the men shouting, but the actual words were difficult to make out. Terry, extremely frustrated, set off to locate Gibbon and script a new plan.

On June 21, Autie joined the two generals aboard the steamboat *Far West* for a conference. Afterward Terry met with his cavalry commander. Tom wasn't privy to the meeting, but afterward Terry left to join the infantry column, leaving George Armstrong Custer in independent command of the cavalry force.

"Be some hard riding the next few days," Otis Turner said when Terry and his escort departed. Already men were packing mules with supplies and extra ammunition. It didn't require genius to realize Custer intended to travel light if he was leaving the wagons behind.

"Do you know what he's got planned?" young Boston asked Tom. "Nobody'll tell me anything."

"Nobody besides Autie needs to know," Tom explained. "Oh, I know the West Point folks expect everything to be written out and all, but Autie doesn't always know what he's going to do until he does it. He's got a knack for carrying it off, though."

"The scouts are talking about a thousand Indians," Boston said, staring anxiously into the surrounding hills.

"Only a thousand?" Tom said, laughing. "Hardly worth the Seventh's trouble. Now, five thousand or ten thousand. That would make for a fair day's fighting!"

The men around him laughed, and the mood lightened. Later Sergeant Turner appeared.

"Your offer of a sip still good, Captain?" he asked.

"Sure," Tom answered, producing the flask

"When this is all over with, we won't all be alive, Captain. If it's my time, you'll let my ma know I was a good soldier?"

"You worry too much," Tom said, retrieving the flask and taking a sip himself. "We've got Custer's luck with us, don't we?"

"It's always good, is it?"

"Always," Tom insisted.

"Better be," Turner said, reaching for the flask again. "I've got itchy toes."

"That mean anything?"

"Last time I had itchy toes, Hood's whole division hit

us at Chickamauga. I spent better than a year in rebel prison camps.''

"Sioux don't take prisoners," Tom pointed out.

"You think I don't know that?'' Turner asked. He took a long draw at the flask and then another. "I had a dream last night. First of the type I ever had. Saw my death, Captain, alongside most of the boys camped here this night.''

"Dreams,'' Tom said, snatching the flask back and screwing on its lid. "You'll be telling me you believe in Sioux spirits next.''

"I wouldn't know of them, sir, but I only met two men during the whole Rebellion who dreamed they would die in battle. Both did.''

"Easy to see why, Sergeant. You get so caught up with worrying that you forget what you're about. Me, I never worry. I should be dead a dozen times. One fool reb shot me right in the face. See the scar there? An inch over and I'd be part of a Virginia cornfield. It's best just to ride hard, yell a lot, and fight like a lunatic.''

"I'm certain you're right, Captain. Thank you for the spirits.''

"Don't worry, Sergeant. I never led a company to its death.''

"Do the Sioux know that?'' Boston asked, joining the two veteran soldiers.

"Why, if they don't, Autie's sure to tell 'em. Maybe they read the *Herald*.''

Boston managed to laugh at the notion. Tom tried to brighten his own gaze, but he, too, felt the awkward solemnity settling in all around them. If the Black Hills had been a haunted place, then this Rosebud country was doubly so. He would be glad when they were riding again tomorrow. Gladder still when the fighting began.

NINE

On to the Rosebud they went. The scenery around them was changing now. The roses blooming along the creek lifted Tom's spirits as he recalled sunlit days sitting with pretty Ohio girls back home. Since he'd turned sixteen there'd been only the army. Still a man needed company, didn't he? Someone always had a daughter around, and some of the enlisted men weren't particular about where their wives spent their evenings. Army posts attracted unmarried women of every type. From the broad-shouldered Martha Jane Canary to the slender Kate Shaw, they had each had their moments.

Tom tried to clear his mind. There was serious fighting ahead. They were all certain of that now. The Rees were jabbering away with Charley Reynolds about some kind of bad medicine while the Crows lent by Gibbon spoke solemnly of their old enemy, the *Lakota*.

"The Indians are spooked," Boston said, joining his brother at the creek's eastern bank. "I don't think Autie's any too happy, either. That young Crow, Curly, says there's a drawing of our camp in the dirt yonder."

There was worse news. The Rees had found signs of

sweat lodges and the poles of a Sun Dance, the great gathering celebration of the *Lakota*, or Teton Sioux, bands. A fresh scalp was tied to one pole. It had belonged to a young white man, according to Autie's favorite Ree scout, Bloody Knife.

"There's already been a fight," Brewer, the tall German, declared. "Could be Crook got here early. Or maybe Gibbon sent the Second Cavalry down here after all."

"To me hair looks like hair," Otis Turner insisted. "Gibbon won't send his cavalry down here while he takes his blamed infantry west along the Yellowstone. They might have had a captive with 'em."

"I hope it was one of those whiskey peddlers," Boston said. "They've been a plague lately."

"Just doing their job, little brother," Tom argued. "Their prices have done more to keep the company sober than all the lectures Autie has given the last ten years. Besides, it's not a single scalp that worries me."

"What does?"

"That," Tom said, pointing to the trampled rosebushes and muddy bank. The telltale signs of heavy pine poles marked the far bank. Dozens of lodge poles had been moved, and recently. That meant hundreds of Indians.

Martini, the little Italian bugler, sounded officers' call, and Tom instinctively nudged his horse into a trot. Soon the company commanders gathered around their colonel, Major Reno, and the regimental adjutant, Lieutenant William Cooke.

"Looks like we've crossed their trail, sir," Cooke said in his odd accent. Born in Canada and trained by the British, he'd come south to join the Union forces during the Southern Rebellion, as he liked to call it.

"They've seen us coming," Lieutenant Calhoun suggested. "Now they're hightailing it west."

Custer eyed Reno coldly, then grinned.

"You might have had the glory to yourself if you'd

crossed over on your own," the colonel said. "Now it looks like you'll have to share it with the rest of us."

"You heard the Crows," Lieutenant Charles Varnum, who oversaw the scouts, objected. "They say there are too many. Five, six thousand."

"They're on the run," Autie said, waving his arm toward the trail. "Look at them. They've broken into small bands. They're not forming up to fight. If we ride hard, we'll find their camps. We hit those villages, and the men will have to stand. We capture the women, the men will come in with their tails between their legs. Did it on the Washita, didn't we? We'll do it here the same way."

"Do you want to send word to General Terry?" Reno asked.

"You asking that?" the colonel responded. "You didn't bother telling us where you went. I don't see any need to tell Terry. He sent us this way, hoping we'd find sign. He'll be coming around on the north side, he and Gibbon. If Crook's up from the south, we've got them. The whole blessed Sioux nation in one valley. You know, this is apt to be the last big fight against Indians. The men that win it will be remembered a long time. Their grandsons will study how it was done in a West Point classroom. Do you doubt God intends it should be me they're studying?"

"Not a bit, Autie," Tom told his brother. The others laughed their agreement.

"Form your companies, gentlemen," their commander ordered. "We've got hard work ahead of us."

"The pack train's fallen behind again," Cooke noted.

"Well, see if they can be hurried along," Colonel Custer grumbled. "I know we're setting a killing pace, but we've got to catch up before they escape."

"Ought to be a trifle careful, too," Reno warned. "If they know we're coming, we could be the ones caught in a trap."

"No, not George Armstrong Custer," Tom bellowed.

"Haven't you heard, Major? My brother's got the devil's own luck."

"Luck can turn," someone said.

"Not Custer's luck," Tom insisted. "I'm ready, Autie. Want my boys to lead?"

"No, I want the whole regiment formed and on the move. Now!"

The shout startled them, and they hurried to reform the column. Soon the whole regiment save for Company B, stuck with bringing the pack mules along, splashed across Rosebud Creek.

They rode with a new urgency that day. It struck Tom as odd that the Rees rode alongside his brother instead of going ahead as the Crows did. There was something else, too. From time to time one of the Rees would ride off alone, dismount, and sit cross-legged beneath a cottonwood.

"They're worried," Otis Turner explained. "Think the Sioux have made powerful medicine. They sing to prepare themselves for the afterlife or whatever they believe follows this one."

"I don't like the notion of scared Rees," Tom confessed.

"The colonel doesn't seem too worried," Turner pointed out.

"Well, he's luckier than most of us mortals."

"Not luckier than you, sir," Turner argued. "I heard about that leap over the rebel works. Shot you point-blank and only mussed your hair a trace."

"Did a hair more than that," Tom said, running a finger along the scar. "There's going to be a battle before this campaign's over, Sergeant. Men will die, but it will bring an end to these hostiles terrorizing settlements, blocking the railroads, and choking off the proper settlement of this country. My brother knows this. He also knows he hasn't got too many more chances."

Tom paused long enough to study his older brother, riding near the head of the column as he generally did. He wore a gaudy buckskin jacket that the men alternately joked about and admired. He also wore a broad-brimmed white hat to protect his head from the blazing summer sun. He didn't like to be seen bareheaded anymore. His hair was growing thin in front, and there was a large patch of bare scalp on top. Libbie had convinced him to trim his flowing locks to make the balding less noticeable.

"You'll prove a poor trophy for a Sioux," Boston had told the colonel.

"Oh, the man who kills me will be remembered," Autie had retorted. "I just hope he's not a Cheyenne. He'd likely cut more than a forelock!"

"Better you than me," Tom had remarked.

George Armstrong Custer, lieutenant colonel and brevet major general, drove his men relentlessly that day. He seemed anxious for battle while at the same time preoccupied with the Rees' odd conduct. Twice he signaled brief halts, but he gave the men few chances to rest or water their mounts. When the regiment finally made camp that evening, Tom couldn't help grinning at the way many of the recruits sat on their haunches.

"Not you, too, nephew," he remarked, noticed a tender-bottomed Autie Reed searching out a soft bit of grass for a chair.

"They say you're a brave man, Uncle Tom," Reed responded. "Think you've got the nerve to ask the general to ease up a bit?"

"He'll kill a lot of horses," Boston added.

"You boys don't understand," Tom told them. "If we're a day late reaching the Sioux camps, we'll have come all this way for nothing. That won't do."

"Well, miserable as I am, it's been worth the trip seeing all this," Reed said, pointing to the wild hills dotted with bushes and the distant crests of the Big Horn Mountains. "We will catch the Sioux, won't we, Tom?"

"I hate to consider otherwise," Tom grumbled. "Don't forget, too, that Crook's down south and Gibbon's to the north. I don't see this big a camp slipping away from the three of us."

Tom Custer believed those words. Toward the end of the day, he'd spied fresh dung left by unshod ponies. The Seventh was closing the distance. Tomorrow perhaps they would spy the camps. The Crows returned while the command was eating its supper of hard biscuit, salt pork, and beans. After a brief discussion, the colonel sent word around that the men should get some rest. They would resume the hunt at eleven.

"We'll be afoot tomorrow," Sergeant Turner declared as he passed Tom's makeshift bed. "Captain, the horses won't manage the trip. They're breaking down."

"I know, Turner, but what else can we do?"

"The men aren't much better," the sergeant explained. "Two of 'em fell asleep in the saddle this afternoon."

Tom nodded. A short while later half the other company commanders appealed to him to speak to his brother. Men and animals were at the breaking point. They needed rest, not a night march.

The elder Custer was past listening to arguments, though.

"We're all tired, Tom," he told his brother. "I had to send the scouts back out with hardly a biscuit to chew or a cup of coffee. I can't risk the Sioux slipping away. Not now, when we're so close."

"Have you considered how poor a chance we stand running them down if we set them to flight?" Tom asked. "A cavalry regiment isn't much use without its mounts. We should hold up and let the pack animals catch up, too. We're short of grain, and we'll need the ammunition if there's a battle."

"Leave me to worry about that. We have to get over that next ridge and have a look. There's a river there, a meandering sort of stream, that's a branch of the Big Horn.

Little Big Horn, they call it. The Crows say that's where the agency Indians have gathered. He thinks Sitting Bull's band is there, too. Most of the Cheyennes may have camped nearby.''

"You figure to strike them tomorrow?''

"Probably later if they don't break down the camp. They give a hint of moving, we'll be on their hides like wolverines.''

"Just like the old Michigan Brigade at Hanover, eh, Autie?''

"More like the way you took to that Cheyenne girl at Fort Supply.''

"I hope to have as much pleasure.''

The brothers shared a laugh. Then they parted company. The colonel continued his planning. Tom collapsed in his blankets and tried to find some rest.

As promised, the buglers roused the command an hour before midnight, and the march resumed. The air was cooler, and Tom noticed the men had donned overcoats or buffalo hides to stave off the bitter bite of a northerly wind.

"Feels odd, riding under a Sioux moon,'' Private Brewer said, clearly unnerved by the experience.

"It's downright foolish,'' Turner added. "Trying to find your way when an idiot knows it's death to enter Sioux country by night.''

"Take care who you call idiot,'' Tom warned. "Sound carries far on a moonlit night.''

The complaints died down thereafter. The men were simply too tired to think. Most closed their eyes and hoped their mount would follow the men beside and ahead of him. Turner rode between ranks, waking a man here and there, but there were too many for a solitary sergeant to keep awake. Company C made its way westward in a daze that grew worse as dust from the horses' hooves obscured the stars overhead and choked both men and mounts. Later the distant flashes of lightning to the south gave faint illumination to the mountains.

"Old George Crook will be dragging himself along there," Tom whispered to his weary horse. Some of the officers had argued for joining the other commands, but that had never been anyone's intention.

"It's fundamental tactics," Reno complained to anyone who would listen. "Never divide your command in the face of the enemy."

Reno was unlucky, though. Custers believed in audacity more than tactics. How else did a man who graduated last in his class at West Point achieve a general's star in his twenties? At Hanover, *General* Custer had committed his brigade piecemeal to a battle some thought needless. And Jeb Stuart, the phantom that had plagued Union armies for two years, failed to reach Gettysburg, where he might have told Bobby Lee what others couldn't, that the enemy was strong and holding all the cards. Instead the Army of Northern Virginia wrecked itself in a charge from which it never recovered.

And what of Sayler's Creek? When others had hung back, Custer had charged, cutting off an entire rebel corps, or at least what was left of it after months in Petersburg trenches.

"Autie knows what he's about," Tom had assured his younger brother and nephew as they prepared for the long night march. If he ignored military doctrine and advice from his scouts, it was because in the end he knew what counted most was the willingness to risk everything on the throw of the dice. Tom knew his brother worried some about the nervous Rees, but hadn't scouts warned of great encampments back in '68 when the Seventh had smashed old Black Kettle's Cheyennes? Nothing was ever won without risk, and the greatest victories were always won when the danger was greatest.

George Armstrong Custer willed his men onward that night. Companies began to spread out on separate trails, and men fought to keep their horses under control. Then came the word.

"Single file now, boys."

Ahead lay more difficult terrain. Still, the dark and the dust that blinded and choked the men also cloked them from prying eyes. If only it could have quieted them as well.

It was a real problem, moving a regiment of cavalry without sound. Tin cups rattled against holsters, and the mules brayed and balked at every obstacle. The civilian packers hadn't given proper care to the packs, and Lieutenant Cooke could be heard cursing each time a mule lost its load. The Seventh Cavalry was leaving a trail of spilled oats, tins of beans, and horse droppings that a blind man could follow!

No matter, Tom thought. *Danger's ahead and not behind.*

Ten miles they rode that night, a full day's march by any normal man's reckoning. Only then did word come to fall out. Tom tried to gather his company into some semblance of order before galloping to his brother's side. Autie was caked in dust except for where he'd tied a kerchief to protect his nose. Tom couldn't help the temptation to whistle a tune. He chose "Garry Owen," the Irish drinking song the regiment had adopted for its own.

"We haven't found much glory tonight, Tom," Autie remarked. "But there's a place close by the Crows say will show the Little Big Horn."

"And maybe the Sioux?" Tom added.

"If they haven't broken camp already."

Bloody Knife and the other Rees shook their heads. Tom knew, too. The droppings on the trail were too fresh. Besides, hauling women and children, the villages could only travel so far in a day's time. Autie had stolen a day's march on everyone. The Seventh would find Sioux to fight.

"Plenty *Lakota*," one of the Crows agreed. "Too many."

"Autie, where are you going now?" Tom asked as his brother nudged his horse into motion.

"To have a look for myself, little brother," the colonel answered. "Get what rest you can and see to the horses. Tomorrow we've got serious business to get done."

TEN

He was called *Pispiza*, the prairie dog. It wasn't a name to crow about when riding through the camp circles of the other *Lakota* bands or even one most took very seriously. His brother taunted him about it.

"What can the old men have been thinking, giving you a name like that," *Hoka*, the badger, complained. "It's no name for a fighter."

More than a fighter, though, *Pispiza* was a watchful sort of boy. And although he had walked the world only fourteen summers, he had won a man's name the week before, driving off the white soldiers coming up Rosebud Creek from the south. It had been a day for which he had long waited, a day when he could count coup and stand among his uncles and older brother as a man of the people. His father, who had remained at the agency with *Sinte Gleska*, Spotted Tail, had warned against fighting the *Wasicum*, the white men.

"Our chiefs have gone to see the *Wasicum* world. They are too many to fight," *Canska*, the red-legged hawk, had warned. "I don't wish to live longer than my sons. Too many among our people have already done so."

Boys rarely listened to the cautious words of their elders, though. Among the young men who had left the agencies were several sons of treaty chiefs. Their fathers' words may have been good, but they also recalled the grandfathers' tales of how a warrior won a name fighting the enemies of the people, not chewing cow meat and drinking *Wasicum* spirit water.

"We must go and fight with our cousins," *Hoka* had told him. "Our father's wrong about the *Wasicum*. We may not kill all of them, but it doesn't matter. Already they are swallowing the world. They will devour us, too."

It was true. The yellow-haired soldier chief, Custer, had broken the word of his chief by riding into *Paha Sapa*, the sacred heart of the world. Custer! He was the one who killed his father's relatives on treaty land at the Washita River. *Pispiza* had hunted rabbits with one cousin who had died that day. An uncle killed there had crafted the boy's first bow.

"What use are treaties?" his own father had screamed when riders brought the news.

Now hundreds of white men came to claw at Grandmother Earth, scarring the land and disturbing the tranquillity of the most *wakan* of all places. If a man wouldn't fight for the heart of his people, he could never number himself among the warriors.

And so *Pispiza* had ridden out with his brother when the first green blades of buffalo grass poked through the snow-covered earth.

"First we'll hunt with our cousins," *Hoka* had explained. "Then we'll fight the *Wasicum* soldiers."

Despite the arguments of the treaty chiefs, most of the *Lakotas* believed the bluecoat soldiers would come out onto the plains that summer to fight the roamers, the bands that had refused to leave the good hunting country and settle near the agencies.

"Why should they?" *Hoka* asked. "We won our fight

with the other bluecoats. The treaty paper promised us these lands.''

Now the white men claimed the paper gave the *Lakotas* only a piece of their old country. Those who remained in the Powder River country or in the Big Horns, where they had always lived, would be punished if they did not come east.

It was crazy, most agreed. Riders went out to tell the roamers. Snows came late that year, though, and even had they wished to come in to the agencies, there was no way to do it.

''If there's going to be a fight, I want to be with the warriors,'' *Hoka* had declared.

Pispiza knew what his brother was thinking. They still had relatives with the *Sahiyelas,* the people the whites called Cheyenne. An unmarried man had a responsibility to protect the helpless ones. There was little danger at the agency. But on the Powder River, their father's sister had only her children, none of them as old as Hoka, to protect her and the younger ones.

The brothers rode as swiftly as the country and the cold allowed. They were nevertheless too late. When they reached the camp of their father's sister, they discovered the bluecoat soldiers had already been there. The *Sahiyela* camp was only ashes, and the woman they had sought was no more. Two cousins were among the *Oglalas* now, their brother *Lakotas*. All *Pispiza* and *Hoka* could do was cut their hair short and sing mourning songs.

They located their cousins in the great camp on Rosebud Creek. The *Lakotas* were remaking the world under the direction of the *Hunkpapa* dreamer, the one the whites called Sitting Bull. He was no warrior, but he had powerful medicine. Once the dancers had completed their suffering, and each part of the deliberate ceremony had been completed, the *Hunkpapa* told of his vision, of soldiers falling into the camps of the *Lakotas* and their relatives.

"The chance will only come once," he warned. "We must be ready."

Even the youngest men took the vision seriously. Scouts kept watch well beyond the lodge circles, and men prepared their weapons. Sweat lodges were set up, and the men cleansed themselves for the coming fight. Old animosities between bands were set aside, and riders were even sent to the old enemy, the Crows, to see if they would join the fighting.

The Crows didn't come, but the *Sahiyelas* formed a considerable camp. Some had even come up from the south country, singing their songs of revenge for the murder of their relatives on the Washita River and before that at Sand Creek. All the *Lakota* bands were there, and even some *Nakota* and *Dakota* people had joined the great village. *Pispiza* had never seen so many in one place.

There was still a chill in the air when scouts brought word that Three Stars, the general called Crook, was coming back to kill more of the people. This time, though, the *Lakotas* were going to be ready for him. Instead of defending a winter camp, with women and children to keep safe, warriors would ride out to meet the bluecoats. *Hoka* and a handful of other *Sicangus* from the agency were going with the *Oglalas*.

"This will be a hard fight, little brother," *Hoka* had explained as he painted his face for war. "You can come and hold our spare ponies, but keep away from the bluecoats. Their guns fire a long way, and their lead kills pony boys as fast as it kills men."

"No faster than it kills sleeping women," *Pispiza* had replied. "I, too, should prepare myself."

"They won't take you if they know you intend to join the fighting," *Hoka* warned. "We have pledged to be decoys, to draw the enemy to our brothers. It's dangerous, and it requires patience."

"I have the patience of a spider," *Pispiza* had replied.

"Then use it and wait for another day. There are many bluecoats. I can't kill all of them."

His brother grinned, and *Pispiza* knew the arguing was over. You couldn't quarrel with *Hoka* once he began laughing at you. *Pispiza* contented himself with holding spare ponies and waiting his chance. It turned out no great patience was required. The *Oglalas* appeared first, startling the bluecoats. When the young riders turned to lure the white devils into the waiting ambush, though, the soldiers failed to take the bait. Instead, one line turned away and headed directly toward the sprawling encampment on the Rosebud.

"Ah, you're alone," an old man said, joining *Pispiza* on the ridge overlooking the scene. "What should we do?" he asked, speaking the language his father's people used.

"I must hurry and prepare myself," the young man replied. "The *Wihio* come this way. We must protect the helpless ones."

"So, you're a man of the people then," the old man observed. "Your hair's cut short in mourning. As mine is. Here, I have some paint. Use the yellow across your forehead. I always do."

"Do you also know the proper prayers?" *Pispiza* asked as he painted his face.

"Ah, they're old prayers, taught me by the *Suhtai* grandfathers."

"You're *Sahiyela* then?"

"You're not?" the old man asked, speaking *Lakota* now. "I thought I remembered you from the buffalo hunt two summers past."

"My brother and I rode with the husband of my father's sister."

"He's begun the long walk now?"

"Yes," *Pispiza* explained. "The Pawnees killed him. Now more relatives are dead."

"Then you'll stand here and fight alongside me?"

"A man can't run," *Pispiza* insisted. The old man nodded. It was foolish, the notion that an old wrinkled warrior and a boy armed only with a short bow could stave off the attack of a bluecoat army. But when the old man started down the ridge toward the approaching enemy, *Pispiza* dropped the ropes of the horses he was holding. Taking up the melody if not the words of the old *Suhtai* song, he followed.

"Ayyyy!" *Pispiza* screamed as he left the ridge. "It's a good day to die."

"A better day to make others die!" his companion shouted.

The old man then charged recklessly at a few bluecoats who had come out ahead. Two fired their rifles at him, but the bullets had no power over the old *Sahiyela*. One struck his shield while the others went high.

"Aim at his horse, you fools!" a big, broad-shouldered brute with three yellow marks sewn on his blue sleeve shouted.

Pispiza strung his bow, notched an arrow, and charged. While fifty feet away, he sent his first arrow flying. It killed one of the lead bluecoats' pony, and the old man whirled past. The boy's second arrow struck the shouting man with the yellow markings on his sleeve. The point went through the neck and emerged in the throat, silencing his words. The shock of the two-man onslaught threw the bluecoats into temporary confusion. Moments later a large band of *Oglalas* struck their flank and turned them from the camp.

Pispiza learned of that later. He was singing his death chant as he heard rifle balls strike his pony's flank. He leaped from the dying animal and slapped his bow against the big *Wasicum*'s shoulder.

"I'm first!" he shouted, counting his first coup. The helpless bluecoat was struggling to pull the arrow from his throat when *Pispiza* drove the blade of a good iron knife into the man's big chest. The boy heard the sound of escaping breath as the edge opened a lung. The big man fell back onto the ground, staring in wild-eyed disbelief at his youthful killer.

A slender bluecoat fired a pistol at *Pispiza*'s head, but the shot went wide. The boy then fired an arrow at the soldier, striking him in the right knee. The wounded man managed to turn his horse and escape before another arrow could finish the task.

By that point the *Oglalas* were pouring out of their hiding places in the ravines and down from the surrounding ridges. Three Stars had a real battle on his hands now, and the fighting was furious. *Pispiza*, afoot, had lost his chance for more glory. He contented himself with taking the forelock of the dead *Wasicum* and stripping the corpse. The boy was especially proud of the fine steel pistol and leather belt. He took the bluecoat's shirt as a reminder of the fight, but he was disappointed to lose the big black horse the man had been riding. It had a good rifle in a sling beside the saddle.

"So, you're not dead after all," the old man exclaimed as he rode up. "See how we two frightened away a whole army?"

"I think it was the *Oglalas*, Uncle," *Pispiza* argued. "I don't scare anyone."

"That was our secret, our *wakan*," the old man declared. "Do you know what they call me?"

"No," the boy admitted. "I don't remember you from the buffalo hunt."

"That's because I am invisible. Ah, you *Lakotas* would call me *Pispiza*, the burrowing dog."

The prairie dog? The boy couldn't help laughing.

"It's a good name for a man who the enemy never sees," the *Sahiyela* continued. "I go where I want, living always among my own kind. No one suspects danger, and yet there I am, bringing down my enemy the way *Pispiza* does with his holes."

That night, when he rejoined *Hoka*, the boy little suspected that he would be summoned by the *Sahiyela* Elk

Warriors. There, before a roaring fire, the old man related the tale of their reckless charge. And when the story was over, the Elks shouted their praise and presented him with a fine spotted pony.

"To mark your coup," another Elk said, tying an eagle feather in the boy's hair.

That was but the beginning of the evening. The old man presented a fine elkhorn saddle and a charm made from the claw of a grizzly bear. Tied to a leather strap, it was to be worn around the neck.

"I've grown old walking the world," the ancient Elk said, studying the proud stance of his young acquaintance. "When I was small, nobody saw me, and I was given a name few thought I would keep when I counted coup. I wear it still, though, as a reminder that it is the unseen, the unexpected, that hazards our people. Now I give this name, which the *Lakotas* would say *Pispiza*, to a young one who will guard the welfare of the people as I have always tried to do."

Again the Elks cheered, and the new *Pispiza* smiled.

There was much feasting that night and more the following day. Three Stars had been driven away, but at a cost. Many brave men limped about the camps, and others lay in their lodges, tended by wives and healers. Scaffolds were raised in the adjacent hills even as young men presented the scalps of their enemies to wives and sisters. *Pispiza* gave the one he'd taken to the *Oglala* woman who had taken in his youngest cousin.

"He, too, will earn a brave heart name one day," *Pispiza* boasted.

Among the *Oglalas*, the youngster was hardly seen. Some older boys grumbled that the pistol he wore was too fine a weapon for one unproven in battle, but then *Hoka* would tell them of his brother's coup.

"You should wear the blue shirt," *Hoka* advised. "It will silence the others."

Pispiza would not do it. He had ridden with the old

Sahiyela, who simply called himself Dust, as the camps were moved to the river called Greasy Grass by the *Lakotas*. Dust taught him the old, half-forgotten prayers and cautioned him to be watchful.

"Don't be like those boasters who sing of their victories and forget Sitting Bull's dream," Dust warned. "Three Stars did not touch our camp. We have killing yet to do."

Stories of more soldiers approaching came from the riders sent to the Crow camps up north.

"Two more soldier chiefs are coming," one of the messengers explained. "Three Stars has not returned to the forts on Platte River. The danger remains."

Remains? Pispiza asked silently. *It grows greater.*

And so when scouts were sought to ride out from the big village on the Greasy Grass, he had offered to go.

"You?" the older men had asked. "A rabbit would be a better scout!"

"Maybe, but rabbits don't have words to tell you the enemy's strength," *Pispiza* answered. "I'm small and I know this country. I have hunted here with my cousins. My brother and I will ride back to Rosebud Creek and keep watch."

Other scouts were sent elsewhere, but it was the two slender *Sicangus* who first heard the noise of jingling tin cups. Concealing themselves behind boulders, they detected the approach of many horsemen led by a pair of Ree scouts. The Rees were particularly wary, and the bluecoats that followed were covered with dust, so that they appeared less men than phantoms.

"Go back and tell the others," *Hoka* urged. "The people Sitting Bull said were coming are near."

"You have the faster horse," *Pispiza* argued. "It's for you to do."

"I can't leave my brother here alone," *Hoka* replied. "Come with me."

"Someone has to stay and watch," *Pispiza* countered.

It was his turn to smile, and his brother swallowed his thoughts.

"I need a brother to craft bows for my sons," *Hoka* whispered.

"First you must use your courting flute," *Pispiza* said, grinning. "Hurry."

Pispiza watched his brother depart. He took a bit of yellow powder from a pouch worn on his hip. Spitting into the powder, he made a paste and drew two yellow stripes across his forehead. He then tied the eagle feather in his hair and donned the blue coat. He had the pistol ready, too, but the only one to come close enough to become a target was one of the Rees. That man had no eyes for seeing prairie dogs. He was muttering his death chant.

It was an odd thing to be doing, *Pispiza* thought. Rees were good fighters, and they had battled *Lakotas* often. The old *Hunkpapa's wakan* must be very strong to drive fear into the hearts of old enemies like these.

As a second line of bluecoats passed, *Pispiza* frowned. He read no similar fear in the eyes of these men. Many were tired, true, but the soldier chiefs, the ones with the yellow bars on their shirts, rode with quiet confidence. One, a yellow-haired man on a tall horse, appeared to be humming a song as he worked his way up and down a column of riders. There was something familiar about this man. He had been at the bluecoat fort when he and his father had gone to search for their relatives.

Yes, he was the one who bothered the girls, wasn't he? Yellow Hair's brother. But where was—

Pispiza stared hard at the man in the broad-brimmed white hat and buckskin jacket. This was the bluecoat soldier who had killed so many *Sahiyelas* at Washita River. There was nothing so remarkable about him. He seemed in command, but he rode with neither the fear of the Rees nor the confidence of his brother. Yes, he was a man between the two.

"He has no *wakan*," the boy observed. There was no aura of medicine, of power. "Come, Yellow Hair, fall into our camps," *Pispiza* whispered to the wind. "Let us kill you."

ELEVEN

For many *Lakotas,* it was a remembered fight, the battle waged on the Greasy Grass, or the Little Big Horn, as the whites chose to call it. For *Pispiza,* who found himself cut off by hundreds of bluecoats, it would be a day of confusion and frustration. He was, as before, prepared to die to protect the defenseless ones in the camp, but he found himself instead listening to the sounds of sporadic rifle fire and shrieks of terror from too great a distance to be of much help. When he did finally approach the scene of the fighting, he saw that mixed bands of *Lakotas* and *Sahiyelas* had encircled one group of bluecoats atop a wooded ridge. They appeared to have the *Wasicum* trapped and well in hand, so he chose to turn toward the sound of gunfire coming from downriver, near the northern edge of the great encampment. Here, too, he was disappointed. Swarms of warriors were picking over the bodies of bluecoats already dead.

"This time you're too late," *Hoka* called from the far side of a nearby ravine. Twenty or thirty dead bluecoats lay scattered in that one place. Once he joined his brother, *Pispiza* saw the magnitude of what had been done that day.

Bluecoats seemed to lay everywhere. Except for a few places, they were alone or in small groups.

"Our *wakan* was strong this time," *Hoka* boasted. "Many of the *Wasicum* went mad and threw away their guns. They weren't hard to kill."

"They weren't?" *Pispiza* asked. That seemed odd. The man he had killed was rarely from his thoughts. He found himself wondering if he had left behind a wife and children who would now know hunger.

"You seem troubled," *Hoka* said, leaning over and touching his younger brother's hand. "Is it because you missed the fight?"

"No."

"Your eyes saw them coming. It was just as Sitting Bull saw it. The bluecoats came at our camps, but we stopped them. Another group tried to come around, but more of us were there to punish these. The first group are still alive, but they will soon be out of water. Maybe we will lead the charge that breaks their line."

"I'm not sure this is a good thing," *Pispiza* said, sighing. "There is a bad smell to this place. No good will come of it."

"Two hundred dead bluecoats isn't good?"

"Look at them!" *Pispiza* shouted. "See what's being done to them!"

Women and even small boys ran around the bodies, poking them with sticks or tearing away their clothing. The *Sahiyela* women who remembered what was done at Sand Creek and at the Washita were cutting pieces from the dead soldiers.

"These aren't the men the Crows spoke of," *Pispiza* muttered. "There are still more coming."

"We will kill them, too," *Hoka* declared. "We have broken the *Wasicum* power."

"Have we?" *Pispiza* asked.

He couldn't find it within him to rejoice at the victory. Perhaps his brother was right. He hadn't shared in the fighting, and so he couldn't celebrate the success. A sudden cry drew his attention. Two old women were chasing a big naked white man across a nearby hill. A clump of small boys were standing nearby, laughing.

"What's happened?" *Hoka* asked them.

"He wasn't dead," one of the boys, a *Sihasapa*, explained. "He was pretending."

"He isn't now," *Hoka* pointed out.

"No," the boys said, laughing.

"It was when they started to cut him," a tall boy said, grinning. "He stayed quiet when they took some of his hair. Then they started to cut him somewhere else."

The boys laughed as they made a cutting motion below the belly.

The brothers nodded. They remembered the stories of Sand Creek that their relatives told. It wasn't a thing to laugh at.

"Stop him!" one of the women shouted as the big man finally slung his tormentors aside. "He's getting away."

Pispiza was tempted to let the man flee. It would be interesting to hear him explain how he had lost his clothes and scalp but escaped alive. The *Wasicum* reached down and grabbed a discarded pistol then, and *Hoka* shouted a warning to the laughing boys.

"Think it's funny, eh?" the big man thundered, firing the gun. The first chamber was empty, though, and the boys managed to scatter before the naked man pulled the trigger a second time. A bullet screamed off a rock and nicked one of the children's left ear.

"Ayyyy!" *Pispiza* yelled as he charged toward the wild-eyed giant. With blood flowing across his face and a gaping hole in one arm, he had the appearance of a demon.

"Is that you, Tucker?" the man cried out. "Have you come to save me?"

Pispiza drew out the pistol he'd taken from the dead bluecoat, but he paused. The *Wasicum* seemed mad, confused. He looked upon the boy as a friend, a savior. Then

Pispiza realized he was wearing the blue shirt. Always light-skinned for a *Sicangu*, he had been mistaken for a friend by the big white man.

"Sergeant?" the giant called. He then spoke a strange, guttural language and dropped to his knees. He had a silver cross in one hand, and he seemed to be praying to it.

"He's making medicine," *Hoka* said, dismounting. "Give me the pistol, little brother."

"No," *Pispiza* answered, replacing the pistol in its holster. Instead he drew out his bow and strung it. He then notched an arrow and approached the praying man. The big *Wasicum* finished his prayer and looked up.

"I'm ready now," he remarked.

Pispiza loosed his arrow, and it tore through the man's bare chest and ended his life. The younger boys then charged the corpse and began stabbing it with their tiny arrows. The *Sahiyelas* also returned, eager to finish what they had started.

"You should count coup," *Hoka* advised his brother after prying the pistol out of the hands of one of the *Sihasapa* boys. "You made the killing shot."

"This one won't haunt me," *Pispiza* replied. "He was ready."

The young warrior then dismounted and led his spotted pony along the ridge toward the place where the last of the bluecoats had fallen. There, in a little circle of corpses, lay Yellow Hair. Blood trickled from his ears.

"It was my people," Dust said, joining the brothers. "It's said they warned him not to come again upon our people. They have cleaned his ears so that he can hear better."

Yellow Hair's brother was nearby. The *Sahiyelas* were cutting him to pieces. They had already pounded his head flat with stone mallets. His clothes were in a pile nearby. Something bright and shiny attracted *Pispiza*'s attention.

"What is it?" *Hoka* asked.

"Some kind of *wakan*. It makes its own sounds."

Pispiza lifted the small, round object to his ear and listened. It was like the heartbeat of a man, only steadier. A part of it opened, revealing arrows that pointed in different directions.

"It's a bad thing, taking things from the *Wihio*," Dust warned. "Look, there's white man's words on there, too. If they catch you with it, they'll know you took it from Yellow Hair's brother."

"If they catch me, it won't matter," *Pispiza* argued. "After what's happened here, there can be no peace with the bluecoats. Only dying."

Sitting Bull's vision had promised victory, but the dreamer could see no great event that would follow that victory. By the time *Pispiza* and *Hoka* returned to the *Oglala* camp, the women were already breaking down the lodges.

"Hurry," they called to their husbands and sons. "More bluecoats are coming. Hurry!"

Pispiza, who had saved his pistol bullets for the bluecoats on the hill south of the great village, was especially downcast.

"We should kill the ones here and then fight the others!" *Hoka* exclaimed.

"It's easy for boys without responsibility for wives and daughters to talk that way," an *Oglala* named *Halhate*, the magpie, argued. His wife had been the one who took in the orphaned cousins.

"Come, brother," *Pispiza* urged. If *Hoka* didn't understand what the man was saying, his younger brother did. "Our cousins are better off with these people. They're right. We must think of the defenseless ones."

The principal *Lakota* left only a small party to watch the trapped bluecoats and sent a second party to keep watch on Three Stars's men camped on Rosebud Creek. A third, somewhat larger group rode north to screen the departing village from the large army of relatively fresh bluecoats coming up the Greasy Grass from the north.

"It's the only thing to do," old Dust lamented. "We've shot our arrows and used all our bullets. We must find another place, another day to fight."

It was a sad admission for them all. Moreover, as the bands split apart to take their separate paths from the place of great victory, of great death, they all knew there would never again be such a large powerful array of the people in one place. No, thereafter it would be a war of ambush and pursuit, of wearing down the *Wasicum* or surrendering to him.

"They're all around us," Dust remarked as he bid farewell to his young *Sicangu* namesake. "There's no longer a place where we can go and be one with the Great Mystery."

"There's one place," *Pispiza* argued. "The other side."

"Yes, and I will soon begin the long climb," Dust observed. "You're too young to speak of death, though. There's hunting to be done, a wife to take, little ones to father."

"That's what our father says," *Hoka* noted. "I wonder if we will do any of those things, though."

That day, when the young men should have been celebrating a great triumph, they found only dread and worry facing them. Some of the young war chiefs continued to talk of killing all the whites, but two hundred had been a lot, and it now seemed as nothing. As *Pispiza* turned north to join the scouts, he lifted Yellow Hair's brother's shiny bauble to his ear once more. It had grown silent.

"The *wakan* has gone," the boy said, flinging it away. "Only fighting and death is left to us now."

TWELVE

Amos Suggs rode into Custer City that August a tired man. Two months earlier, serving as chief scout for John Gibbon's Montana column, he'd felt like a young forty-seven. Not now. He was caked in dust and weary from head to toe.

"Custer City," he mumbled. "Only dead a month and they're already naming places after the man."

Of course, calling *that* particular place a city was a stretch by anybody's calculation. There were only a few buildings up with walls. Mostly it was a universe of miners' tents, clapboard saloons, and fancy houses. Ever since a few miners had struck genuine veins of gold, white men had poured into *Paha Sapa*, the sacred heart of the Sioux country. "Black Hills," it was loosely translated. Well, the hills weren't half black. They were mainly green with tall pines and blue with flowing streams. Black? Not since buffalo had covered the land.

Things change, old-timer, he told himself. When he was a nineteen-year-old hero of the fighting with Mexico, he could have ridden all day and all night for half a week. Now six hours in the saddle left him fatigued. And what

had he gained for twenty years' service with and for the
army? Not so much as a thank you or the offer of supply
clerk for one of the new Montana posts!

If only Charley Reynolds hadn't ridden off and got himself killed with the Seventh Cavalry! Lonesome Charley
would have found his old friend work somewhere, somehow. With the whole U.S. Army off shooting hostile Sioux
and Cheyenne, though, they didn't need old hands like
Amos Suggs to talk to the scouts or treat with the hostiles.
No, after Custer's death, nobody wearing blue was very
interesting in talking.

There were reasons, Suggs supposed. He remembered
that bright morning when he and the vanguard of the Second Cavalry had approached the Little Big Horn. Young
Curly, the teenage Crow, had been waiting for them. Even
before the young man began jabbering about a big fight
and many dead soldiers, Suggs had known that Custer's
luck had run out. Circling buzzards and a sickly sweet odor
carried on a southerly breeze marked a place of much
death.

That same day Suggs had stood beside Gibbon, watching the surviving members of the Seventh scratching out
shallow graves for the bodies of their slain comrades. It
was an awful thing to behold, those bodies. Suggs had seen
carnage in Mexico, and he'd been with John Buford when
General Henry Heth had broken his ranks against two bri-
gades of cavalry that first day at Gettysburg. He'd witnessed Pickett's Charge and seen Grant kill off a division
at Cold Harbor. Before, there had seemed a purpose to the
dying, if such a thing was possible. The men had at least
died in line, facing the enemy. On the Little Big Horn the
men of the Seventh had often fought their own private
wars against small parties of Indians, and they had all too
often died alone, to no purpose whatsoever.

And the bodies! Even before the birds and animals had
started picking at them, those men had been battered and
mutilated. Most were stripped, and some had been torn into

so many pieces it was impossible to be sure that all the parts of the same man were being put in his grave. With the afternoon sun putrefying the remains, nobody spent a lot of time worrying over such things. They merely covered them up the best they could and tried to identify the officers.

Custer himself hadn't fared too poorly. Nearby young Boston Custer and the other boy, a nephew according to Marcus Reno, had been fairly easy to spot, too. Their hands and paler flesh set them apart from the five companies of veterans scattered along the ridges above the river. Tom Custer, too, was located. He'd been fond of tattoos, and despite being disemboweled and having his face pounded to mush, the men knew it was him. The tall Canadian, Cooke, had distinctive whiskers. Still there were several officers and nearly fifty men unaccounted for.

"Take the Crows and have a look," Gibbon had ordered, and Amos Suggs, as always, had gone. It was across the river, near the poles of an abandoned lodge, that Suggs had seen a flash of light.

"What is it?" Stalking Wolf, another of the boy scouts, asked.

"A timepiece," Suggs had answered. He dismounted and had a closer look. It was a good one, too. Likely gold. It wasn't ticking, but—Suggs had only to wind it a few times before the watch came to life. There was something peculiar about the sound, though. Amos had grown up at his grandfather's place in St. Louis. The old man, like many of the Germans who had settled there, was a craftsman. His specialty was clocks, and he'd showed young Amos a few things before the boy had broken his family's heart and ridden off to be a soldier.

Suggs examined the casing first. It had an inscription which, though scratched a bit, betrayed the name of its original owner. Lucius Bratton? He wasn't with the Seventh anymore, was he? A colonel? Maybe old Bratton had

the watch engraved to fool the girls, make him appear
more important.

Suggs hadn't paid much attention at the time. His job
had been to find survivors, not pick up souvenirs. They'd
found no white men west of the river. There were a few
Lakota burials here and there. The Crows tore down two
of them out of pure spite. They had little love for their old
enemies, but Suggs put an end to it before they destroyed
a third.

"Won't do to stir up their ghosts, boys," he told the
Crows. "There was strong medicine used here. You don't
want it to find you, do you?"

The Crows weren't certain they cared, so Suggs produced a pistol. A shot fired into the rocky ground between
the scaffold and the Crows convinced them. They rode
only until they spied the distant dust thrown up by the
fleeing Indians before turning back to report to Gibbon.

"Nobody that way," Suggs explained. "Maybe to the
east."

"We're sending the wounded out that way," Gibbon
explained. "They can search that ground. I don't think
anybody rode away from here. More likely the Sioux took
captives."

Suggs thought it unlikely. There were dense nests of
brush and wicked ravines everywhere. Fifty men could
easily lie there, hidden from easy viewing. There was no
point in trying to educate generals, though. Suggs had
worn the eagles of a full colonel a dozen years before, but
he'd lost any chance at a regular's commission when he
challenged the wisdom of torching the Shenandoah Valley.

"Most of these poor folks are simple farmers," Suggs
had argued. "Makes no sense slaughtering their animals
and burning their fields. The rebs are done for, sir. Old
Stonewall's not going to rise up out of his grave and come
marching back up the Valley!"

Amos Suggs might have told a soldier like John Buford
such a thing. The words were directed at Little Phil Sher-

idan, though. Suggs was half a foot taller, and Sheridan wasn't tolerant of volunteer officers, especially tall ones, questioning his orders.

"You're relieved, sir," the little general had responded. "Major, burn those farms!"

His second in command, Joe Watters, had done as he was told. Watters likely would have gotten at least a captain's bars if the rebs hadn't killed him outside Richmond. Amos Suggs had passed two weeks in close confinement before being assigned duty overseeing the hundreds of prisoners who were returned when the exchange was resumed. Those scarecrows weren't fit for more combat. It was a worse sort of prison than a jail, drafting discharges while his old command died burning farms and ripping up railroad track.

Sheridan was said to have a long memory. His mood wasn't made any better when word reached him that his pet monkey, George Custer, had lost half the Seventh and himself along with it fighting Sioux at the Little Big Horn. It wasn't but a week later that Suggs found himself unemployed.

"Sir, you'll need men who know the Crows," he'd told General Terry. "I lived with 'em, you know."

"I know, Amos, and I'm sorry I can't do better by you," the soft-spoken general added. "I follow my orders, though. Apparently better than you do."

Sure, it was Sheridan, Suggs thought. But in the end he'd still been only a scout. And now—

It was the watch that had brought him to the Black Hills gold camps. Lucius Bratton's watch. Chatting with the survivors of the Seventh on the long voyage down the Yellowstone aboard the *Far West,* he'd learned the tale. Lucius Bratton had found the mother of all gold strikes. He'd died with nuggets the size of a man's fist in his pockets. They'd heard as much from Isaac Pettis, the corporal from Company C who had left the army to hunt the place on his own.

And the watch? Tom Custer had bought it, but it hadn't held any clues to the strike. Any secrets Lucius Bratton had died with him.

But then Tom Custer didn't know timepieces. Neither did Pettis.

"You were a wise old bird, Grandpa," Suggs had whispered as he examined the watch closely. There had been the usual cover that lifted, exposing the face. On the back side, a watchmaker would pry open the cover to work on the wheels inside. But there was a third, cleverly hidden, panel. It might normally have held a photograph, but instead Suggs had found a bloody scrap of thin paper. At first he wasn't able to restrain his glee. Surely it was a map. Bratton was giving up his secret after all!

It wasn't. There were only dots and dashes faintly scrawled by a feeble hand.

"Likely a code," a telegraphist in Bismarck had suggested. "Doesn't mean anything in Morse. Must be some private sort of message. He have friends? Family? Might be they'd know."

That was the trouble, though. Suggs had the treasure chest, but he didn't know who had the key to unlock its mystery. Who was supposed to find that message? Bratton would not have been so cryptic if he hadn't wanted to make certain only that person found the gold. Who was it, though, and why?

Bratton was dead. The men of the Seventh were certain of that. Two had even helped bury what was left of him. They swore there was no gold nearby. Only Sioux.

Pettis? Now there was a possibility. That fool never showed any glimmer of intelligence, and he wasn't schooled enough to scratch his name on a pay voucher. The men said Bratton had given Pettis the watch. Was it the truth? Only Pettis would know.

Suggs had spent ten days riding from one camp to the other in search of Ike Pettis. He had been through most of them, but a pretty Irish girl named Shannon said he was at Custer City now, drinking up his latest diggings.

"He's found gold, then?" Suggs asked.

"Enough for a bottle and a bed for the night. Could be he's headed back for more, but I think he was looking for partners. Claims to know where's there's a real strike."

"You believe him?"

"If I believed everything men have told me," the girl said, "I'd be the queen of England and the richest gal in San Francisco, both at the same time."

"So you don't much believe Pettis's big talk."

"He's still wearing his cavalry boots and trousers. If he had money," she added, "I'd be busy, and you'd be talking to Kate or Josie."

It seemed to add up. Pettis didn't know everything, but maybe he knew enough. Suggs located the Iron Horseshoe, the saloon Pettis reportedly favored. It was little more than a big tent with a raw timber front. Suggs dismounted and tied his horse to a log rail provided for that purpose. Then he walked inside.

Pettis was playing cards in one corner, next to a piano player. A tent saloon with a piano player! It was beyond imagination. So, too, were the pouches of gold dust changing hands on that table.

"Suggs!" Pettis exclaimed, spying the weathered scout. "My old friend. Come join us. You finish your hitch, too, did you?"

"I did," Suggs confessed. "Didn't pick my time as wisely as some, though."

"Yes, sir," Pettis agreed. "I'm the last living, breathing man of Company C, Seventh Cavalry. Pure blind luck, it was, my time coming up before old Custer could get me killed."

"Mind your talk there," the bartender growled. "Whatever Custer was or wasn't, this town's named for him. He's surely paid for his sins, and I won't have a dead man talked down in my place."

"No offense intended," Pettis insisted. "I wasn't speaking of the general anyhow. I rode with his brother, and a better man for killing horses or men you'd never find. He's dead, too, though, and as you say, it's best to leave the dead to others.''

"Indeed," the bartender added.

"So, what's sent you to Custer City, Suggs?" Pettis asked, pulling a chair over for him. "Come to see if a bit of Custer's luck hasn't rubbed off on you?"

"I'm alive, aren't I?" Suggs asked, grinning. "Many aren't. I came to have a ride through these hills, a last look at the land of the Sioux, before going home to St. Louis."

"That where you're from?"

"Born there in my grandpa's house a mile from the Missouri," Suggs explained as he joined Pettis at the table.

"You still playing, Pettis?" a bewhiskered man wearing a dirty flannel shirt asked.

"Afraid you've done for me, boys," Pettis explained, showing the others his empty pockets. "Maybe my old friend here's got the price of another game."

"I haven't had you boys' luck," Suggs replied. "I heard about this fellow with the Seventh, name of Braxton, who found pay dirt, and I thought maybe I knew the spot the boys were talking about, but there wasn't anything but water and rocks there. No gold."

"Wasn't any Braxton," Pettis said, licking the lip of a whiskey glass. "Bratton was his name. Lucius Bratton."

"The Illinois colonel?" one of the cardplayers asked. "The one who got his regiment shot up and hightailed for the rear?"

"Yeah, that's the very one," Pettis said. "Wasn't much of a soldier, and he took French leave in the Black Hills. Some say he found gold. One of those boys sure did. I went out with a pair of Rees to find him."

"And did you find him?" Suggs asked, nodding to the bartender.

"Got a thirst?" the man called out.

"My friend here does," Suggs explained.

"Already owes me twenty dollars. Another bottle makes it thirty."

"Another bottle?" Suggs asked. "And a glass?"

"I don't sell sips here, mister," the bartender explained. "We're men here. Miners. We buy a bottle at a time."

"Yeah, and what we get's more water than whiskey," Pettis complained.

"Tell you what, sir," Suggs said, rising. "I've got a double eagle, fresh out of Denver, that I say buys my friend and me a bottle. Got a second one if you'd like to wager both against the bottle and Ike here's debt."

"Wager on what?" the bartender asked, growing interested.

"That I can take the knife out of my boot here and put it between the eyes of that mountain cat you've got painted on your wall yonder."

"That's a good twenty feet," Pettis warned. "I never knew a white man could do that."

"I don't want my painting marked," the bartender argued. "How about you hit the second board of my side door there, just above the knob."

"That's closer to twenty-five feet, Bannon," Pettis objected. "Besides, how are we to know what mark he's to hit."

"He's going to draw it for me," Suggs said, tossing a pencil on the bar. "You make it the size of a quarter, and I'll hit it."

"You're crazy," the fellow in flannel declared.

"Can't be done," a miner on the other side of the saloon insisted.

"Then you've got little to risk," Suggs said, nodding to the door. "I've got a good blade, and it'll come out of the wood neat and clean."

"More likely out of one of my customers," Bannon muttered. "I'm game, but show me your money first."

"Fair enough," Suggs said, producing the two gold pieces. The bartender marched to the door and marked a small circle. It was smaller than a quarter, but before Pettis could complain, Suggs rose. The men near the door scattered, and Suggs laughed. "Count me down from five, bartender. I'll let her fly on one."

The bartender began counting, and the customers made their way around and behind the bar to safety. When Bannon shouted "one," Suggs drew out his knife and hurled it underhanded across the saloon. It split the mark perfectly, and the others stared in amazement.

"Must be part Sioux to do a thing like that," Bannon grumbled as Suggs slipped the gold pieces back into his pocket.

"A Sioux would have done it with an arrow," Suggs argued as the bartender produced the promised bottle. "To learn the use of a knife, find a Cheyenne. They're fewer of them these days, so they have to move quietly and do their killing quick and sudden."

"You know Cheyennes, do you?" Pettis asked.

"Was one of 'em for a time, Ike. Too short a time, it turned out. They were good people, but they had too many enemies."

"Amos?"

"Ah, no point in recalling such times now," Suggs said, picking up his chair and moving to the corner of the saloon. The others kept a respectable distance after the former scout retrieved his knife. Only Pettis followed, carrying the fresh bottle.

"Amos, you feel all right?" Pettis asked as he handed over the bottle and sat beside his old comrade.

"Tell me about our old friend Lucius Bratton," Suggs urged as he filled Pettis's glass. The former corporal nodded, then drank.

"Was me found him, you know," Pettis said, savoring the taste of the whiskey.

"Alive?"

"Well, he was for a time. The Sioux put an arrow in his side, and he was half bled to death. Funny how he was, though. For a man never known for bravery, he fought well enough at the end. Gave me a chance to get away."

"Why'd he do that?"

"Oh, it was foolishness. He had a watch with his name scratched on it. He wanted his boy to have it."

"A boy, you say."

"Won a Medal of Honor in the war. Just a youngster, to hear tell. Funny thing. Bratton says he's a gunsmith in St. Louis. At McNamara's, on River Street."

"I know that place."

"I do, too. Anyway, I thought to speak with the boy. I promised, didn't I? Then I talked with Tom Custer. He argued against giving the watch to the son. The captain said it would likely just bring back his pa's disgrace. Besides, I'd be asked how I come by the watch, and I'd have to lie or tell the boy his pa deserted. Hard thing to tell anybody."

"Bratton say anything about why he wanted the boy to have the watch?" Suggs asked, refilling Pettis's glass.

"Oh, not as I recall. I know there's talk Bratton had gold on him, too, but I was there. He didn't have a trace on him. I was there, wasn't I? Anyhow, I suspected there might be a map hidden inside, but there wasn't. Ted O'Hare, sutler at Fort Lincoln, took the thing apart and put it back together."

"How'd he come by it?"

"How else?" Pettis asked, emptying his glass. "Traded me whiskey for it. Only the captain found out and got it back from Ted. I think he planned to have the writing scratched off and something else put on it. Fancied himself up for a redheaded little gal. Had that watch when I left the regiment, so a Sioux's likely got it now. From what I heard, they didn't leave much of the captain for the buzzards."

"He wasn't any too popular with the Cheyennes," Suggs said, refilling Pettis's glass once again. "Must've been quick, though. One of the Crows said the whole thing was like a big wind come up out of a thundercloud. No more'n an hour at best.''

"Got five whole companies, did they?"

"Except the men who'd fallen out sick or went back with lame horses. Reno and Benteen lost some of their boys, too.''

"The general split the command again, eh? Like at Washita, only instead of the other batch getting hit, the general got himself killed. Well, I won't lie and say I'm sorry. You know officers, Amos. I heard you was one yourself, but not a bona fide West Point gentleman, I'd bet. Up from the ranks is different.''

"Like Tom Custer?"

"I never took to him, not after his doings with those Cheyenne gals. Everyone knew he was forcing them, but he was the general's brother. You or me did that sort of thing, we'd be scratching the walls of a stockade. I won't say I'm sorry the Cheyennes found him, but I do wish I'd had some time with Bratton. I'm tired of being poor, Amos. I wouldn't mind striking gold.''

"Nor would I," Suggs agreed.

"I've got a few boys rounded up. We aim to trace the Seventh's route through the hills, find Bratton's spot. You know that country, and if there's any Sioux still about, you'd be able to treat with them. Join us?"

"No, thanks the same, Ike. It's been too long since I was home.''

"You're going to St. Louis then?"

"That would be home, all right."

"Maybe you'd stop by McNamara's, at least tell the boy his pa's dead. I know I should go myself, but if you're bound there anyhow—"

"I am," Suggs said, passing the bottle over to Pettis. "Have another drink, Ike, and trust me to do what's right by the boy. You know his name?"

"I only remember he's a gunsmith. Sorry, but I was in a bit of a hurry, and old Bratton didn't write it down.

Shouldn't be too many gunsmiths with a Medal of Honor, though.''

''Not likely,'' Suggs agreed. ''I'll find him.''

''Shame about the watch, it being lost, but the captain was likely right. It would just bring up memories best forgotten.''

Or reveal secrets best shared, Suggs imagined. He rose slowly and withdrew from the saloon. Even as he mounted his horse and rode eastward, away from the Black Hills, he knew he would return. He was as ready as Isaac Pettis to be rich.

III

TORY

THIRTEEN

Hector Bratton could never remember a time of such wild excitement. War! The Carolina rebels had fired on the flag at Fort Sumter in Charleston harbor. President Lincoln, his fellow Illinoisan, had taken the oath of office only a few weeks before. Now he was calling for thousands of volunteers to restore the Union!

"Hooray for Lincoln!" Patrick Harper had shouted after school was let out. "What do you say, boys? Shall we all sign up and march down south?"

Pat was known to boast a bit now and then, and he never did anything halfway. If he was for doing something, he let you know. If he was against it, heaven help anyone who wasn't on his side. He was near as good a two-handed puncher as Peoria had ever known. For a fourteen-year-old, anyway.

Hector, on the other hand, was barely thirteen. On a good day, when it suited him, he might pass for older, but most times he was content to mind his tongue and stay in the shadow of his older brother Achilles. If there could have been a king of schoolboys, it would certainly have been Achilles Bratton. Tall for fifteen, with dark brown

eyes and light brown hair, he was first choice on every
team and the favored dance partner of every girl at Mr.
Parker's school.

"Why can't you be more like your brother?" the teacher
had often asked. "Apply yourself, Tory. Diligence is its
own reward."

Tory was far from satisfied that diligence was any use
at all. Already the boy had mastered every math problem
his headmaster could imagine. Tory had read all three
shelves of Mr. Parker's books and most of the fifty vol-
umes his grandfather owned. Tory had read the *Bible* from
cover to cover—twice! Even when his father gave him
cryptic puzzles to solve requiring the study of verses, Tory
had them solved in an hour's time.

"Boy ought to go to Chicago or Philadelphia," Mr. Parker secretly told his parents. "He's wasted here."

No one, of course, ever uttered such praise in Tory's
presence. Still, the boy could hear when he wanted to.
When he couldn't, his sixteen-year-old sister Emiline usually filled him in.

"They're going to send me away?" he asked when she
repeated Mr. Parker's words.

"Ma said they'd have to kill her first," Emiline added.
"She'd let you if you wanted, though. Maybe you could
go to a fine boy's college or even one of the academies."

That talk had predated Fort Sumter. Now everyone
spoke of raising regiments and enlisting soldiers. His
neighbors naturally turned to Lucius Bratton. Hadn't he
led a company into Mexico? He knew what fighting was
about, and he'd soldiered with the state's top soldier, Ulys-
ses S. Grant.

Tory should have guessed something was wrong when
he got home from school that afternoon. For one thing,
Achilles wasn't at his accustomed spot on the study bench
they shared. His mother was red-faced angry, and his father seemed to be the target of her heated words.

"What about me?" she asked. "I'm your wife, after all.

Don't you feel I should have a say in such matters?''

"We're at war, Eliza," Tory's father had answered. "A man has to concern himself with the needs of his adopted state. Sam Grant needs men of experience to train these tinsmiths and carpenters. He asked me to form a regiment and bring them to Cairo. What could I do?''

"You could have talked to me!" his wife barked. "You could have declined. In a month's time Father will have you named a general with your own command. Be patient.''

"My own command? On which side? Your father's sentiments are known, dear. He may well have been the only man in Peoria to vote for that fool Breckinridge!''

"You may recall he was the vice-president?''

"As big a fool as Buchanan, too. I could see a man supporting Douglas, but a Kentucky weasel like Breckinridge?''

"You won't reconsider?''

"I'm for the Union, Eliza," Lucius Bratton declared. "A man is either for her or against her. The sooner we field a proper army, the sooner we'll bring the rebels to heal.''

"Then go if you must, but you won't take my son.''

Tory's ears perked up at the notion of soldiering with his father, but those hopes were quickly crushed.

"It was Achilles asked," Bratton explained. "There are others even younger going. How could I deny him his place?''

"His place?" she asked. "When did any fifteen-year-old have a place in the army? I've read the proclamations. They say no boys under sixteen will be taken.''

"But that doesn't apply to musicians and orderlies. Eliza, you have to understand the way it is with boys like Achilles. They have to be first in everything. He's expected to enlist. If he stays behind, his friends will wonder why. Is he somehow lacking the sand? Does his father find him lacking?''

"You can assure him—"

"Eliza, speak with him. If you can convince him to remain at home, then I'll support your decision. We need good men in the ranks, though. I don't know a finer youngster than Achilles."

"Well, Hector certainly won't go," she insisted.

"Did I suggest he would?" the boy's father asked. "He's smallish and studious. Later he might make a fine cadet at West Point, but for now he needs to stretch himself, put on some pounds."

Hector sighed. He knew his father was right, but he also hated the notion of being left out of a fight his father and brother were rushing to join. And that night, when Achilles told their mother he couldn't stay home, that avoiding his duty would make him no better than a coward, he heard his mother cry for the first time in recent memory.

"Ma, I might as well wear a skirt," Achilles declared. "My whole class has enlisted. Boys as young as twelve and thirteen have signed on as drummers. How would it make Pa look, me holding back?"

"Your father will survive," she told him.

"I wouldn't. I swear, if you try and hold me back, I'll run off to Cairo and sign up there. I've got the price of a ticket. You know I can pass for sixteen, and if I join up down there, Pa won't be close by, looking out for me."

It was that argument that overpowered her. Soon Achilles was packing the fine wool uniform Lucius Bratton had brought home from the tailor.

"Ax, it's not fair," Tory had complained. "You're leaving me at the mercy of Grandpa and two females!"

"Not sure who'll have the tougher fight," Achilles said, pulling his brother close. "Watch out for Ma, little brother. You know Grandpa's got a mean streak, and she's apt to catch the sharp end of most of his musings."

"Those that miss me, you mean."

"Em'll take up for you," Achilles assured him. "She's solid enough. Rely on her."

"And when the boys pick on me at the school yard?"

"It's time you learned something," Achilles said, resting Tory's chin on his chest. "They go after you, just stop, ball up your fist, and get one good whack in. Hit 'em in the belly, where's they're soft. Won't hurt your hand as much. May not stop 'em, but it'll get their minds to working."

"You'll be careful?"

"You haven't been listening, little brother," Achilles said, gazing hard into his brother's eyes. "You don't have to win, but you have to hit 'em hard. You can't do that being careful. I expect we'll be in the heat of it, Pa and me. I wouldn't welcome a rebel ball, but if that's what's coming, I won't turn from it. Most likely they'll see the Illinois infantry marching south and hoist the white flag. If they try and fight, we'll soon turn them around."

Tory had fewer words from his father.

"Mind your ma," the newly commissioned colonel admonished his younger boy. "Keep at your lessons, son, and make us proud of you."

"I'm proud of *you*, Pa," Tory had replied. "Leading the whole regiment off to war."

"It may not be as simple a thing as everyone expects," the colonel said, bending down and kissing his son on the forehead. "I expect some hard fighting. I mean to come back to you, son, but if I don't, do what you can to ease your ma's heartbreak. And if it lasts so long that your term comes, bear your obligations as a Bratton should."

"Yes, sir," Tory replied, saluting.

Even his father-in-law had surprised Lucius Bratton that day. He had provided a fine gold watch to honor Peoria's first colonel.

It had been a hard thing, watching the regiment marching off to the train depot for the trip south. Pat Harper had been out in front of Company A, drumming proudly. Achilles had come later, banging away on a fine drum supplied by his grandfather.

"It's all foolishness, this war," the old man had argued later that same week. "Let the South go her own way. What good ever came out of those fools anyway?"

The war news was surprisingly good, though. At least in the beginning. Grant had fought the rebels hard at Belmont, then forced them out of strong positions on the Mississippi at Columbus, Kentucky. Next came the brilliant victories at Fort Henry on the Tennessee River and Fort Donelson on the Cumberland. A whole rebel army had surrendered, and Grant was the hero of the day.

"Nashville is ours!" Tory shouted when he met his stern-faced grandfather on the front steps of the house he shared with his daughter's family. "Grandpa, Tennessee's near captured."

"Well, near isn't the same as captured," the old man muttered. "That General Johnston's a real soldier. He had the Mexicans running from him, and he put a kink in the Mormons out in Utah."

"Pa'll put the fear in him," Tory boasted.

"He did fair at Donelson, to read the papers, but that isn't the same as driving the Rebs out of Tennessee. Look on the map there. Corinth, down in Mississippi's the key. It's where the railroads cross. They take that place, and Memphis won't hold. Nothing to keep us from marching all the way to New Orleans."

Actually New Orleans, the largest city in the whole Confederacy, fell fast enough. Tory might have celebrated the victory more if it hadn't been for the rebels striking Grant's army at a little log meeting house called Shiloh near Pittsburg Landing on the Tennessee River. The rebels emerged from the morning mists, screaming and shooting, and they set the better part of two whole divisions to flight. Before it was all finished, though, Buell had come out from Nashville to reinforce Grant, and the fresh troops had made the difference. As for the famous Albert Sidney Johnston, he would trouble the Union no more. He'd died at the height of the fighting April 6. The disorganized Confederates had been outfoxed and outfought thereafter.

The Peoria regiment was hit particularly hard. As telegrams arrived with details and the names of the wounded, Tory scanned the lists with great care. Pat Harper was listed there. No Brattons, though.

It was a lonely time but a good one. Tory walked about the town feeling ten feet tall.

"That's the colonel's boy," shopkeepers would whisper.

"Won't be long before we've three Brattons in the field. Nothing can save the South when that happens."

But even as Tory pushed pins into the map board in his grandfather's study, he sensed something was terribly wrong. His mother was oddly quiet. His sister grew teary-eyed.

"What's wrong, Em?" he finally asked.

Emiline motioned him to her side and hugged him hard. "It's Ax," she whispered.

"I read the lists," he declared. "He wasn't wounded."

"There was another list," she explained. "This one went up this afternoon, after the families were notified."

Tory felt his knees wobble, and he leaned on his sister for support.

"No!" he shouted. "Can't be. No reb could kill Ax. Not *him*! Not *my* brother."

"They've buried him on the battlefield," she explained. "Didn't even take the trouble to ship the body home. You'd have thought the new colonel—"

"*New* colonel?" Tory had exclaimed. "Is Pa hurt, too? Not him, too!"

"He wasn't hurt, but he probably wishes he was. Ma will. Once word gets around, we all of us will wish he was dead."

"That's crazy," Tory objected. "I could never wish him dead."

"You just wait and see if you don't," she said, hugging him desperately hard. "Soon we'll just have each other,

Ma and Grandpa, Tory. It's not too comforting a thought."

The third week of April a train brought wounded men home to Peoria. Tory saw the train arrive and rushed to the station. The shopkeepers continued to whisper as he passed, but they had no smiles for him. The barber, Jack Boone, whose son Jim died beside Achilles, told Tory that Brattons weren't welcome in his shop. Tory was stunned and confused. Then he located Pat Harper on the platform. It wasn't until Pat turned that Tory saw the slight-shouldered boy's right arm was missing at the shoulder.

"What's happened, Pat?" Tory asked.

"We run across some rebs who could shoot," Pat explained.

"They got Ax, too, I hear."

"Killed him, Tory," Pat said, frowning. "It was a mess, that fight. Nobody had pickets out save a regiment or two. The rebs flat hit his with our pants down and eggs on the skillet."

"And Pa?"

"Don't ask *me* that, Tory," Pat said. "Not me. I was your friend, after all."

"*Was* my friend, Pat?" Tory gasped.

"Oh, to blazes," Pat said, offering his remaining hand. "Isn't your fault. You never had a cross word for anybody I can remember, and you sure got me out of a scrape or two at Mr. Parker's school."

"Tell me," Tory pleaded.

"You won't like it, Tory. Not a bit of it."

"Will I like it better tomorrow?" Tory asked.

"No, I guess not," Pat confessed. "Let's take a walk, the two of us."

"Don't you have somebody coming for you, Pat?"

"Tory, you know there's just my pa, and he's a drunk. I can take care of myself."

"I could carry your trunk," Tory offered, gazing at a pile of baggage.

"I've only got me and twenty dollars, Tory," Pat explained. "We'll talk as we walk, okay?"

"Nothing else?"

"Tory, I'm mighty lucky to have my life. Let the Rebs have my extra drawers and blanket!"

"And Pa?"

"Tory, this is going to be hard to hear. You might better ask your ma."

"If it's hard for you to tell me, Pat, it'd be twice as hard for her. Lord knows you've got your own troubles, but I swear, I'll owe you for telling it. Don't hold back. Must be pretty bad. Mr. Boone near took a razor to my hide."

"Well, you know they killed Jim. He's likely upset's all. It'll pass."

"He was drunk, wasn't he?" Tory asked. "We heard stories about Grant. They were friends, he and Pa. They took to the bottle, didn't they?"

"I don't know what the general was up to, but your pa wasn't sipping any whiskey at Shiloh, Tory. I wish it was as simple as that. I mean, my pa's drunk more often than not."

"Then I don't know what's happened!" Tory exclaimed. "Tell me, Pat."

"He ran away," the one-armed boy answered, lowering his eyes. "That's the long and short of it both, Tory. He took to his heels when the shooting started, and we didn't any of us see him for better'n three days."

"What?"

"It's the Lord's own truth, Tory," Pat swore. "I hate like the devil to say it, but it's what happened. Might be he wasn't feeling proper. Who'm I to say? He was steady enough at Fort Donelson, but he took off like a scared rabbit at Shiloh."

"And Ax? Did my brother prove to be a coward, too?"

"Lord, no," Pat said, shaking his head. "He was a fireball, just like always. Corporal Finch had the colors. The

first volley put two holes through his forehead, and the
flag went down. Wasn't an instant later that Achilles took
up the banner and waved us on. We hit those charging
rebs like a thunderbolt, and they fell back for a time. Gave
us a chance to catch our breath. Then more rebs hit our
right flank, and we fell apart. Five balls hit Achilles, just
tore the life right out of him. Jim Boone grabbed the flag,
but he was killed, too. By then I was down myself. I don't
know who dragged me off the field and cut off my arm,
and I don't know what happened to anybody else. They
sent me upriver to Cairo. I suppose I fared better'n most.''

"My brother led a charge while Pa ran," Tory said,
allowing the truth to take effect. He wanted to die.

"Tory, you've got to understand," Pat pleaded. "It
wasn't like any fight we'd ever seen. Rebs were everywhere. We couldn't see more'n a few feet ahead because
of the trees. It was all smoke and confusion and—"

"Achilles didn't run, and neither did you, Pat."

"If I had," the maimed drummer said, "maybe I'd still
have two arms. What difference did I make to anybody? I
didn't have a rifle to shoot, and once they hit me, I wasn't
any use as a drummer. I might as well have not been
there."

"So might be said of Pa," Tory added. *Better he had
stayed out of it,* Tory told himself silently.

It was later that afternoon that Lucius Bratton appeared
in Peoria. Sad-eyed, without his uniform, he walked up
Main Street, stopping to speak to relatives of the wounded
or dead. Most simply turned their back and closed their
doors. Tory saw it firsthand. Even drunks like Horace Harper ignored the cashiered colonel. The next day, when
Tory met Pat on the way to Mr. Parker's school, they
walked for a time in silence. Pat finally broke it.

"You can't take it to heart, Tory," Pat argued. "You're
always telling me how a man makes his own way. I don't
walk the same places my pa did. Just because he's a drunk,

I don't have to be. Seems like it ought to be the same for you."

"I always believed that, Pat, but today? How can I be sure?"

"I don't suppose you can."

"How do you feel on it, Pat? He ran and you lost an arm. You hold him accountable for it?"

"I've been afraid, Tory," Pat said, pausing. "Of Pa, lots of times. If I'd run, what would've been the harm? A company missing its drum? But when the colonel runs, your whole regiment unravels. He's the man everybody counts on. They look to his example. He turned and ran, Tory, left us on our own. The rebs came on then, and nobody knew what to do. They caught us in a cross fire and tore us to pieces."

Pat Harper wasn't the only one with an opinion of Lucius Bratton, either. The newspapers were full of the tale, how Grant's own friend, the colonel of the Peoria Rifles, had run like a jackrabbit.

"You have to understand what this means," Tory's grandfather explained that night after dinner. "There can be no more talk about West Point. No academy's going to take in the son of a coward."

"Pa, that's unfair," Eliza Bratton argued. "It's got nothing to do with Tory."

"That's far from certain, dear," the old man warned. "Hector, you'll discover as most do that life's a disappointment at the best of times. People rarely measure up to your expectations. Sooner or later you have to make your own way, and you might as well study the possibilities now. A college might take you if you adopted your mother's name. What would you think about that?"

"I don't see my name as the problem, Grandpa," Tory complained. "If no school wants me, then I'll find something else to do."

"Your grandfather's made you a generous offer, son," Eliza argued.

"I can only be who I am, though." Tory said, "No matter what name I carry, I'll always be Tory Bratton, son of Lucius. I'll just have to live with their whispers and the sneers until I have the chance to disprove others' opinions."

"And when will you do that?" Emiline asked. "How?"

I don't know, Tory told them with the sorrow in his eyes. But he was already formulating a plan.

FOURTEEN

It was simple, really, Tory convinced himself. He would find some regiment to join, maybe one in another state. Then he'd have a chance to redeem himself. But each and every time he tried to slip away, someone spotted him. His grandfather appeared twice at the train depot, frowning.

"Do you have no conscience, boy?" he howled. "Do you think your mother's ability to bear grief is boundless?"

Tory shook his head each time. Inside he knew that it wasn't his mother's grief but the family's shame that worried his grandfather. Sometimes, long after a boy should have been fast asleep, he overheard voices exchanging sharp words downstairs.

"You vouched for him, John!" one might shout. "I thought you said he knew war, could stomach a hard fight."

"I supposed he was good at something," the old man had replied. "How was I to know he was spineless? Grant himself thought the man worthy of command, didn't he?"

In the days that followed, rumors of the colonel's cowardice grew. Pat stuck to his story, but other men wrote letters home hinting that Lucius Bratton had Southern sympathies, that his real plan was to pull the whole regiment back and open the way for the rebel army to crush Grant and invade Illinois.

"No truth to it," Pat insisted when Tory raised the subject.

"Then why say it?" Tory asked.

"There were lots of boys that turned tail at Shiloh," Pat said, frowning. "Lots. May comfort some to think the colonel ordered 'em to retreat, but that didn't happen. No, they just got scared and ran like rabbits."

Tory found little solace in the truth, though. Rumors continued to circulate. Boys he'd known all his life called him coward. Girls scorned him. His mother and sister walked about dressed in black, but that didn't bring them any kinder treatment.

"Eliza, we'd be better off if you had never met that scoundrel of a husband!" Mrs. Henry Lawler, wife of the minister, shouted one afternoon. "I'd be ashamed to show my face if I were you."

The following Sunday, when Tory's grandfather drove them to services, they discovered the reverend felt much the same. The pew they had occupied all Tory's life was full of sad-looking lilies.

"Where do we sit, Grandpa?" Tory whispered.

"We don't," he'd answered. The tall, stiff-backed man turned and slowly led the way outside to their carriage. Outside, he turned and looked at Tory and Emiline with what could only be called hateful eyes. "This is your father's doing," he told them. "Curse him!"

That same afternoon a knock at the door interrupted Tory's thoughts as he stretched out, sobbing, on his bed. Below he heard heated words once more, but he recognized the bark of his father. Somehow, despite the pain and the shame, he still longed to see the man. He bolted out the door and raced into Emiline's hip.

"Go back to your room," she scolded. "You won't want to hear this, Tory."

He *did* hear some of it, though. He father's quivering voice begged for forgiveness.

"It was only an instant, Eliza, an instant. I was bone tired, and I panicked. I—"

"Where is my boy?" she asked. "Where's Achilles?"

"You know, dear," Lucius Bratton answered. "He fell on the field and was buried there."

She turned and started up the stairs. When Tory's father tried to follow, servants blocked the way.

"I don't believe you're welcome here, sir," Tory heard his grandfather boom. "Now, do I summon the sheriff?"

"No need," the former colonel said, surrendering. "I won't trouble you hereafter."

Tory started to race after the man, but Emiline stopped him.

"Leave it be, Tory," she pleaded. "Look at Ma."

The boy froze as he watched his mother ascend the stairs. Her face was ghostly pale, and her eyes were burning red from the tears that flowed down her cheeks and stained her ebony dress. Tory was shocked to see her so, but he was desperate to speak with his father. He raced back to his room, closed the door, and hurried to the side window. Opening it, he slipped out onto the wide limb of a great oak tree and scurried down to the ground. He managed to catch up with his father ten feet from a waiting horse.

"Pa?" the boy cried. "Pa, wait."

Lucius Bratton halted, shuddered, and turned. Tory saw another haunted face, and it staggered him.

"Pa, where's your uniform?" he asked. "What's happened?"

Lucius Bratton stepped to the boy's side and clasped his frail shoulders.

"Tory, I'm sorry," the father told his son.

"They say you ran," Tory said. "They're wrong, aren't they?"

"Lord, Tory, you have to understand. I'd had little sleep that last week. I took a fever at Donelson, and I wasn't well. I shouldn't have been with the regiment, but I couldn't leave Achilles there on his own."

"You did leave him, though," Em declared, joining them.

"I did," their father admitted. "I wish I hadn't, but there it is. Wish I could take it back, make the pain of it vanish. It was only an hour of weakness, after all, but it's destroyed us all. Don't you think that if I could give my own life away to bring Achilles back, I'd do it?"

"I know *I* would," Tory said sadly. "Ma'd rather lose me, I think."

The words shattered his father, and he fell to his knees.

"Forgive me, Emiline. Forgive me, son. Give me a chance to undo the harm, won't you?"

It was then that the first of what was quickly turning into a mob appeared.

"Didn't we make it clear, Bratton?" someone shouted.

"No? Then we soon will," another added.

Someone arrived with a torch, and another brought a bucket of tar.

"Quick, Pa, go!" Tory said, spotting young Jack Evans with a tub of chicken feathers. "Hurry."

Lucius Bratton also realized what was about to happen. He stumbled to his feet and mounted his horse. With the shouts and curses of twenty hostile neighbors following him, he fled.

Emiline tried to drag Tory inside, but the boy remained rooted where he stood.

"Others ran, too!" he hollered as loud as his young voice could. "He was sick! Haven't we suffered enough? My brother's dead, remember!"

The crowd turned away from the fleeing horseman, and

for an instant Tory thought they might leave, shamed by his words. Instead they turned toward him.

"That's it!" Jack urged. "One Bratton's same as another, isn't he?"

A shotgun blast halted them in their tracks. Emiline marched out with the smoking weapon and glared at them.

"I've got another barrel," she warned, "and a pocket full of reloads. You people! How many of you are in the ranks? My brother's not even fourteen yet, and he's harmed nobody. You touch him, and you'll have need of a casket before nightfall!"

"You heard her," Sheriff Gordon King declared, working his way through the crowd. "Get along home, people. I may be nigh on seventy, but I've got my pistol primed and ready. Get!"

The mob dispersed, but the sheriff lingered. Emiline kept the shotgun ready the whole time.

"I'll trouble you for that, young lady," the sheriff said, nodding toward the weapon. "You know I won't abide gunfire in Peoria County."

"No?" Emiline said, stepping an inch closer to her brother. "You'd let them tar and feather a small boy, but you won't let me keep my means of protecting my home?"

"It's not for you to do, young lady," the sheriff insisted.

"And just who else is there to do it, Mr. King? My grandfather, who can hardly bear the sight of us? Our neighbors, who brought the feathers? My little brother, who would let them torture him rather than back away? Can't you see what's happened here? This town's turned its anger on us, Sheriff! It's the rebels that are the enemy, not us!"

Sheriff King nodded and frowned. He made no second effort to take the shotgun. Instead he retreated to the street and walked away.

"Thanks, sis," Tory said, leaning against his sister's side. It was only then that he realized that she was trembling from head to toe. "Em? he asked.

"We can't all run away," she told him.

It was later that evening, after supper, that Tory was led into his grandfather's study and left alone opposite the old man's large walnut desk.

"Who's this?" the old man asked, holding up a small tintype of drummer Achilles Bratton of Company C.

"It's Ax," Tory answered.

"Who?" his grandfather growled.

"Achilles," the boy replied. "My big brother."

"Have you heard how he led the men back when your father ran?" the old man stormed. "Have you heard how he stood his ground with three rebel musket balls in his body?"

"Yes, sir," Tory said, stifling the urge to cry. "It's how he was, Ax. Always first at everything. They killed him, Grandpa!"

"There are worse things than dying, Hector. Dishonor. A man's reputation is all he has when it's all said and done. Fortune? Family? Both can vanish in an instant. But a man with a proud name can hold his head high. You understand that, don't you?"

Tory managed a slight nod.

"Do you read your *Bible*?"

" 'Most every night, Grandpa."

"Pay particular attention to Job, boy. A man has burdens to bear in this life and few rewards. You understand?"

"Yes, sir."

"I want you to remember the face of your brother. See his eyes?"

"Yes, sir."

"Let your brother's example be a light and your father's shame an admonition, young man. Take heed of both. Be a better person for the knowledge you receive."

"Yes, sir," Tory said once again. "Sir?"

"Yes?" the old man asked, glaring down at his grandson.

"Is Ma all right?"

"She's bearing twin sorrows, Hector. She's lost a fine son and discovered that she has a coward for a husband. That's more than most women can manage."

"Can't we help her, Grandpa?"

"Nothing can help her but the Lord above, Hector. You can pray she has the strength to endure the torment that is life."

"Sir, I do, too," Tory added.

"You do what?" the old man stormed. "Pray?"

"That also, but I meant that I suffer. I miss Pa. I miss Ax. I hear what people say behind my back and even to my face."

"You can expect little else after what your father's done. You suffer? Why not? I've worked my entire life to build this family up, and your father's torn it up by the roots. Why shouldn't you suffer, boy? You're Lucius Bratton's son!"

Things got little better that summer. By the time of the annual harvest dance, few souls other than Pat Harper would acknowledge that Tory was alive. His grandfather grew more sour by the day, and his mother rarely left her room. Worse, the rebels had found themselves a new general to lead their army in Virginia. With federal forces on the doorsteps of Richmond, Robert E. Lee threw them back to their bases and was now storming north toward Washington, D.C. Another reb army under Braxton Bragg was in Kentucky, and it looked as if all the dying and suffering would be for nothing.

Tory didn't want to attend the harvest dance that year despite the fact that it was always held in his grandfather's ballroom. He was tall as most thirteen-year-olds, but still a thimble shy of looking a girl eye to eye. He wanted and needed Emiline's advice, but she had tired of their grandfather's scorn and left to nurse wounded soldiers at Cairo. When he finally walked downstairs to join the celebration, the girls turned their backs to him.

"You're not wanted here," Jack Evans growled.

"It's my house, isn't it?" Tory replied.

Rough hands seized him and dragged him outside. There, surrounded by ten boys, most of them older and bigger, he heard the now familiar taunts. "Turncoat Tory! Coward!"

"Prove it!" Tory answered, balling up his fists.

They didn't come at him one at a time. No, hands reached out and tore at his clothes. Someone kicked him behind his left knee, and he fell. Strong wrists clasped his arms while others pinned his legs. A boot came down hard on his stomach. A fist bloodied his nose.

"Give it to him good," he heard Jack yell. "Give it to him like the rebs gave my pa!"

Hands clawed at him, ripped his coat, stripped his shirt until he was left, bare-chested and bleeding. They were tugging at his trousers, laughing about leading the naked coward back inside, when Pat Harper dragged the first of them off and slammed a knee into a second.

"Coward, you say?" Pat shouted so loudly that Tory thought the sky itself might open. "Coward? I don't see him running anywhere. Have any of you stood in the ranks? No! Ten of you it takes to whip a snip of a boy. Maybe you'd like to try me on instead. I've only got one arm, so maybe you have enough courage in your pitiful souls to face me?"

Pat stood three inches shorter than Tory, but he was wearing his only decent clothes, the bloodstained tunic and blue trousers he'd worn returning from Shiloh. Maimed and smallish he might have been, but the whole bullying lot of them weren't a match for the pure anger blazing in Pat Harper's eyes. They slunk off like a pack of dogs caught barking at a farmer's chickens.

"Tory, you all right?" Pat asked, helping the battered boy to his feet.

"I've looked a bit better at times," Tory confessed. The

knees of his trousers were torn, and his coat was a mere rag. He felt low as a worm.

"It's not your fault, Tory," Pat said, frowning. "Don't I know better than anybody that a fellow can't do a thing about who his pa happens to be."

"I'd join up tomorrow, Pat," Tory said, rubbing the redness out of his eyes. "I'd march off and never think twice, but who'd accept a son of Lucius Bratton in their ranks?"

"Be glad of that," Pat said, shuddering. "You can read a thousand books and not know anything about what a war is. It's your good fortune to be free of the army. Battle's no parade. It's death and dying."

"At least you're judged on your own merits, Pat, and not on what your pa's done."

"It's poor compensation for an arm, Tory!"

"It's easier to live with only one arm than be the son of a coward! Pat, I wouldn't be afraid. When have I ever backed away from a fight? Oh, I never ducked my head and butted my way into the middle of one the way Ax used to do, but I wouldn't run."

"You don't think I know that?"

"I'm not sure of anything anymore. I mean, I used to have a pa people nodded to on the street, who was looked up to. Now . . . And Ma! She won't even come out of her room to eat breakfast with me. She doesn't say anything. She just stares at a picture of Ax and sings baby songs."

"So? I never had a pa anybody thought was worth the cost of a funeral."

"Were you ever ashamed of him?"

"More than a few times. More than a hundred, if the truth be known. But you can only be yourself, Tory, not your pa."

"Sure," Tory said, sighing. "Only people won't let me be myself anymore. Did you know they won't let me go to school anymore?"

"What?"

"That Mr. Greene, the new teacher, said I cause trouble."

"You don't."

"Pat, it doesn't matter what I do anymore. I'm Lucius Bratton's boy. People can drag me out of my own house and tear my clothes to shreds. Just look at me! What'll Grandpa say when he sees my clothes? You know if Em hadn't come out here with a shotgun, there were folks ready to tar and feather me? Mr. Tolliver, over on Elm Street, spit at me day before yesterday."

"Tory, listen hard," Pat said, growing grim. "You don't know what it's like, fighting a war. You think having a shirt torn off you or being spit at's bad. Nobody's shooting cannon balls at you. I saw a boy no older'n you with his head taken plum off by a cannonball. It's not the same as ducking a fight to stay home and grow older."

"You don't think I could hold up to it, do you, Pat?" Tory asked, rubbing his eyes again.

"Sure I do," Pat said, resting his remaining hand on Tory's tattered shoulder. "There's nothing to standing in line and getting shot except not caring whether you're alive or dead. It's easy enough. There's no courage to it. Now, staying here and showing these folks you won't back down takes real sand."

"You believe that?"

"Tory, the truth is that it doesn't matter what anyone else believes. It's what *you* believe that counts. It's all that matters in the long run. Not your grandpa, nor your ma, nor me, nor some fool like Jack Evans or Mr. Greene."

Tory searched his friend's face for some hint of pretense. He found none.

"Just what I think, huh?"

"Just that, Tory."

Pat gave him a final nod and turned back toward the door.

"Pat?" Tory called. "You going back in there?"

"Sure I am," he said. "Don't you know the girls like

a fellow in uniform, even if he's only got one arm?''

"Well, I guess if Jack gets after you, I can come rescue you.''

"I don't figure he'll have much cause to mess with anybody else tonight," Pat argued. "You coming along?''

"No, I'd better skin up the oak and sneak into my room. Grandpa won't like seeing my clothes in tatters.''

"Well, you figure what you're going to do, you let me know. They go to kicking you out of that school, they'll sure find a reason to boot me. I'm the worst reader and the poorest speller in the place.''

"You watch out, Pat," Tory warned. "Somebody's apt to mistake you for my friend and start spitting at you, too.''

"I been spit at since I was walking," Pat boasted. "Never took an arm off me. As to being your friend, I been that since you, me, and Ax got caught peeking in Miss Agnes Cooper's back window.''

Pat laughed, remembering. Then he returned inside the house. Tory took a deep breath and started up the oak. It wasn't until later, when he was safely out of his rags and in a nightshirt, that he thought some more about what Pat had said.

It doesn't matter what anyone else believes. It's what you believe that counts.

But what did he believe?

"Pa, why'd you go and put me in such a fix?" Tory whispered to the emptiness all around him. "Why'd you turn the world upside down on me?''

It wasn't supposed to be that way. Fathers were supposed to look after their sons. But when you considered Pat—

"Doesn't always work the way it's supposed to, does it, Ax?" Tory whispered. "You'd know what to say to 'em, wouldn't you?''

Downstairs the orchestra was playing a waltz, and Tory remembered that last harvest he stood in for his pa and led his ma out to open the dancing. The top of his head barely touched her chin, but she had worked with him a week, practicing the steps, and he managed it decently enough.

There had been no Brattons opening the dancing this year.

Oh, Pa, why'd you do this to us? Tory wondered.

He was still wondering an hour later when he fell asleep listening to the notes of another waltz.

FIFTEEN

As the war continued, the enlisting officers in Peoria grew less choosy. Younger, less healthy boys joined the ranks of the new Union regiments while others filled the gaps left vacant by fathers and brothers and cousins left dead on battlefields from Virginia and Maryland in the East to Missouri and Arkansas in the West. Illinoians took pride that their state's soldiers fought and died well. Sometimes Tory lingered near the gates of cemeteries, listening to the haunting notes of bugles playing their sad refrains as honor guards lowered caskets occupied by the bodies of husbands and sons into their graves.

He never dared to join any of the funeral parties, not even when neighbors or schoolmates were buried. No son of Lucius Bratton was welcome in the company of the brave.

Bad as it was for him, it was doubly difficult for his mother. She never left her room anymore, but she couldn't ignore the scornful faces of neighbors who avoided walking past her father's house. She faded like thin paint on a sunlit barn until there just wasn't anything left of her. A year and seventeen days after her favorite son fell on a

battlefield she never visited, she welcomed her own end
on a rainy April afternoon.

"Now I've lost them both," Tory's grandfather said,
dropping his head into his hands. "I've lost everything!"

What about me? Tory wanted to scream. He held his
tongue, though, even when the old man ordered Eliza Bratton buried by torchlight, with only the family present.

"Nobody would have come anyway," his grandfather
declared.

"Em would have been here," Tory argued. Secretly the
boy had hoped Lucius Bratton would return for the burial,
too. Pat Harper came without being asked, and he stayed
even when instructed to leave.

"I've come to be with my friend," Pat announced.
"I've got just one arm, mister, but it's mostly Irish and
strong enough to deal with a bitter old man."

"I wish I could ask Ax what I should do," Tory told
Pat afterward. "Nobody brought him back to bury, though.
He's off in some cold, muddy field in Tennessee. Now
Ma's gone, too. Should've been Pa they buried today. Or
maybe in Tennessee."

"They're burying him in a different way," Pat noted.

"Yeah, and me along with him," Tory added bitterly.

The local recruiters were offering hundreds of dollars in
bounty money to induce recruits, but even when Tory told
them they could keep their money, they refused to admit
him to their ranks.

"Son, even a one-eyed man can tell you're not of age,"
a scarred veteran told him that dreadful summer of '63
when it seemed everything was going wrong for the
Northern cause. Grant was failing to take Vicksburg and
Bobby Lee was up in Pennsylvania, spreading panic everywhere.

"They'll be marching into Peoria next," Emiline said
sourly during a rare visit home. "Can't the generals figure
it out? You win by advancing, not pulling back!"

"It only serves to show them I was right all along,"

their grandfather replied. "Thousands will fight and die, all for nothing."

"There are some who believe in the cause, Grandfather," Em argued. "If a people won't fight for freedom, what *is* worth fighting for?"

"Freedom?" the old man cried. "For slaves? I've never owned a slave, nor met one, either. I've lost my grandson! *He* was worth more than all the slaves in the blasted South! And Eliza! These people from town with their black armbands walk around, weeping over some fool boy of a shopkeeper's son. I've lost my whole family! Who's suffered half as much as I have?"

"I have," Tory mumbled.

"You!" Grandfather Drury raged. "You? It's your father brought all this down on us, Hector. Your father got Achilles killed, and the sorrow carried off my Eliza. You! What have you suffered? You're fed well enough. You have a warm bed."

"Don't you?" Em asked. "Do you think he doesn't feel the loss of his mother? His brother?"

When their grandfather ignored the remark, Tory rose from the table.

"Sit back down, young man!" his grandfather shouted.

"If you hate me so much, Grandpa, why won't you sign the army's paper and let me go off to make amends for Pa?" the boy asked. "You don't want me here. The town doesn't want me here. I don't want to be here, either. Seems to me it would be a reasonable solution for everyone."

"You're too young," Emiline declared. "Our family's paid its price."

"Don't you mean to say we've done our share?" Tory argued. "It's fine for you to say so, but what have I done? I'm almost as old as Ax was when he left. I can beat a drum, too. Pat Harper's showed me."

"You stay away from that boy!" Grandfather Drury demanded. "Son of a drunken oaf! He should be the one dead."

"Grandpa, Pat's pa died last December of pneumonia," Tory said, digging his fingers into the back of his chair to control his fury. "His ma's off in Chicago, living with a sister. Pat's just got one arm, but the army took him back. He's helping the quartermaster down at the depot. Couldn't I at least do that?"

"No," the old man growled. "Now sit down and finish your dinner. I know it's difficult, considering your blood, to act like a gentleman, but do try."

Tory just glared at the old man. Later he tried to coax Emiline into signing his enlistment papers.

"You're of age and my sister," he pleaded. "They don't look too hard at those things anyway. I've heard of boys signing themselves up."

"Tory, if you saw half the carnage I see down at Cairo, you wouldn't ask such a thing," she told him. "There's no glory to dying slow of a fever or withering away after a surgeon's cut off a limb. Ask Pat if he would be so eager to join, knowing what he does now."

"But he's doing something, Em! I have to get out of this place. Can't you see Grandpa's smothering me? Can't I come live with you in Cairo?"

"You couldn't feed two snails on what they pay me, Tory," she explained. "I would take you if I could, but I live in a room with three other girls. There's no room for another body, and no money for a room of my own. I would come back here to see you no matter what, but I have to confess I also need Grandpa's financial help. Be patient. That war won't last forever. After it's over, people will forget and forgive."

He doubted they would.

By mid-July, though, the fortunes of war had turned against the enemy. Lee's army was slaughtered at Gettysburg, and Grant's columns were parading through the shell-torn ruins of Vicksburg. Victory seemed more certain than ever. The casualties continued to mount, and hard-pressed recruiters came weekly, accompanied by little drummers on leave from the fighting. Men boasted of the proud records of this regiment and that. And Tory? He lay on his bed, reading books and writing essays his grandfather assigned.

In August the first rays of sunlight began to crack through what had become a dismal world. George McNair, formerly a captain in the Pennsylvania infantry, arrived in town with his young daughter, Victoria. Captain McNair had been a teacher before the war, and when a rebel cannonball shattered his left hip, he sought refuge in Peoria.

Tory was at the depot, helping Pat, the day the captain arrived.

"Excuse me," the hobbling man said, breaking into their conversation.

"Sir?" Pat asked, offering a crisp salute to the man leaning on one crutch and still wearing his officer's frock coat.

"I'm not in the army anymore," Captain McNair had explained. "I was hoping to find someone here to help with my baggage, though. As you can see, I'm little use where carrying things are concerned."

"I have the same problem," Pat said, gazing at his empty sleeve.

"And is there no one else about?" the captain asked.

"The men are mostly in the army," Pat explained. "Or crippled up. Or dead."

"It's the same everywhere," Captain McNair said, sighing. "I hoped farther west things might be better, but—"

"There's nothing wrong with me," Tory volunteered. "I'd be happy to help."

"Oh?" the captain said, sizing up Tory. "You don't work here?"

"Only when I can talk him into it," Pat said, grinning. "Most days he's got his face in a book or else his grandpa's got him at some chores."

"Well, if I could pry you away from the depot, I'd gladly pay the going rate," McNair offered.

"You might find the company more appealing, too," Pat added, grinning at the shy, graceful girl about their age who appeared at the captain's side.

"I'd be honored to help," Tory said, shaking away the greenbacks Captain McNair offered. "Seems the least a fellow can do for a veteran. Where did it happen?"

"Gettysburg," the girl announced proudly. "Papa was in the thick of it the last day when the whole Rebel army came charging at the center of Meade's line."

"This is Victoria," the captain said, nodding to the girl. "My daughter. She likes to exaggerate my role in the fighting. Actually I stood with thirty or forty thousand others and shot bullets at Virginians and Carolinians that could well be cousins of my late wife."

"Your ma's dead?" Tory asked Victoria.

"A month now," she replied. "Influenza. I nearly died myself. It's why Papa's brought us west. The climate favors recovery."

"My ma died in April," Tory explained. "Grief for my brother, I think."

"Oh?" Victoria asked, her eyes growing more animated. "And what keeps you from the ranks?"

"My grandfather," Tory said, sighing. "I'm too young to join on my own."

"We're all of us too young for *this* war," Captain McNair added. "I helped bury a boy not as tall as you, son."

"My name's Hector," Tory explained as he followed the captain out onto the train platform. "My friends call me Tory, though."

"I'm glad to have met you, Tory," the captain said, offering his hand. "You listen to your grandpa and stay home. A battlefield's no place for a scholar."

"He should know," Victoria added. "Pa taught at Pennsylvania College and before that—"

"You keep talking, dear, and it will be nightfall before we're home," McNair complained as they reached a waiting wagon. "We can just as easily talk as we go."

"Sure we can," Tory agreed as he began picking out valises and parcels on which the captain had written his name. "Best get the work done before the day gets away from you."

Tory proved more than a help loading the wagon. The McNairs knew only that they had arranged to board with old Mrs. Fitzhugh, who was a widow before Tory had been born. Her youngest son was in the navy, and Tory suspected there might be grandsons serving as well. The Fitzhugh house was not so grand as the Drury place, but it was nevertheless a substantial brick residence two stories high with additional rooms on either side of an attic. Over the years Tory had been inside three or four times, mostly delivering parcels or apologizing for trampling flowers. The house was only half a city block away, and Achilles had been fond of racing through its side garden on spring afternoons. Where his older brother went, Tory was certain to follow.

It was a relatively brief journey to Widow Fitzhugh's from the depot, and Tory sat in the bed of the wagon with the McNair family belongings. Occasionally Victoria would flash him a smile. Otherwise father and daughter talked about beginning life anew in Illinois or remembered better days before the war. It was only after reaching the house that Captain McNair asked Tory about his schooling.

"For a boy whose friends say he's fond of books, I can't help wondering why you aren't attending school," the captain said as he limped to the rear of the wagon.

"I suppose you'd learn sooner or later," Tory said, sighing. "I'm none too welcome at school or most other places in Peoria."

"Oh?" Captain McNair asked. "And why is that?"

"My pa," Tory said, staring at his shoes.

"Is he an outlaw of some sort?" Victoria asked, joining them.

"Worse," Tory explained. "When the local boys formed up a regiment, they asked Pa to take command. Made him colonel because he served in Mexico. He knew General Grant there."

"And?" the captain asked.

"When the rebs attacked at Shiloh, he lost his nerve," Tory said, biting down on his lip until a droplet of blood appeared. "He ran away. My brother stood with most of the others and died. People here know that plenty of men turned tail that day, but a colonel's supposed to be an example to his men. Pa wasn't, and they hold it against him."

"You never ran away, Tory," Captain McNair said, squeezing the boy's shoulder. "Life is a heavy burden without carrying your father's shame around with you."

"I don't have much choice," Tory explained. "You won't find this a forgiving sort of place. People hold it against Pat because his pa drank. Well, Pat's lost an arm and, even so, works every day at the depot. People rarely give him the time of day. As for me, they cross the street so they won't have to ask me to step out of the way. Pat's the only single person in this whole town who has a kind word for me, and I figure he's got the best reason for holding a grudge, losing an arm at Shiloh and all."

"Well, you've got other friends now," the captain declared. "I've come to Peoria to read the law with Judge Miller. You come over any evening you choose, though, and I'll help you with your lessons. We'll have our own school, so to speak."

"I'll have to ask my grandpa," Tory explained. "I don't think he'll favor the notion."

"He holds your father against you, too, does he?" Captain McNair asked. "Well, you let me speak with your grandfather. I can be persuasive. After all, arguing is the business of lawyers, isn't it?"

Tory couldn't resist returning the kindhearted man's smile.

It took the captain only three trips to convince Abner Drury to allow his surviving grandson to study at the Fitzhugh place. The fierce Widow Fitzhugh soon softened her gaze and even insisted Tory call her Granny. For the first time since he watched Lucius Bratton march away to war, Tory felt himself a member of the community. Perhaps most important, Victoria became a soul mate. The two motherless children seemed to understand each other in ways no one else could. In the afternoon Tory walked with her through the Fitzhugh garden. He helped pluck weeds and cut roses. When he received an invitation to the 1863 harvest dance, moved to the Fitzhugh home, Tory mustered enough nerve to ask Victoria to attend with him.

"I'm not altogether certain that it's proper," she answered. "You're only fourteen, Tory."

"Oh, Victoria, it's just a dance," he responded. "There's nothing we're going to do in Granny's ballroom that we haven't done in the garden."

"Meaning?" she gasped.

"Meaning we've held hands before," he told her. "Please agree, Victoria. No one else will go with me. The boys came close to killing me last year just for going, and it was at Grandpa's house."

"Maybe you should stay home."

"Victoria?" Tory asked, growing nervous. "Are you afraid of what people will say?"

"I'm afraid of lions and tigers, not gossip," she insisted. "I just thought, well, maybe we could just meet here. In Philadelphia no girl of fourteen would attend a dance with a man."

"My ma was married at fifteen," Tory said, shaking his head. "I'll do whatever you say, though. Can I at least bring you a flower from Grandpa's garden?"

"I think Granny would let you cut a yellow rose," she

said, cracking a smile. "It will match my dress."

"Then I'll see you at the dance," he said, grinning from ear to ear.

Tory rubbed polish on a new pair of black leather shoes until he could see his face in the shine. He practiced tying and retying a string tie. He borrowed Achilles' old church coat and bought a fine new pair of trousers from money he'd saved from the nickels Granny gave him for helping in the garden.

He walked to the Fitzhugh place the night of the dance with Pat Harper. Pat was also wearing one of Achilles' old coats. The old uniform had long since failed to fit, and his new one had grown thin in the seat.

"One good bow, and I could embarrass myself," Pat had remarked the week before.

Once they arrived, Granny Fitzhugh greeted them with a broad smile and made a point of welcoming them. Tory knew it was her way of announcing to everyone that no nonsense would be tolerated toward the two of them. But when Tory approached Victoria, she shied away. Three dances came and went, and she managed to find a partner for each before Tory could reach her side.

"Maybe we should dance together," Pat whispered.

The offer only heightened Tory's confusion. Pat wasn't having any difficulty finding female partners. Each time Tory even stepped close to a girl, a brother or father managed to block the path. Finally Major McNair took his daughter's hand and led her to Tory.

"You two seem to be having difficulty finding each other," he said, placing his daughter's hand in Tory's fingers. "Dance!"

But when the music began, Victoria stormed off the dance floor and marched outside. Tory found her sitting on the porch.

"I don't understand," he said, the hurt flooding his face. "Does what the others think matter so much?"

"The others?" she cried. The scorn in her voice tore at him like the claws of a bear.

"What's wrong?" he asked.

"Follow me," she said, taking his hand and leading the way inside the house and down a side corridor toward the sitting room. "Look!" she commanded. "Look there!"

Tory followed her pointing finger to a small table. Six small tintypes of soldiers formed a half circle there. Nearby was a larger photograph of her father wearing the uniform of a captain.

"Those two on the ends are uncles," Victoria explained. "The others are cousins. I write to each of them every week. Their replies speak of hardship and suffering. They talk of shirkers and cowards, too. Sometimes I sit with Pa and pray that they will be safe. And do you know what I think about when I go to bed?"

"Them?" he asked.

"You," she said, shuddering. "You, Tory Bratton. You've been a cross to bear. We work in the garden and you talk about suffering. What do you know about it? You're safe enough!"

"Do you think that's my choice?"

"Oh, I forgot. Your grandfather won't sign for you. Well, two of my cousins signed the papers themselves. Who signed for Pat Harper?"

"His father was glad that he went," Tory said, swallowing his hurt and anger long enough to respond. "I'm as big a fool as Grandpa always told me. I trusted you. I told you my feelings. All the while you were no different from the others except maybe they were honest enough to let me know how they felt. Don't worry about seeing me out, Victoria. I know the way, don't I? I hope you'll apologize to your pa for me. I wouldn't want to bother you by coming over to study. I'll ask Pat to bring back the books I borrowed."

She reached for his arm, then pulled it back. With a move that was both graceful and final, she turned her back

on him. Tory turned and ran. He didn't stop until he
reached his grandfather's door.

"Tory?" a voice called as he stepped inside.

It was Emiline, home on her monthly visit. Her eyes
were unusually tired, and he suspected the stories of hard
fighting near Chattanooga were true.

"Em, I don't feel like talking," he said, pausing only
long enough to catch his breath. Then he hurried upstairs
to his room. She entered a few minutes afterward to find
him staring hard into a mirror.

"Tory?" she asked, resting her hands on his shoulders.
He was only three inches shorter now, and her grip lacked
the firmness he had remembered.

"What's wrong with me?" he asked.

"Nothing in this world," Emiline assured him. "I
thought you were meeting the McNair girl at the dance.
Your letters spoke of little else."

"I'm not welcome in her company anymore," he said.
Tears welled up in his eyes, and he wiped them away with
his sleeve. "If it weren't for Pa, I'd be in uniform, Em.
I'm not a coward. Can't they see me for who *I* am."

"You can't blame Pa for this," she said, kissing his hair
the way she had the day their mother had died.

"Can't I?" Tory asked. "He got Ax killed. That finished Ma. Everyone hates me because Pa ran away at Shiloh. Then he ran away again and left us on our own. I
can't fight everybody, Em!"

"You really believe Pa left us here on our own?" she
whispered.

"Look around, Em. You see him?"

"There's something you *should* see," she announced.
With a determined gaze, she steered him down the hall to
their staircase. They continued downstairs to their grandfather's office. They stopped when they reached a small
bureau that had been locked for as long as Tory could
remember. Emiline took a pin from her hair and jiggled it
until there was a distinctive click. She pulled out the

drawer. Inside were dozens of opened letters, most of them addressed to Hector Bratton. They contained brief notes and money.

"Read this one first," Emiline suggested, handing him one that bore traces of gunpowder.

My dear son,
    It pains my heart that you don't return my affec-
tion. Every day I think of you and your dear sister.

The letter spoke of a better future, promised a new home away from Illinois and a fresh start.

"Grandfather poisons your thoughts, Tory," Emiline explained. "Take the money and go see Pa. He's at Alton, working at the railroad depot."

"All this time," Tory said, eyeing the letters. With great care he collected each and every one of them. There was also close to two hundred dollars.

"Go tonight," Emiline urged. "Go before you lose your nerve."

"I'm not the one who loses his nerve," Tory explained. "Em, thank you for showing me these. I guess Ax wasn't the only Bratton to understand courage."

"No, he wasn't," she said, hugging him tightly.

Tory waited only long enough to turn over Captain McNair's books to Pat Harper. He left half the money with Pat, too.

"Just in case," he explained.

He left on the late train that very night. It wasn't bound for Alton, though. It carried him instead to Chicago. He was certain he could locate a recruiting officer who wouldn't examine him too closely there. He might pass for sixteen now, even if he wouldn't need a razor for another year. If he couldn't, he had a letter penned and signed with a fair representation of his grandfather's signature by a one-armed quartermaster's aide.

"If I get through this, I'll write you where we can meet," Tory had told Pat. "I won't ever be coming back to Peoria, though. At least not alive."

SIXTEEN

Chicago was the grandest city Tory Bratton had ever seen. That early autumn day when he stepped off the train, he could scarcely believe his eyes. The station—you couldn't call it a depot—was full of soldiers. Some were veterans arriving or returning on furloughs. Others were fresh-faced recruits bound to "see the elephant," as people had taken to calling one's baptism by fire. There were a fair number, too, of sick and dying, not to mention the ones who had lost limbs to a surgeon's saw.

"Where are you bound?" a husky voice called from his left. Tory turned and saw the words were directed not at himself but toward a pair of broad-shouldered young men who had arrived on a westbound train.

"Nowhere particular," one answered in a heavily accented brogue.

"County Cork," the husky voice pronounced. "I'd know it like my own mother, wouldn't I?"

The deep voice belonged to a bewhiskered scarecrow of a corporal. He had adopted a similar accent and was in the process of offering the newcomers a fine bounty to sign up with his regiment.

"No, thank you just the same," the second Irishman said, leading his companion away. "We've done our fighting in the East. My brother and I've come west to find some peace."

The disappointed corporal growled and turned toward another newcomer. This one shook his head and continued on.

"It's getting harder, ain't it, Will?" a boy of perhaps fifteen said, joining the corporal and handing over a half loaf of bread and a pair of German sausages. "They get first crack at 'em in New York. I told the lieutenant we'd be better off going through the farm towns. A fellow used to working the fields all summer won't shy from a fight. Lots of men looking for work when winter comes, too."

"You recruiting?" Tory asked the pair.

"We are," the corporal answered. "You have a pa around someplace?"

"Know where we can find a man?" the youngster added.

"I know there are a lot of dead ones buried around Shiloh Church," Tory replied. "One's my brother."

"I hope and pray he was older'n you, boy," the corporal said, laughing.

"He wasn't by much," Tory boasted. "Wasn't any taller."

"Well, it isn't the inches that make a man," the boy answered, stretching himself. "I signed on at twelve to beat a drum, and I've managed to grow an inch or two since."

"Get along with you, son," the corporal said. "It's not infants we're seeking."

"I was told a fellow of sixteen could sign up," Tory said, staring hard at the corporal. "Of course, if you fellows don't need men, I suspect somebody will."

"Son, you couldn't pass for sixteen on a cloudy day," the corporal replied. "We sign drummers at sixteen, and I've already got one more of them than I want. I'll tell you the truth. Last time we took in a few youngsters, they were all dead of measles by July. Uncle Billy don't need babies.''

"He's got enough already?'' Tory asked the youngster. "Anyway, I've got my grandpa's permission to join. Doesn't that count for anything?''

"Let me see,'' the corporal asked.

Tory turned over the forged paper, and the two soldiers shared a laugh.

"Nobody's grandpa signed this,'' the corporal declared. "Good effort, though. You write the note and let somebody else sign it, did you?''

"Next time have 'em mark an *X*,'' the drummer suggested. "That's how I got in.''

"You got in because you could pick up a tune,'' the corporal argued. "And because the colonel was along, and he didn't know how hard war is on boys.''

"Oh, Will, you're closer to seventeen than seventy yourself,'' the boy complained. "This one here's got a little size. How're your teeth?''

"Sound,'' Tory said, opening his mouth so they could inspect.

"Open up your shirt,'' the corporal ordered.

Tory gave him an odd stare but complied with instructions.

"Don't look like a woman to me,'' the drummer observed.

"What?'' Tory cried. "A woman?''

"Caught two trying to join the Fifteenth,'' the corporal explained. "You've got no whiskers. I suppose there's the other way to check.''

Tory scowled, and the corporal laughed.

"The surgeons'll look you over,'' he explained. "So if you don't have all the proper parts, best step aside now and avoid the embarrassment. You sure there's no ma going to come to our camp and want you home.''

"My ma died of grief last summer," Tory explained. "Lost her oldest boy and husband both."

"Oh?" the corporal said, studying Tory's eyes. "That ain't entirely true now, is it?"

Tory dropped his gaze and tried to avoid the corporal's eyes.

"Spit it out," the corporal urged.

"My brother died at Shiloh, and it killed Ma," Tory told them.

"And your pa?" the drummer asked.

"You had one?" the corporal wondered.

"I sometimes wish to heaven that I didn't," Tory told them. "Look, I had the measles and mumps both before I was seven years old. There isn't anyone back home going to miss me. I'm used to work, can march to Florida if need be, and I won't run from a fight."

"Can't anybody be sure of that," the corporal insisted. "A man who's been in battle doesn't even know that. Each time's different."

"And if he did run?"

"That's it, Will," the drummer declared. "His pa's a deserter."

"Is he?" the corporal asked.

"Be simpler if it was," Tory said, sighing. "No, he resigned."

"Was an officer, then," the drummer observed. "Ran at Shiloh? Half the army did that. What made him different?"

"He was his regiment's colonel," Tory explained. "My pa's Lucius Bratton."

"Sure, we heard about that, all right," the drummer said, nodding his head. "Back then it was quite a stir. Now, well, we all of us done a bit of running at Chickamauga. Old Rosy, General Rosecrans, beat the army by a good twenty miles, the way I heard it. They took his army away from him, but I suspect he'll live. Your pa?"

"He's alive, all right," Tory admitted. "Probably has an easier time than I do."

"Plenty of poor boys in Billy Sherman's army," the corporal declared. "Not many admit to being rich. We started out with some bad officers, but they mostly fell out. Uncle Billy made himself a mistake or two early, but he doesn't make 'em often now. You sign up with us, life won't be too easy, but the food's regular as the fighting. Can you cook?"

"Some," Tory said, remembering the times he had helped in the kitchen. Dora, the Irish cook his mother had hired when he was eight, had taught him to bake biscuits and scramble eggs. He and Achilles had roasted a few chickens and one wild turkey they shot south of town.

"Well, Bratton, we can sure use a cook," the corporal announced. "Welcome to the ranks. Name's Will Hutchings. This fellow beside me here's Napoleon Brooks. He's Company A's drummer for now, but he expects a transfer to brigade. The general favors his singing voice. You don't sing, do you?"

"Used to carry a tune, but now I'm all squeaks and whines," Tory confessed. "Hector's my Christian name, but nobody much calls me that. I'm Tory."

"Will," the corporal said, shaking Tory's hand.

"Nobody calls me Napoleon, either," Brooks said, shaking Tory's hand next. "Poke's what my baby sister named me, and it stuck."

"Will you teach me the drum calls, Poke?" Tory asked.

"If you can cook better'n Will, I'll even teach you to sing," the youngster replied, grinning cheerfully.

"I can't promise you a full bounty, Tory, or even that we can take you," Will added. "That's the lieutenant's say-so. He's around someplace."

"Mostly some other place," Poke said, glancing around. "Anyway, he's no more'n seventeen, but when your daddy's a general, you can come by a lieutenant's bar easily enough."

"That the same general that likes you to sing?" Tory
asked.

"No, that'd be General William T. Sherman himself,"
Poke boasted. "And he don't like much, so I take it a
particular compliment he likes my voice."

Will laughed, and Tory decided that for once fate had
dealt him a fair hand, putting him in the company of such
good spirits.

Lieutenant Luther Berry was another matter. The youthful officer was all frown and temper. He scolded the others
for not buttoning their tunics, and he was less than delighted to find Tory there.

"I remember meeting your father," Berry said, frowning. "He appeared to be directing half his regiment in the
wrong direction."

Later Will Hutchings told Tory that the lieutenant had
been at school in Indiana until early 1863.

"What's he know of Shiloh?" Poke muttered. "Or any
other battle. He's spent his war at headquarters, writing
out dispatches for Rosy. Uncle Billy swept him out of
headquarters with a new broom."

"Shaped like a toe, I believe," Will added.

Tory refused to judge the lieutenant, though. He knew
how hard it was to overcome a reputation. To be truthful,
though, Berry wasn't much of a recruiter. He passed his
time in Chicago in the home of an aunt, and later, when
they took a train to Nashville, he stayed busy making an
inspection tour of the brothels set up along the Cumberland
River.

Tory, meanwhile, studied the drum calls hard. By the
time he and the thirty-four other recruits arrived at their
regiment's camp near Knoxville, Tennessee, Tory was the
equal of any drummer in his brigade. As expected, Poke
Brooks was ordered to Sherman's headquarters, and Tory
was officially mustered in as a replacement.

His first weeks of army life were full of routine drill
and tending the score of sick who daily reported them-

selves to the surgeon. Poor food and cold weather made things worse in November, and things became desperate when the regiment, reduced to a mere four hundred of its original thousand men, entered Chattanooga. Braxton Bragg's rebel forces surrounded the beleaguered Union army. Thousands of rebels supported by powerful batteries of artillery occupied a long ridge east of the little railroad town. The ominous gray bulk of Lookout Mountain towered over a bend in the Tennessee River, threatening the city's narrow supply lifeline.

Tory did his best to cheer the men of Lieutenant Berry's Company A. With the aid of Mary, a runaway off a Georgia plantation, he took over the cooking. He lacked Poke's singing voice, but he entertained his companions with readings from a handful of bawdy tales smuggled out of Nashville and "borrowed" from the lieutenant.

As for Berry, he kept himself occupied writing letters to his father requesting promotion and reassignment.

"As company commander, I deserve to be a captain!" he shouted at Will Hutchings one morning. Of course, Company A had once numbered a hundred effective men. It did well at Chattanooga mustering forty men healthy enough to form a skirmish line.

The plight of the army boxed in at Chattanooga could not continue forever. Sickness was killing more men than rebel artillery and rifle fire. With the twin victories at Vicksburg and Gettysburg that summer, the people back home had expected total victory by Christmas. Bragg's sudden and unexpected attack at Chickamauga in September had proven that the South still had muscle, and Lee continued to outfox larger armies in Virginia.

In December the weather worsened, but the federal generals were tired of stalemate. Bragg seemed none too eager to resume the fighting, and patrols observed that the rebels on Mission Ridge were growing careless.

Orders to attack finally came from headquarters.

"Our job's to distract the rebels in the center," Berry

told his ragged company. "No need to expose yourselves recklessly. Just keep up a fire and let Sherman outflank the ridge. Then we'll chase the blasted rebs all the way to Atlanta."

The recruits, Tory included, cheered those words. The veterans just shook their heads.

"Uncle Billy's a good man," Will said, "but that's Pat Cleburne holding the rebel flank. He's no Irishman to trifle with. He'll hold."

Tory didn't know one rebel general from another, excepting maybe the now dead Stonewall Jackson and that terror of the east, Bobby Lee, and he left the strategy to the generals. If he had learned anything since joining, it was to do your job and grumble quietly.

"You keep out of trouble, youngster," Mary warned when he took his place at the end of Company A's thin line. "You cook biscuits near as good as I do. Shame to waste such talent killing those poor boys atop that hill."

"That hill" was actually a long ridge that dominated the federal positions below. How anyone could safely distract an enemy perched up there was a mystery beyond Tory's comprehension. What soon became clear, too, was that Will was right about the rebel Irishman holding the right flank. His men weren't yielding ground, and that stymied the entire attack. Rebel cannons rained down shot and shell all along the center of the federal line. Exploding shot ripped men and animals apart. Couriers racing down the line drew the ire of sharp-eyed rebel riflemen.

The need for new messengers arose, and Poke Brooks apparently offered to ride to his old brigade with new orders. He arrived on a tall white horse that made him appear like a mouse atop an elephant. He was preparing to dismount when a well-placed shot fired from three hundred yards away tore through the back of his neck and passed downward through both lungs. The boy died in Will Hutchings's arms.

"Lord, Poke, you've gone and got yourself killed," the

corporal yelled. "Lord, what'll the general do for music?"

The noise drew more fire, and Lieutenant Berry's nervous horse bolted, carrying its rider within range of a rebel battery. The same shell that killed the poor horse carried away the hapless lieutenant's head.

"Enough!" Will shouted angrily.

Men up and down the line similarly cursed the rebel fire coming from the heights. Then, without orders or seemingly any sense, one regiment after another began snaking its way up the ridge.

It was an odd thing, everyone agreed afterward. The "soldiers' fight," they called it. While colonels and captains met to decide what to do, enraged corporals and privates headed for the enemy.

"Might as well die up there as down here," Will told Tory.

Now Tory knew that his duties did not require him to advance in the first rank of battle. In fact, he was supposed to stay behind and tend the wounded. There were no wounded men from Company A below the ridge, though. There were three dead men. Those still alive were trudging uphill. He went with them.

"Go back, youngster," a German private named Hohenhof yelled.

"Boy, stay to the rear!" Will hollered.

Tory couldn't do it, though. For the first time he knew how Achilles felt. And when the national colors carried by an adjacent regiment went down, he discarded his drum and raised the flag.

"For Poke!" he shouted.

Company A surged upward with a cohesion they had never demonstrated in drill. After them came the rest of the regiment, and then the brigade reserve. The shout spread up and down the line. Men who had never met the sweet-voiced little drummer fixed bayonets and charged when they learned of his death.

It was exhilarating. Tory felt reborn. He could hear mus-

ket balls and conical bullets whining past his ears, but he
never hesitated. Instead he waved the big flag and beck-
oned his companions onward. Will was on his left. Hohenhof was on his right. Men who had been strangers a
month before were now brothers. Together they reached
the halfway mark.

For a few moments they paused to catch their breath. It
was another oddity, but the Rebel cannons, placed as they
were atop the crest, could no longer hit their attackers.
Except for a sporadic rifle fire, the onrushing federals were
immune to harm. Realizing this, an Indiana sergeant
shouted and motioned his regiment toward the summit.

"Well, do you want to live forever?" Will called.

Company A resumed their advance, led by Tory and the
big flag. The banner had begun the fight with two small
round holes. It now had more than twenty. A minié ball
ripped Tory's hat from his head. Another shattered the
flagstaff. Tory adjusted his grip and continued. Then a
fiery sensation sliced through his left thigh, and he stumbled.

"Tory, you all right?" Will called.

In that instant a rebel rifleman shot the corporal through
the right arm. Hohenhof made certain that graycoat never
harmed anyone else. A single shot struck the rebel's forehead.

It seemed to Tory that the world slowed down. He didn't
remember it all. His head was full of pain, and he saw
blood spreading across his left leg. He thought of poor Pat
and suspected they would share the same fate, amputation.
Screaming like a banshee, Tory threw himself forward.
The rebels suddenly bolted, and Tory had the satisfaction
of planting the colors beside the still-smoking barrel of a
captured rebel howitzer. He then collapsed.

For a time he was in a fog. Then he saw the big German,
Hohenhof, binding the bloody leg with what was left of
Tory's left trouser leg. That seemed to ease the pain, and
Will's grinning face restored his spirits.

"Ball passed right through," the corporal said, raising his arm to show the white bandage he'd applied himself. "We've broken their whole line, Tory, cracked Bragg's army right in the middle. He'll never get 'em formed and ready to fight now. It'll be Chickamauga all over again except they've got no George Thomas to stop the rout. Lord, look at 'em run!"

Indeed, the former defenders of Mission Ridge scrambled down the far slope, abandoning their heavy guns and running as if the devil himself was in pursuit. Perhaps he was, for the half-starved federal army, bottled up in Chattanooga for months, was out for blood. Unfortunately, the stubborn Irishman, Pat Cleburne, was every bit the equal of George Thomas and stopped the Union army in its tracks a few miles down the road. The rebels got away, and the war continued.

SEVENTEEN

By an odd quirk of destiny or coincidence, Tory and Will Hutchings found themselves in a sprawling new hospital recently relocated from Cairo to Nashville. In beds placed on either side of a pleasant window, the two young men received the particular attention of the ward's chief nurse, Emiline Bratton.

"Somehow I just knew you were going to do this," Em scolded Tory shortly after his arrival. "You just had to go and prove you weren't like Pa when everyone who cared about you already knew it."

"I didn't just have to prove it to everybody else," Tory tried to explain. "I had to know myself. It's hard to explain how it all happened, that charge. It just did."

"You should've seen him!" Will piped in. "It was magnificent. The generals spotted him with their telescopes, that fool boy with the big flag! He carried the day, you know."

"It's like him," Emiline observed. "I work all these years patching up boys and then find my own brother's gone and got himself shot, too."

"Was only the one shot, through the thigh," Tory argued. "I heard the doctors. As clean a wound as they've seen."

"You remember it, do you?" she asked, scowling. "With a chloroform mask on and your head light from loss of blood! They were talking about the corporal here, shot through the arm. A miracle wound for certain, what with two bones there to fracture."

"My leg," Tory said, paling with a sudden rush of fear. "They didn't—"

He fingered the side of his leg with his fingers, but he was stiff and sore. He couldn't feel anything below mid-thigh.

"It's still there," his sister told him. "Mind you, I saw to it Dr. Polk took the ball out. Nasty thing, too, big as the end of your thumb. Nicked the bone, so he took out a sliver of that as well. You've also got yourself a nice notch in the left ear. Bled some, but it shouldn't be much trouble to you later. Another ball lodged in your right boot, but it hardly broke the skin."

"That all?" Tory asked, aghast at the notion that he'd been shot three times.

"Not quite," she said, sliding the sheet down from his side and lifting a nightshirt to reveal a heavy white bandage wrapped around his ribs. "That was the close one, little brother. If it hadn't deflected off a rib, it would have torn right through your heart. You remember that one, will you? Don't go leading any new charges. Promise?"

"I can't," he said, growing solemn. "I signed on for the balance of the war, Em. It's not over. I'll be going back."

"You lied to get in," she declared. "I plan to get you discharged as underage."

"Don't," he pleaded. "I finally found something I can do right."

"I've spoken to the other men, Tory," she said, sitting beside him. "What you mainly did was cook. I've made friends here. If you're determined to stay in the army, why not serve out your time here?''

''So you can keep an eye on me?''

''Would that be so bad?''

''It would,'' Will broke in. ''Excuse me for entering a family argument, ma'am, but when a boy sets his feet on a man's road, he can't go turning around. Tory's a soldier now. Anyone on that charge knew it the moment he snatched up that flag. It's a hard thing, being called son of a coward. Sometimes it's every bit as hard to be called a hero. You find a lot's expected of you either way.''

''And not just by others, Em,'' Tory added.

''Well, you'll not be rejoining anybody's army for a time,'' she insisted. ''Mr. Hutchings here can leave in another week, but you'll stay longer, Tory.''

''Ma'am, there's never been any mister to me,'' Will said, laughing. ''My sainted mother called me William, but no one since has done it. I'm Will.''

''Mr. Hutchings, you had better get used to titles of respect,'' Emiline warned. ''That's expected of an officer.''

''Ah, I'll never make an officer,'' Will complained. ''I hardly deserve two stripes.''

''Nevertheless, your colonel sent over a new tunic with a lieutenant's bar sewn on,'' Emiline explained. ''I understand they've got a little something planned for you, too, Tory.''

''Maybe I'll be named corporal in place of Will,'' Tory said, laughing at the notion.

''Why, you've spoiled the surprise,'' she said, matching his grin.

Tory passed the rest of December and most of January in the hospital, mending. He was back in the field that spring, though, helping drive through one rebel defense line after another toward Atlanta. In May, at an obscure little Georgia crossroads called New Hope Church, Sherman's attack was thrown back with heavy losses. Four companies of fresh Alabama troops managed to cut their way through the federal line, and in the swirl of smoke and confusion, Tory found himself trapped with three wounded men behind the enemy lines.

"What should we do?" a youngish recruit named Pohlman asked. His right arm was broken, and he was of little use is a fight. His cousin, a Chicago shoemaker named Robeson, had his left ear shot away. Only Lars Hohenhof had seen battle before, and he was looking to Tory for leadership.

"You fellows can all walk, can't you?" Tory asked.

"If they can't, I'll drag 'em," Hohenhof growled. Despite taking a rifle ball through the upper arm, he was showing no inclination to surrender.

"Then I say we make a run at that right earthwork there," Tory told them. "I saw a flag up there a minute ago. Maybe our boys are coming back for us."

It was a long chance, but the Alabamans had seemingly passed by, and nobody was in a hurry to stop the little band. Tory led the way, but when he reached the work, he found no welcoming Illinoians. The flag belonged to the Alabamans, and there were close to thirty of them milling around there.

"Made a bad bargain this time, Corporal," Robeson declared.

Tory never hesitated. He pointed a Colt cavalry pistol he'd picked up weeks earlier at the nearest rebel and fired. He shot a second one before the others had a chance to react. Hohenhof swung his rifle at a third, and the little rebel line melted like butter under a summer sun. In one of those blind flashes of instinct a soldier scarcely remembers later, Tory wrenched the Alabamans' flag from their color-bearer and dashed off toward the nearest line of blue-clad soldiers.

Now, there were smarter things than charging your lines carrying an enemy battle flag, but Tory's foolish act was abetted by Will Hutchings, who recognized the foolish youngster with the flag as his own lost corporal. Hohenhof and his two companions trailed along behind. It would have been amusing except that the Alabamans' major had recovered from the initial shock and was ordering a volley.

"Down!" Will shouted. "Get down!"

The volley came thundering out of the shell of the old federal defense line, knocking limbs from trees and shattering the wing of the eagle atop the flagstaff. Tory raced on, unhurt, and an Iowa battery opened up on the Alabamans, sending them scrambling for cover. Tory returned with his little band unhurt and turned over the flag to Will.

"They'll likely give you my job if you keep this up," Will declared, slapping the young man on the back.

"Thanks, but I'd as soon stay a corporal," Tory replied. "I get lost as it is."

A half hour later, trying to recover the lost trenches, Tory received a musket ball through the meat of his lower leg. Three days later he was back in Nashville.

"Missed me, didn't you?" Emiline asked as she changed the bandage on his leg. "Just couldn't stay away."

"Just wanted some rest," he told her. "I have to admit it, though. I'd take an ounce or two of lead in return for your smile and some clean sheets."

"I told you to stay home," she said, touching her hand to his forehead. "The fever's passed. I suppose that means they'll have to schedule the parade now."

"Down Illinois Avenue, most likely," Tory said, laughing at the notion.

"They've told you?" Em asked. "I thought it was only decided yesterday."

"What exactly are you talking about?" Tory asked. "I wasn't serious."

"Well, you're going to have to be soon," she said. "If you thought a corporal's stripes were a surprise, you'll never believe this one. No one in Peoria will. That much is certain."

She was right about that. Three days later a hospital steward changed his bandages, bathed him in a tub, and shaved the first few hairs from his chin. That afternoon a train from Washington brought a delegation to Nashville that included a representative from the War Department. After a speech that Tory considered far too long for the occasion, the roundish, balding man pinned a bright ribbon bearing a distinctive star to Tory's tunic, the Medal of Honor.

The fanfare embarrassed Tory, and he found it hard to lie in bed as other, more seriously wounded men looked at the bit of a soldier with the medal pinned to his chest. As soon as the dignitaries left, Tory asked Emiline to put the medal in its case and keep it with her belongings.

"Won't you want it for the parade?" she asked.

"You were serious about that?" Tory asked. He could feel a tremor winding its way through him.

"Why, the mayor himself's ordered it," Emiline explained. "General Sherman's offered your whole company a week's furlough so they can march through Peoria with you at the head of the column."

"Small parade," Will observed. "Not many of us left."

"They've recruited fifty men to restore you to strength," Emiline continued. "What's more, the governor's sending one of the new regiments to join you. How's that for a welcome home, Tory?"

"Are you coming?" he asked her.

"I have my work here," she said, growing serious.

"Then you understand how I feel about a parade," he grumbled. "I've got soldiering to do."

Part of soldiering was following orders, though. So it was that Tory and Will Hutchings boarded a northbound train, rolled through Louisville, passed Indianapolis, and continued all the way to Chicago. There they transferred to a military train carrying the new regiment and most of

Company A. In Peoria a band played when they arrived, and the mayor spoke for an hour about how the town was honored by the presence of its young hero.

During the parade, Tory saw few familiar faces. Later, when he limped out of the carriage provided by the mayor and knocked on his grandfather's door, a new maid tried to turn him away.

"Tell Mr. Drury his grandson is here to see him!" the mayor barked. The chagrined maid tried to explain, but before she finished, Abner Drury appeared.

"He left this home without my permission," the old man said. "His father's brought shame to a good name, and nothing can erase that."

"Look at him, Abner," the mayor, a newcomer Tory didn't even know, urged. "I've seen the portrait of your daughter hanging in your study. This boy's her very image. Don't you see her in him?"

"That only reminds me of my loss," the judge declared. "Hector understands, don't you?"

"I understand that I'm not welcome," Tory replied. "I know you kept my father's letters from me."

"*That* was a service," the old man insisted. "It's true what he says, though. You do have your mother's eyes. But they're set in your father's face, and I won't have a trace of that man in my house."

"Good-bye, Grandpa," Tory said, making a slow turn and trying to avoid revealing the pain brought on by his yet-to-heal leg. That evening he begged out of a party thrown in his honor. The wound had begun to bleed again.

The day he was scheduled to return to Chicago en route to Nashville, Captain McNair and Victoria appeared. The captain offered him the gift of three favorite books. Then he excused himself, leaving Victoria and Tory alone.

"I joined up," he told her. "I don't understand. I looked for you as we made our way through town. I saw your father, but you—"

"Tory, I'm supposed to apologize for treating you

rudely at the harvest dance. I suppose, in a way, I'm responsible for your wounds. I'm not sorry, though. You needed spurring, and I'm proud to have done it.''

"I don't understand."

"Yes, you said that," she pointed out. "Did you expect me to rush out and embrace you? You don't remember much, do you?''

"I remember every word we've ever shared," he insisted. "I love you, Victoria."

"You wouldn't know the meaning of the word. I suppose you have our whole life planned, how you'll pin your medal on my chemise and sweep me away to a happy ending.''

"I gave Em the medal," he told her. "I didn't earn it. I was just trying to get through to my regiment. There were four of us did it. I picked up a reb flag. I suppose that got noticed. I didn't expect, didn't even want this fool parade. I did think you might manage a smile for me.''

"Tory, what would be the point? What future could you and I have together? Could I in good conscience subject my children to a life you yourself described so vividly, so terribly as cruel injustice? Could I condemn us all to a future of poverty and—''

"And what?" Tory asked with wide eyes.

"Disgrace," she said, sliding away when he reached for her hand. "You remember my photographs."

"Your uncles and cousins?"

"Both uncles are dead. Two of the cousins are gone, too. John, the youngest, is crippled. Jacob, the other, is missing in Virginia. My entire family, Tory! They're dead or maimed! What do you expect me to feel for you? Your father's a coward and you're only here because you disobeyed orders and enjoyed rare good fortune.''

"Is that what it was?" Tory asked. "I'll have to remember. Here I thought I was doing what you wanted, serving my country and erasing the dishonor placed on my name.''

"Some shame lingers," she argued.

"I can see that!" he cried. "Victoria, I've done nothing wrong!"

"I wish you well, Tory," she said, turning to leave. "Go back to the army. Do something useful. Save yourself some grief and don't return to Peoria."

Tory frowned. It hadn't been his idea to return. Except for a brief visit with Pat Harper, he had found no solace and no comfort in the trip. He welcomed a return to the fighting.

He had to wait for that, though. The train journey did nothing to improve his health, and Will Hutchings had Hohenhof, now wearing sergeant's stripes, carry the young corporal back to his sister's hospital ward. By the time he was walking properly, Sherman was at the gates of Atlanta.

Even after John Bell Hood took over what was left of the rebel Army of Tennessee, it was clear Sherman had all the advantages. Hood didn't help himself hammering away at powerful Union positions. By September the city was in Union hands, and what followed was a few final months of lingering death for the Southern Confederacy.

Tory saw Georgia and South Carolina plundered and burned. If it was true that Sherman boasted he would make Georgia howl, then the general was as good as his word. It was little better in the Carolinas. By the time Joe Johnston surrendered his outnumbered shell of a Confederate army, Lee had already given up. Only a few insignificant fights followed.

With little future awaiting him in Peoria, Tory pondered a future that lacked easy answers. At one time he had considered a career in the law like his grandfather or perhaps becoming a teacher like Captain McNair. Two years in the army changed him. He had become adept at repairing guns, and he was more comfortable around the machinery and gunpowder than he was sitting on a bench with his nose in a book.

"What do you figure to do now?" Will asked after they

marched through Washington in the grand parade of the Western armies.

"Don't know," Tory confessed.

"Me, I've saved my pay, have no wife nor children, no kin to bring over from Ireland. I thought I might go west, explore the rest of the country. I'm tired of cities. I want to find some place to make my own."

"I wouldn't mind that, Will. Mind some company?"

"Hoped for some, actually. Mind, you know by now that I snore, and you'd have to do the cooking."

"Then you'll have to provide meat for the pot," Tory insisted. "Fair's fair."

They laughed, shook hands, and headed for St. Louis. They never got past River Street.

It was funny in a way. For days Will Hutchings had been recounting his first two years in the country, working in a mercantile store in Chicago.

"There's a fortune to be made in such a store," Will had boasted.

They had scarcely left their seats when Tory spied the small red placard in the window of McNamara's Mercantile Store. FOR SALE, it read.

"Will?" Tory asked.

"He'll want too much money," the former lieutenant declared.

As it turned out, though, McNamara had died, and a German banker was eager to sell. For five hundred dollars the two discharged soldiers managed between them and a five-year mortgage, they took possession of the business.

It was almost a week before the partners realized they needed help with the business. Neither was half the clerk who was needed.

"I know who we need," Tory announced.

"Yes?" Will asked.

"Pat Harper. He spent the war's final three years as a quartermaster's clerk, and he'd welcome the chance to leave Peoria."

"Send a telegram," Will replied. "And tell him to hurry."

Pat was there within the week, and he surprised his employers by making sense of jumbled accounts and providing an intimate knowledge of supply sources. The three partners quickly established a reputation for fair prices and honesty.

Tory devoted most of his time to setting up a small repair shop for firearms. Westbound pioneers and Mississippi travelers kept him busy. When not repairing rifles and pistols, he tinkered with his own designs. He was altering a notoriously unreliable Henry rifle when Emiline arrived.

"Haven't you had your fill of guns?" she asked.

"I'm not shooting them," he pointed out. "Truth is, I rarely shot anybody in the war. Most days I cooked and beat a drum. Managed to get some people killed, but most of them wore the blue."

"I suppose it's as peaceful here as anywhere," she admitted. She then passed over a small parcel. Inside was the small case containing his medal, an envelope with money he'd asked her to keep safe, and two letters from their father. There was nothing particularly new in the few lines he had written in the first letter. Lucius Bratton was down in Texas, looking for property to buy.

"Dreaming again," Tory observed.

"He's trying to rebuild his life," Emiline argued.

"We're all of us doing that," Tory told her.

The second letter asked his children to join him in Kansas.

"Did you read this?" Tory asked.

"He didn't know how to reach you, Tory," she explained. "I don't suppose you want to go farther west?"

"We have a business here now," Tory said, frowning. "To be honest about it, I wouldn't go anyway. Pa would expect the boy he left in Peoria. I'm not the same now, Em."

"Don't you think I know that?" she asked. "I've seen the aftermath of battle myself. You don't fight a war and come home the same."

"You're talking about Pa, aren't you?"

"Remember, he was in Mexico and came back. Then it started all over again. Aren't you a little more compassionate toward him?"

"I try to be, Em, but I can't help remembering those long months in Peoria. There are things I've lost forever."

"Things or people?"

Tory frowned. Pat Harper had brought the painful news that Victoria had wed Martin Carpenter, a young Chicago lawyer who had passed the war as a clerk in the War Department. Tory couldn't help feeling a little bitter. Apparently she had forgotten about her dead cousins.

"Em, I try not to blame anyone for anything. It's hard, though."

"At least answer him."

"I will," Tory promised.

It took him a week to think of the right words to write. He had come of age on the battlefield, and his literary skills had not improved there. Tory never did express his real feelings. He finally scripted a brief note detailing the success of the mercantile and closing with the hope that his father might find peace with a new start.

The next letter Lucius Bratton sent came a year later. If peace was to be had in Kansas, it seemed odd to Tory that his father should have enlisted with George Custer's Seventh Cavalry.

Tory, on the other hand, prospered in St. Louis. He enjoyed the bustling city situated at the confluence of the Missouri and Mississippi rivers. The whole world seemed to pass up and down those two waterways. Months passed, and things only got better. Profits increased, and the partners paid their mortgage. Pat Harper took a Missouri Street chorus girl, Flora O'Hara, for a bride. They then began populating the West.

Will Hutchings selected a solemn young former nurse who had been working at the St. Louis Soldiers' Home for his bride. Tory served as best man at his sister's wedding.

"You should find yourself a good woman and start a family," Pat advised afterward. "Forget that sour-faced girl from Pennsylvania. She was never half good enough for you."

"Is that all there is to life, finding a wife and bringing children into the world?"

"It has its rewards, Tory," Pat said, smiling wildly.

"They aren't all Flora," Tory said, sighing. "You've been lucky. I'm afraid I used every ounce of good fortune due me at Mission Ridge."

"You're right about Flora, my friend. She's the finest woman I've ever known. But, Tory, if you close your eyes, you won't ever find a rose, not even when it's growing in a bed of briers. I know you feel a weight left by your father, but don't you think you've proven yourself? You've won the Medal of Honor, Tory, and look what you've made of this business! Oh, I keep the books, and Will enchants the ladies, but it was all your doing, bringing us together. The ladies may buy a bit of lace and fabric, but it's the sale of those rebuilt Henrys of yours that produce our profits."

"It's a thing I can understand, Pat. You don't need to believe in anything to fix a machine. Cold steel doesn't ask questions about your family. It doesn't hold the past against you."

"Tory, nobody's come of worse roots than I have. Flora's not spoken of her parents, and I've not asked. When a person doesn't speak of a thing, sometimes it's best to choose another subject. I have my boys and girls and the friendship and respect of my friends. I can't think of anything more I will ever need."

"Nor can I, Pat."

"But you need more, eh? Is that it?" Pat asked.

"I don't know what I need or even what I want," Tory

confessed. "I just know I don't have it yet."

"You're not yet twenty," Pat said, laughing. "There's time perhaps."

I hope so, Tory thought. But life had its own way of hurrying things. He wondered if there was, after all, time.

EIGHTEEN

In the years immediately following the Civil War, the country experienced a great surge westward. Disheartened Southerners, Union veterans, and freed slaves passed through St. Louis on their way to new territories in search of fresh opportunity. For six years McNamara's Mercantile grew and prospered because of that movement. Then, in 1873, everything changed. Banks and railroads collapsed in oceans of debt. Farmers lost their land. People who had once been so full of hope and expectation began to despair.

McNamara's did not escape the depression. Pat Harper was the first to notice the problem.

"People aren't paying their accounts," he told his partners. "We have to be careful not to overextend ourselves."

It was difficult, though. Affable Will Hutchings had trouble saying no to old friends of the store, especially those widowed during the war and burdened by responsibility. Another troubling trend was the increasingly large number of war orphans crowding the river area streets. Raised by relatives or in soldiers' orphanages, they often found themselves homeless when homes closed their doors or relatives grew desperate. Some flocked to the cities, hoping to find work. Others, hungry and cold, appealed to the charity of veterans. Those who couldn't earn or beg turned to thievery.

"What's this?" Tory noted after catching a boy of fourteen with a small pair of denim trousers under his shirt. "They're not even the right size!"

"For my little brother," the boy explained. "He's near naked."

When Tory followed the youngster to a home the boys had made from two old pickle barrels, he shook his head and handed over the trousers.

"When was the last time you ate?" Tory asked.

"Yesterday a lady gave us an apple," the smaller boy answered.

"Come along, then," Tory urged.

"No, sir, please," the older boy pleaded. "Don't turn us over to the sheriff."

"I'm not so old as I seem," Tory explained. "Wasn't long ago I was in the army, half-starved myself. Even an apple would have seemed like a feast. Come along. I'm certain my sister can spare some supper."

But as the situation worsened, the partners' soft hearts began to harden. By late 1873 Pat had six children, and Emiline had delivered two boys to Will. They, too, had to eat, and the store often failed to produce any profit for weeks at a time. Worse, the Winchester Company had manufactured a new repeating rifle that made Tory's rebuilt Henrys next to worthless.

"What do we do now?" Pat asked. "In six months we'll be broke."

"Nonsense," Will complained. "We sell more dry goods than ever."

"Yes, but it's mostly on account," Pat pointed out. "On paper, we're rich. But our customers are facing the same trouble. If Dr. Mueller's patients don't pay him, his wife can't pay us for their daughter's dresses. No one seems to have any money.''

Amid the terrible depression, rumors of new gold strikes seemed to crop up everywhere. Armies of hopeful men set out for Colorado only to discover news that a bigger strike had been made north of the Yellowstone. Then there were the Black Hills.

''It's said Custer's taking his whole regiment up there, looking for gold,'' Will said. ''Isn't that the outfit your pa's riding with, Tory?''

''You know it is,'' Tory replied. He didn't like to be reminded of the fact. Once a colonel, Lucius Bratton had turned to service as a meager private in order to feed and clothe himself. The old man had written glowing letters about Colorado, but Tory had looked past the words at the growing desperation behind them.

I'll make it all up to you, son, Lucius Bratton wrote often. Sometimes the notes were scribbled in the old Bible code Tory and Achilles had invented when they were small boys. Using compass bearings and Bible verses, they could direct anyone almost anywhere. More than once the path led them through Widow Fitzhugh's garden and into trouble, Tory remembered.

Bad as times were, Tory found them easier to accept than the recollections of veterans who had fought with Lucius and Achilles Bratton at Shiloh. Old soldiers would appear like phantoms whenever Tory felt the last of them had finally vanished.

''Spare us something, son,'' they pleaded. ''Do it for your poor brother's sake. We were with him when he waved that flag. We weren't the kind of men to run away like your father!''

If their words didn't bring back the Peoria years to his mind, then the small army of orphans and the parade of one-armed and one-legged men walking the streets of St. Louis did.

''There but for the grace of God,'' Will often remarked.

Pat just gazed at his stump and frowned.

It was late the following year when a man dressed in the blue trousers of a cavalryman appeared, bringing news that Lucius Bratton was dead.

"Must have been a time dying the way I heard it," the soldier explained. "He and a pair of others set off from the regiment, likely looking for gold. Some say they found some. Who can know for sure? One thing's certain, though. The Sioux caught 'em and made 'em suffer for it. By the time we found the bodies, wasn't much left. We buried all three, or at least what we found of 'em."

It was bitter news for the children of a despised man.

"I thought maybe he had changed," Emiline remarked. "I hoped he would redeem himself somehow."

No, Tory thought. *He died as he lived, chasing dreams while avoiding his real responsibilities.*

Tory couldn't help but worry he would do the same. Whenever Pat and Flora had him to dinner, some young Irishwoman always appeared.

" 'Tis my cousin Kate," Flora would announce. "She's just come out from Chicago."

Another time it would be an old friend from County Cork.

"I was thinking about the store," Tory told his partners early the following year. "We are doing better, but only slightly. I don't feel like I'm holding up my part. No one brings their rifles in these days. What little work I do get is from Pinkerton agents or army officers. It's not enough to justify keeping a gunsmith. If I left, the store would support you two."

"Lord, Tory, what sort of survival's that?" Pat asked. "Cutting out your heart to save your liver?"

"You're not just a partner," Will reminded him. "You're family."

In the end the store was saved by the death of Abner Drury. He may have been happily ignorant of the fate of his grandchildren, but he had provided for them in his will.

Captain McNair arrived in St. Louis in June 1876 to present a bank draft for twenty thousand dollars.

"Our firm has handled all the details," he explained. "You'll be pleased to know I bought the house myself. I think Victoria was especially pleased. She always valued your friendship, Tory."

"Did she?" he asked.

It was more than a week later that they learned the McNair-Carpenter firm had assets to cover only half of the draft. Victoria's husband had run off with the bulk of the funds. He was later spotted with a Chicago dancer in New York.

A hard blow, Captain McNair wrote in a letter.

"I never wanted his money," Tory said, handing over his share to Emiline. "Pay the debts. I think I'll head west, maybe see the Pacific Ocean."

"I don't want the money if it means you're leaving," Emiline replied. "I have no other family left."

"You have two sons and Will," Tory reminded her. "I'll be back one day."

"Pa used to say that, Tory. He didn't always make it back."

"I'm not Pa," he told her.

"You still might not make it back," she argued. "A lot can happen to a man, and not all of it's planned."

They were at the New Western Theater, watching a dance revue, when a newsboy dashed across the stage announcing that Sioux Indians had wiped out George Custer and most of the Seventh Cavalry. The audience laughed. Most had read of the new expedition to round up hostiles, and they thought it was but another act. It wasn't.

"I'm sorry," a swollen-eyed actress declared moments later. "Many of us performed for the general last month, and some had sweethearts with the Seventh. We simply can't continue."

The notion of a whole cavalry regiment slaughtered by

Indians only days before the country was to celebrate its
hundredth year was beyond imagining. When Tory read
the story in a special edition of the newspaper early the
following morning, he couldn't very well deny it. A list
of the dead appeared, but they were faceless. Lucius Brat
ton had mentioned a few men in his letters, but they
weren't listed.

"Probably the ones he ran off with," Emiline suggested.

"Could be," Tory admitted.

Custer's death gave new impetus to mining operations
in the Black Hills, and many St. Louis merchants loaded
up wares and headed for the gold camps.

"We might have a try ourselves, eh?" Pat asked.
"Your pa must have written something about that country. Maybe he gave you a clue as to where the gold can
be found."

"Pat, there's honest work here in St. Louis," Tory objected. "I don't need to be rich. I have what I need here.
That's enough for me."

The next day Amos Suggs appeared.

The first hint of his arrival was a lingering odor of
horseflesh and wet leather. Tory didn't see the man until
later, when Will led him back to the corner of the shop
where Tory was repairing the shattered stock of a carbine.

"This fellow says he knew your pa, Tory," Will explained.

"Oh?" Tory asked, glancing up from his work.

"That's not exactly it," Suggs said after Will returned
to the other end of the store. "I'm Amos Suggs," he
added, offering his hand. Tory ignored it. "I come across
him a time or two out west. When he was with the Seventh
Cavalry."

"That would have been a time or two more than I saw
him," Tory replied. "We weren't all that close, mister."

"Still, he was thinking of you at the end," Suggs said,
producing the watch. "Gave the man that found him dying
this watch to bring you."

"It took you a long time," Tory observed as he examined the watch. It was badly scratched, and the rear panel didn't close tightly the way he remembered. It sounded odd, too.

"I wasn't the man who promised to bring it to you," Suggs explained. "If I had been, you'd had it earlier. I found it near the Indian camps on the Little Big Horn River. Just this June."

"You were with the Seventh at Little Big Horn?" Tory asked.

"I was with the other column. Civilian scout. I've scouted and traded with half the tribes living west of the Mississippi. I talk with the Crows for the generals. Did anyhow. The days of talking are long past."

"Well, I thank you for bringing the watch," Tory said, sighing. "Should have gone to my brother, but—"

"He got himself killed," Suggs broke in. "I know the tale. You say you weren't close, you and your pa. Odd he'd send you the watch, then."

"Was his effort at making peace, I suppose. Look, Mr. Suggs, I don't know what you came here for, but if it was for some sort of gratitude, I don't have much to spare. We're having a hard time these days, my partners and me. The watch just doesn't mean that much to me."

"That's what old Pettis figured," Suggs said. "Hard times, you say? Ever consider trying your hand panning for gold?"

"I repair guns and sometimes tend a store counter," Tory explained. "I don't know that country. Last I heard Sioux Indians were killing people there."

"Still may be, but I do know the country, and I'd see we weren't troubled too much."

"I'm sorry, but I don't see where I'd be any use to you. If it's partners you're seeking, you'll find a hundred men better able to work a gold claim than me."

"Maybe not," Suggs said, reaching deep into the pocket of his buckskin jacket. He produced the series of odd scratchings Lucius Bratton had hidden in the watch. "Your pa fond of codes, was he?"

"This was in the watch?" Tory asked.

"Found it there. Don't figure any Indian did that."

"No, it's Pa's work," Tory admitted. "You didn't figure it out, did you?"

"Makes no sense to me nor anybody else I showed it to. Like Morse code, but different. What's it about?"

"It's about why you're here," Tory said, waving Will back over.

"No need to involve a lot of people in this," Suggs warned.

"Yes, there is," Tory insisted. "Will, get Pat."

"I'd give some thought to what you're doing," Suggs said, drawing a Colt revolver. "I didn't come here to get myself cornered by a bunch of shopkeepers."

"If you know my brother died at Shiloh, then you know I've done some fighting myself," Tory replied. "I'm not going anywhere or doing anything without my partners knowing about it. I don't know what happened to Pa, but I'd be surprised if he was thinking of me when he deserted the cavalry."

"Maybe he was thinking of you and maybe he wasn't," Suggs said, lowering the pistol when he noticed one-armed Pat Harper arrived with a double-barreled shotgun. "I can't know for certain, and I don't see it matters. I can tell you he come across gold in the Black Hills, and most men that rode with him believe he left a fair amount of it up there someplace. I suspect those scratches are some kind of map. Now, you might make sense of it and get up there on your own, but if there's as much gold as I think, there's plenty for everybody. You don't know the country. I do. I don't know old Bratton's code. You do. So, we can make a bargain, the two of us, or we can neither of us find it."

"Don't trust him, Tory," Will warned.

"You'll get yourself killed up there," Pat added.

"Well, it's possible," Tory said, studying Suggs's eyes. "What he says is true, though, and we could sure use gold."

"I thought you just said you had all you needed right here," Pat objected.

"And I thought you were all for trying your luck up there even without a map, Pat, Look, if this fellow's agreeable, we can leave Will to tend the business and have a try. I can figure out the map. It's just directions and distances. We go, have a look, and come back. We either find gold or we don't."

"You got it all figured, do you?" Suggs asked.

"Not a bit of it," Tory answered. "I don't know you, mister, and I don't trust what I don't know. You hand me Pa's watch, knowing all the time it was the map he intended me to have."

"And how do you see it that way?" Suggs asked.

"Because I made that code up myself when I was nine years old," Tory explained. "My brother and I used it to track each other in the woods. This way we always had a meeting spot if one or the other got lost. We showed it to Pa after he got on us about going off on our own."

"Isn't anybody else knows it?" Suggs asked.

"Nobody," Tory insisted.

"Now that Tory's put his cards on the table, why don't you go and do the same," Pat suggested. "We're not the brightest of fellows, so make it easy to understand, will you?"

"Easy as I can," Suggs agreed. "The gold's there. We go get it. I split it even with you, boy."

"The split's three ways," Tory said. "Pat's to have a share, too. I'll want him along."

"Him!" Suggs exclaimed.

"He's right, Tory," Pat said, frowning. "You don't need half a man. Take Will."

"Em'll never let him go," Tory declared. "And I don't

plan on riding into hostile Indian country with a man that keeps secrets. If Pat goes, though, he gets an equal share.''

''You're a tough one to figure out,'' Suggs said, shaking his head. ''There's enough gold and plenty of work for three, but a one-armed youngster like him's not much use in a fight.''

''You only say that because you haven't seen him fight,'' Tory said, turning to Pat. ''Me, I'd rather have half of Patrick Michael Harper than a dozen of anybody else. So, Mr. Suggs, what's your answer?''

''Guess I've got partners,'' Suggs grumbled. ''Take me a day or to arrange pack animals. We can get a train as far as Bismarck. Then we head to Fort Lincoln. That's how the Seventh started, so I suspect it's the best way to follow your map.''

''It isn't,'' Tory said, studying the letters. ''I can tell that much. I'll need a Bible for most of it, but I recognize the first passage. It talks about heart, heart of the world.''

''Harney Peak,'' Suggs declared. ''That would be the right area, all right. Wasn't too far from there the Seventh found what was left of the other man. It's a powerful medicine place for the Sioux, though. Won't be easy slipping in and getting away.''

''I never found much easy in this life,'' Tory said, turning to Pat. ''Well?''

''Heart of the world, eh?'' Pat asked. ''Bet it's a pretty place.''

''You're going, then,'' Will said. His eyes were full of disbelief, and Tory knew there would be trouble convincing Em about the trip. As for Flora, he deemed that to be Pat's business.

''Get your Bible and start to work,'' Suggs urged. ''Isn't just a few miners up there eager to take our gold. There are whole camps of them.''

''We're not much different,'' Tory observed.

''We're a world away from them, boy,'' Suggs argued.

"We have a map and a direction. For once the luck's on my side."

Tory wasn't so sure. He figured the odds better that they'd all end up scalped the first week.

IV

THE BLACK HILLS

NINETEEN

Tory Bratton wasn't at all certain what led him to accompany Amos Suggs into the wild, untamed country that the Sioux called *Paha Sapa*, the Black Hills. Perhaps even after years of disappointment and disillusionment, some glimmer of faith in his dead father had survived.

"You're only giving him another chance to get you killed!" Emiline had complained the night before he and Pat left. "Can't you see it's the same as when Ax grabbed that flag and tried to steady the regiment at Shiloh? Pa's dead, Tory. Even if he found gold, there's no guarantee it's waiting up there for you!"

Flora had been slightly more understanding. With a brood of children and a failing business, Pat wasn't the first Irishman to take a wild gamble.

As for Amos Suggs, the man seemed alternately a worn-out rag and a whirlwind of motion. As awkward as the old-timer had seemed at first, Tory developed a grudging respect for his skills as an organizer. His knowledge of the country was legend. While dozens of others were turned away from a Missouri River steamer hauling supplies to

the army, Suggs managed to gain permission for the three
of them to travel as far as they cared.

"I showed that captain his first buffalo," Suggs explained. "We've faced some hard times, the two of us,
and a man never forgets the people who stand by him at
such times."

Tory sensed Suggs wished he had more reliable men
with him now. The former scout later found himself leading a pair of tenderfoots south from Fort Lincoln into the
heart of Sioux country. The one-armed Irishman and the
scowling war hero inspired little confidence. Suggs inten-
tionally set a hard pace those first few days. To his surprise, and perhaps his relief as well, his young companions
kept up every step of the way.

At night Suggs and Pat took turns keeping a wary watch
on the surrounding countryside. Tory busied himself trying
to match his father's coded references with the hand-drawn
map of the area Suggs had provided. The first references
were plain enough, but as the trail continued, the cited
verses became muddled and difficult to sort out.

"You're sure you haven't changed any of the marks?"
Tory finally asked Suggs. "There are things that don't fit."

"I turned it over to you the way I found it in the back
of that watch," Suggs explained. "I can't promise you
nobody tampered with it before I came by it. That timepiece was two years in the hands of other folks."

In the end Tory decided his father must have forgotten
parts of their code. N, S, E, and W were easy enough.
They marked the cardinal points of a compass. The biblical
references, though, were complicated. Tory couldn't even
interpret all the book and verse citations without gazing at
his Bible from time to time, and he doubted that his father
carried a Bible into the Black Hills.

As they made their way closer to their destination,
Tory's mind rested no easier. He couldn't ignore the
throngs of hopeful miners crowding into the small mining
camps. Some were little more than children, while others

might well have had a firsthand look at Noah's Ark. Every sort of human condition was represented in those crowded camps. They had only one thing in common, a desire to be rich and a tendency to regard any stranger with suspicious eyes.

Eventually the three wayfarers reached Custer City. It had changed little since Amos Suggs's earlier visit. Oh, there might have been another saloon or two and a half-dozen extra tents at the edge of town, but otherwise it remained a stopover and supply base for prospectors. A man here or there had panned a bit of color from a stream, but no one had yet found the mother lode. Suggs secured two rooms in a clapboard structure that passed for a hotel. He was off tending to the mules and supplies when Tory and Pat entered the Sundown Diner.

"Isn't possible," Pat said when he saw the menu. A buffalo steak went for five dollars, and potatoes were two dollars each. Even a bowl of beans sold for three dollars, and fruit and vegetables were beyond reason.

"We'd best find gold before we starve," Tory added, checking the time by opening his father's watch. "Somebody must be making money."

"Should've brought dry goods to sell and forgot all about gold," Pat grumbled. "These traders will be the only ones to get rich."

"No, lots of us will," a gruff voice argued. "You only have to know where to look."

"I suppose you have a map," Pat said, laughing.

"No, but I thought that you might," the stranger continued. "Nice watch you have there. I used to know a fellow had one like it."

"Oh?" Tory asked. "Who would that be?"

"Man I served with in the cavalry. Bratton. Lucius Bratton."

"And what would your interest be in his watch?" Tory asked, glancing around in hope of Suggs's arrival.

"Well, if it's Bratton's watch, I always figured there

was a map of sorts hidden in it. Maybe some other sort of message. I never found a trace of one myself, but then I only had it for a few days. I figure you're the boy, Hector, up from St. Louis. Old Suggs gave you the watch, did he?''

"Might have," Tory confessed. "Who are you and what business have you for asking?"

"I'm Isaac Pettis. I was a friend of your pa."

"Oh? I didn't know him to have many," Tory declared, examining Pettis's evasive eyes.

"Actually," Pettis said, taking a deep breath, "I was the one who found him."

"Found him?" Pat asked. "What do you mean, found him?"

"Didn't anybody tell you?" Pettis asked. "Old Bratton and two others took French leave of the regiment. Scattered the company's horses and took off into the hills on their own. They found gold, I'm pretty certain. Then the Sioux found them."

"I thought you said *you* found Pa," Tory said, giving Pettis a cold stare.

"Custer sent me and some Rees after the three deserters," Pettis explained. "We found Bratton last. The other two, well, the Indians got to them first. Wasn't much left of 'em. One young fellow had gold flakes on his trousers, though. That's why I always figured they found a paying stretch. When we come on Bratton, he was half-dead of an arrow wound. Then the Sioux hit, and my Rees managed to get themselves killed. I would have shared their end but for your pa, Hector. He made a stand, gave me time to get away."

"My pa did that?" Tory asked. "The deserter? The coward? Pardon me for saying so, but it doesn't exactly fit."

"He found courage that day, boy. Maybe it was dyin' gave it to him. Who can say? I do know he was thinkin' mostly of you, wanted you to have his watch, to think better of him. He gave it to me to bring to you, but, well—''

''You didn't,'' Tory observed.

''I did my best to try and find you, but St. Louis's a big place. The Seventh never was generous with furloughs, either. Then Tom Custer come along, insisted on takin' charge of the watch. He was a captain, and you don't argue an officer out of anything. You were a soldier once, as I heard it. You understand how it is.''

''I understand that Pa traded his life for yours,'' Tory pointed out. ''You promised to take the watch to me, didn't you? It was always important to him. He tried to give it to me once before, but I wouldn't have it.''

''That's how Tom saw it, too. He said you wouldn't want a reminder that your pa was a coward.''

''He didn't sound like a coward,'' Pat argued. ''Staying behind to fight while you ran away.''

''Well, he might have known Custer'd find him. Even if the Sioux arrows didn't finish him, a rope would.''

''I really don't understand why you're telling me all this now,'' Tory said, frowning. ''You didn't bring me the watch. According to you, it was to spare my feelings. Now you've changed your mind. Why?''

''I figure maybe you know somethin','' Pettis admitted. ''Where the gold is maybe. I've got two partners. We've been all through these hills, tryin' to figure it. Together we might put the pieces together.''

''I have my own partners,'' Tory replied.

''Him?'' Pettis said, turning to Pat. ''A cripple?''

''I figure he was thinkin' of me, too,'' a deep, half-threatening voice, announced. Amos Suggs had managed to slip into the diner quietly. He stood behind Pettis, fingering the hilt of his knife. ''You fellows will excuse us now, won't you, Ike?''

Pettis slowly backed away. The others moved a hair more swiftly. All three betrayed anger and disappointment. After they were gone, Suggs joined his young companions and called for buffalo steaks and potatoes for all three,

"I hope we're not staying here long," Pat said, shaking his head at the prices once again. "I don't think we can afford to eat, and I don't favor the company, either."

"You've got a right to be nervous," Suggs replied. "Those three are trouble for sure. I can read men's eyes. Don't go trustin' that Pettis, son. I've known my share of snakes, and I'd trust any one of them above Ike Pettis."

"If he thinks we know where to find the gold, he'll follow," Pat observed.

"You leave that to me," Suggs suggested. "I've dodged Sioux and Rees and Pawnees more times than you could imagine. Won't be much of a trick losin' three white men. Now settle down and have a good feed. We'll likely be chewin' cold beans till I shake Pettis and his friends."

Suggs proved prophetic. Isaac Pettis and two other rough-looking men followed Tory's little band as it left Custer City for Harney Peak and the start of the cryptic map Tory had finally managed to decode. Suggs did his best to avoid established trails and use old Indian paths, but Pettis seemed to know each one.

"Why wouldn't he?" Pat asked one night. "Those three have been searching this country for months."

Tory nodded, but Suggs stormed off, kicking rocks at trees and muttering to himself. When he came back he packed the mules and ordered his weary companions to saddle their mounts.

"I should've thought of that," Suggs remarked. "Only way to lose those three is to take off by night and steal a march on them."

And so, four days out of Custer City, Amos Suggs led the way by twilight into the heart of Sioux country. They wove their way through the pines and spruces, up shallow streams and past scampering jackrabbits, though rocky notches scarcely wide enough for a horse and rider, until they came upon a moonlit clearing. Glancing back, Suggs ordered a halt.

"This is a fair place to camp," he announced. "Not even a Crow could track us through all those streams and up that rocky trace."

Tory hoped the veteran scout was right. Pettis had left him with a lingering sense of danger. He didn't doubt the ex-cavalryman would kill to achieve his fortune.

That night as the three of them settled down together to chew cold beans and what was left of biscuits brought along from the diner, Pat scribbled a note to Flora. The sight of the one-armed Irishman writing home touched Suggs, and the old-timer stared dreamily off into the distance.

"You have family?" Tory asked Suggs.

"Married a Cheyenne woman twenty-three years ago," Suggs answered. "Red Clay Woman, she was called. As pretty as a prairie flower, and as good a cook as I'll ever know."

"My Flora's handy in the kitchen," Pat said, putting his letter aside for a time. "I'll bet she could turn even these fool beans into a feast."

"Red Clay Woman would cook up a trout so that it melted in your mouth," Suggs said, sighing. "She took a skin I brought in from a doe and chewed the hide till it was soft as a baby's cheek. Made my elk robe, too. Brought three sons and a daughter into the world, and each one was smarter and prettier than the one before."

"You have four children?" Tory asked.

"I've got a brood myself," Pat boasted, "and another on the way."

"I've got no children," Suggs said sourly. "Not anymore."

"And your wife?" Tory asked.

"She's started the long walk, too," Suggs said, gazing up toward the sky. "There's the Hangin' Road, what white men call the Milky Way. It's the path a Cheyenne walks to the other side. It's a hard walk for some, though."

"They're dead?" Tory asked.

"Killed," Suggs said, grinding his teeth. "Down on Sand Creek, in what's now Colorado. Odd thing is that I went east to fight rebels. I thought a fellow ought to stand by the country that raised him, and I had a brother who was raisin' a regiment. We beat the rebs, all right. But what did that matter?

"Was a colonel named Chivington down in New Mexico, stopped the rebs from takin' Santa Fe. He burned their supply wagons and forced them to retreat. Later he went out to Fort Lyon and took charge of the Third Colorado Cavalry. I was still up in Virginia. Next thing I know my brother tells me Chivington's attacked Black Kettle's camp and killed close to five hundred Cheyennes."

"I heard about that," Tory said, sighing. "I was in Georgia. Even there, people were talking about it. At first they said it was a regular battle. Then we heard talk the cavalry rode down women and children."

"I found my oldest boy hidin' in a cave twenty miles north of Sand Creek," Suggs went on. "He told me what happened. Red Clay Woman shielded the youngest, my little girl, with her own body. They shot her and the baby both. The younger boys got clear of the camp, but there was nothing to eat. Snows came down, and they took a fever. They're resting at peace now on a hill overlookin' the Arkansas River. I couldn't find my wife or the girl. By the time the snows melted, was only bones left."

"And your boy?" Pat said, growing angrier by the moment.

"Killed at the Washita River four years later by George Custer's men," Suggs explained. "Only sixteen, but he died fightin'."

"I know about that, too," Tory said, shuddering. "Pa was with the Seventh by then."

"I did no weepin' when I rode up the hill where the Sioux slaughtered Custer," Suggs said, turning away a moment. Even in the faint moonlight Tory could see the man rubbing tears from his eyes. "No, he finally found himself some men to fight. My boy, well, I guess you fellows weren't much older, and you went to war."

"I was a little younger," Pat explained, "but I hadn't seen my ma killed."

"I lost my brother at Shiloh," Tory said, sighing. "Saw plenty of boys no older'n sixteen killed in Georgia. Lots of young rebs there. Me, I mostly beat a drum or waved a flag. Didn't do much shooting."

"You're lucky," Pat observed. "Easier to sleep at night without their ghosts chasing you."

"You don't have to kill people to see their faces in your dreams," Tory argued. "I see Ax every week. I see plenty of those young rebs, too. I helped carry an Indiana boy back off Mission Ridge who had both his legs shot away. Died on the way. If he was sixteen, I'd be surprised."

"Told you to stay home," Pat reminded his old friend. "A family shouldn't have to lose more than one brother."

"I came back, didn't I?" Tory asked.

"Sometimes I wonder," Pat said, gazing overhead as a cloud swallowed the moon. The sudden darkness seemed to envelop them, and they remained silent until the cloud passed on, and the light returned.

"You never took a wife, eh?" Suggs asked Tory.

"I only ever knew one girl I took to heart, and she married a Chicago lawyer," Tory explained.

"Victoria," Pat whispered.

"She couldn't forgive Pa's deserting," Tory explained. "Thought I wouldn't amount to anything. Well, I haven't, have I?"

"Seems a bit early to tell that," Suggs said.

"You ever take another woman?" Pat asked.

"Never found anybody like Red Clay Woman," Suggs replied. "I could never really let her go, you see. Oh, I know I ought to leave her to walk the other side, but I can't. I never saw her die, nor my baby girl, either. I've been to see my boys' scaffolds, but there's nothin' left of them now. Time carries away everything but the memories.''

"Sure," Tory agreed.

"Never mated with a white woman?" Pat asked.

"None I didn't pay for," Suggs said, cracking a smile. "There was a little gal in Dodge City I was half tempted to court, but she had her eyes set on a rich cattle buyer. Now, well, I've grown old and weary. Still, with a pack full of gold nuggets, I might find a willin' woman."

"What about you, Tory?" Pat asked. "Made any plans what you'll do when we get back to St. Louis with all that gold?"

"Best get back first," he replied.

"But if we managed it?" Pat asked.

"I think I'd like to go to Philadelphia and see the Centennial Exposition. Maybe see Boston and New York. Pa has brothers there. Wouldn't mind settling in a place where nobody knows where I come from or what my pa's done."

"Ah, you'd miss Will and Em," Pat insisted. "My boys, too. You could be happy enough in St. Louis. People won't always remember your pa. They forgot mine quick enough. You let 'em know about that medal of yours. Nobody who sees that will think you a coward."

"Medal?" Suggs asked.

"Tory won the Medal of Honor," Pat explained. "He was a real hero in the war. Not that there was much of him at the time, but he picked up his flag and charged up Mission Ridge. Later, in Georgia, he captured a reb flag."

"Mostly got myself lost," Tory declared.

"You didn't run, though," Suggs pointed out. "That's a good thing to know if it comes down to a fight."

"You won't find us wanting," Pat boasted.

"It's easy enough to be brave when you've got nothing to lose," Tory told them. "I'm not altogether sure I would have picked up the flag at Mission Ridge if I had a wife and young children back home. I saw men shy from the front line after hearing a baby was born."

"Did it do them any good?" Suggs asked.

"No," Tory confessed. "Bullets found them anyway."

"It's not courage a man has to have to make his stand," Suggs argued. "I've known plenty of men in my life to run when the day turned against them. No, a man stands because he feels the obligation, because he realizes it's no easier for the next man. He owes his brother soldiers, so he stays. The Seventh made a stand of sorts on the Little Big Horn. Was interestin'. Some ran away and died alone, out in the open. Others formed a line and made their lives count for somethin'. I know my boy gave up his life because he hoped others could use the time to get away. Many did. I don't figure a man can give a greater gift than his very life. I would have died to protect my family. Never had the chance, though."

"It's why I came out here," Pat said, gazing into the stars overhead. "So we might have money enough not to worry. So nobody ever again could treat us like useless Irishmen. I've spent all the days I ever intend as a penniless fellow. I want to earn respect."

"Money won't bring it," Tory objected.

"Maybe not," Pat confessed. "But it doesn't hurt. You can't tell me it was only your pa's running that soured her on you, Tory. It was knowing she would have to give up some of her fancy dresses and fine ways. You come back with gold nuggets in your pockets, I expect she might find a way to see you."

"Money can make a difference," Suggs agreed.

"Maybe, but that's not why I came," Tory told them. "I came to make peace with my pa. If I can only do that, I'll be happy."

"Maybe so," Pat agreed. "Lord knows I never managed it myself."

TWENTY

They were up before dawn that next morning and already on their way deeper into the hills as dawn's first rays illuminated the fog-shrouded hills. Amos Suggs led the way, as was his custom, but he rarely left his companions far behind.

"We're apt to come across visitors hereabouts," the old-timer explained. "Sioux and Cheyennes camp this country once summer's done. Some may have headed out onto the plains to avoid cavalry, but I wouldn't wager everyone has. Keep your eyes and ears alert for trouble. I wouldn't be surprised if we run across some."

Pat tied the pack mules to his saddle horn and supervised them while Tory hung back, keeping an eye out for pursuers. He couldn't shake the sense that someone was watching.

"It's just the hills," Suggs said more then once. "There's an unreal feel about the place."

Tory wasn't so sure only spirits were watching, though. Twice he thought he spied a horse or a bit of cloth. He couldn't help recalling the determined look in Pettis's eyes. Sooner or later that man would cross their path.

It turned out that the first humans to be encountered were neither Pettis and his friends nor Sioux warriors. Instead a party of bare-chested young men appeared in front and along both flanks of the gold seekers.

"*Tsis tsis tas,*" Suggs declared, waving a greeting and speaking to the strangers in their own tongue. "Cheyennes."

Tory was instantly nervous, and only a quick glance from Suggs kept him from drawing a revolver. Pat was likewise anxious, but the riders were calm enough. After Suggs showed a necklace of bear claws, the Cheyenne riders seemed close to joyful.

"It's all right," Suggs announced to his partners. "Tie your horses up and come along. We're goin' to do a bit of treatin' with them."

It turned out that one of the Cheyenne leaders was related to Suggs's dead wife, and the two passed half an hour catching up on the plight of friends and relatives. Finally Suggs engineered a trade of several knives and a barrel of gunpowder for some dried meat and two buffalo hides.

"You'll be glad of them as the weather turns chill," Suggs told Tory and Pat. "What's more, we've made friends. Never hurts to have some of them."

Suggs added that he hoped the Cheyennes might spread the word that a friendly band of whites was in the country, but it soon became clear the trading had its limits. Later that afternoon three Sioux passed by on the far side of a shallow stream. Their faces were painted, and their ponies' tails were tied up in preparation for war.

Suggs waved toward a dense growth of pines, and Tory watched the Sioux pass without attracting any attention. Less than an hour later Suggs signaled it was time to resume the journey.

At first nothing particularly eventful happened. Later that afternoon, though, Pat pointed to a group of circling buzzards. Suggs urged caution. They crossed a small hill and descended toward a muddy stream. Two lumps lay near a canvas tent. When they approached the spot, Tory recognized the remains of two miners. Their hair had been cut away, and their stripped bodies were gashed in a number of places.

"Guess we ought to bury 'em," Pat said, hopping down off his horse.

"Leave 'em be," Suggs advised. "No need for us to advertise our arrival. Besides, those fellows got what they deserved."

"How can you say that?" Tory asked. "They're doing nothing we aren't."

"Maybe not now, but you can bet your life they did more than pan gold," Suggs declared. "See how their noses are cut? Look where else they've been cut. These men bothered somebody's wife or sister or daughter. Sioux don't bother taking a man's privates off him. Cheyenne might, especially after Sand Creek, but I'd bet you a year's pay these fellows were up to no good."

Pat remounted his horse, and the trio resumed their ride. A quarter mile away they found proof of Suggs's suspicions. A girl no older than fourteen lay atop a burial scaffold. Although she was covered in a fine elk hide, anyone with half a mind could see she'd been bloodied. Her face was bruised and swollen, too. Tory lost all feeling for the dead miners. Men who would harm a woman like that deserved anything they received.

Nevertheless, Suggs was clearly nervous as they approached Harney Peak. Tory identified the first clue left by his father, but Suggs signaled a halt.

"Best we rest the horses and start fresh tomorrow," he announced. "With angry Sioux about, it won't do to continue, tired as we are."

Tory gazed at the older man with surprise. Tory wasn't tired, and Suggs appeared capable of riding past sundown. It was when Pat virtually fell out of his saddle that Tory realized how weary his old friend had become. It wasn't just looking after the mules, either.

"Couldn't help thinking of my children," Pat explained as he freed the mules of their burdens. "I don't know how I'd act if one of my youngsters received such treatment. And if it was done by an Indian, I fear I'd blame every man that looked halfway like a Sioux."

"You think we're in for trouble?" Tory asked.

"Wouldn't be surprised. We know there's Sioux about, and we're leaving a pretty clear trail, Tory. How long do you figure it will take us to track your pa's stash?"

"A few days, maybe more," Tory estimated. "If we go slow, it could take even longer."

"We'd best find the gold before the Sioux find us. I'm in no favorable mood to get myself killed."

"Isn't why we came here, Pat," Tory observed. "But gold or no gold, I'll see you get home to Flora and your kids."

"You can't promise a thing like that, Tory," Pat insisted. "If it's my day to die, then you leave it be. Try and get back so at least they know what happened."

"I told you, Pat," Tory said confidently. "I won't let anything happen to you. I *can* promise that, and I have. So you rest easy on that account at least."

Pat started to argue, but Tory turned away. Sometimes it was best to leave things be, and it appeared to Tory that Pat at least understood that much.

That night it turned cold, and Tory was particularly glad of the Cheyenne buffalo hides. Suggs had brought his own, together with the fine elk robe his wife had crafted for him. He seemed oddly quiet. Pat stirred a bit, but he was fairly well rested when Tory woke him to take the second watch.

As for Tory himself, he slept fitfully. The sight of the miners caused him to wonder about the horrifying fate his father might have suffered. The dead girl weighed on his mind, too, and he awoke screaming twice after finding himself back on Georgia battlefields.

"You all right, boy?" Suggs called the second time.

"He had a touch of pneumonia down in Georgia," Pat explained. "Chill nights trouble him."

Suggs marched over and draped his buffalo hide atop Tory. The extra warmth was welcome, but it did nothing to stop the nightmares. Tory saw himself at his father's side, facing a savage attack by a horde of vengeful Sioux. His father stood a moment before turning to run.

"Pa?" Tory called.

But he was left alone to face his enemies. He awoke before he could feel their knives and arrows ripping at his flesh.

"Tory, shake it off," Pat urged, rousing him. "Put it behind you."

"Pat?"

"I know what it's like, remembering. It happened to me all the time when I first came home from the war. Pa made me sleep outside, in a shed. Sometimes I still see myself there at Shiloh and feel the pain when that rebel ball halfway took my arm off. But it's a long time gone, and we've got serious work to do tomorrow. You need your rest."

"Sure," Tory agreed. But he was less than certain he could find rest with his mind so troubled.

Perhaps that was just as well. It was only a few moments afterward that Tory heard twigs snap near where he'd tied the horses. Pat noticed, too, but he headed to check on the mules instead. Tory pulled on his trousers, wrapped himself in a buffalo hide, and grabbed his pistol. He walked to the horses in time to see two very young boys trying to free the animals from their ropes.

"Hold on there," Tory called, pointing his pistol at the closest one, a boy of perhaps fourteen with deep brown eyes and long, raven-colored hair. The second boy, even younger, froze.

"What's happening?" Suggs called.

"Nothing," Tory said, stepping up to block the boys' path to the horses. "Do you understand English?"

The oldest boy stared hopefully at Tory and managed to make a slight nod. The younger one moved to his companion's side.

"Children," Tory muttered to himself. "Why is it we hurry ourselves so? Going to war when you ought to be content to stay home and play."

The young Sioux failed to comprehend the words, but when Tory waved his pistol at the nearby pines and shouted, "Go!" the youngsters turned and raced away. Suggs arrived seconds later, just in time to see a bit of buckskin vanish into the trees.

"What the blazes was that about?" the older man stormed. "You let 'em go?"

"They were just boys," Tory explained. "I wasn't any older when I joined the army. One day I walked right up on a rebel patrol, just me and my drum, without any way at all to protect me. Know what they did?"

"Well, they didn't shoot you," Suggs noted.

"Could have, though. Instead, they laughed, told me to get a compass, and hooted me back toward my own lines."

"Sioux won't do that. No, they'll go get their brothers and papas and be back here by dawn."

"I came here to make peace, not shoot little boys," Tory growled. "If you want to break camp and move, I'll help. I don't see much to be gained by killing children. Your own boy was about that age, wasn't he?"

"Was," Suggs admitted. His tone seemed to soften, and he rested a hand on Tory's shoulder.

"You've got a good soul, son, and I confess I've spent so much time around war and cruelty that I can't even recognize compassion. You should know, though, that in this country, it's rarely returned. Tomorrow those same boys may be cuttin' pieces off you."

"I can live with that," Tory confessed. "But I won't abide shooting boys for raiding ponies."

Suggs shook his head and led the way back to camp. They found Pat Harper standing over a half-conscious young Sioux in his late teens.

"Caught him trying to take the mules," Pat explained. "The others got away."

Suggs asked the captive a few things, and the startled young man responded.

"What did you tell him?" Pat asked.

"I told him he was lucky," Suggs said. "I've got a fellow with me touched by spirits. You, Tory," he added, laughing. He then spoke a bit longer with the would-be thief before waving him off into the pines.

"I thought—" Tory started to say.

"No point to shooting one when you've already let the rest run away," Suggs argued. "Anyway, he said he'd leave us be. They don't care to be around crazy men. Besides, there are other whites nearby with better horses."

"Glad to hear we're not hindering commerce," Pat said, breathing a sigh of relief. "Do we stay or move camp? I'm tired, and I don't know that I care to fight off a band of their brothers and cousins tonight."

"We won't be troubled here," Suggs assured them. "Not by those fellows. A Sioux can be a devil to fight, but when he says somethin', you can count on it. I've never known one to lie to me. No, they'll go after the others."

"You figure it's Pettis?" Tory asked.

"If it is, he'll find the going harder than he ever imagined," Suggs said. "There are two hundred *Sicangu Lakotas* camped a half mile from here. I don't know where you get your instincts, Tory, but they served you well tonight. If you'd fired that pistol and killed one or both of those boys, we'd be lucky to get the treatment afforded those two miners. Those two you chased away are sons of Tall Bull, a hard man by anybody's reckonin'. He takes it into his head to kill you, you're a dead man."

Odd as it might have seemed, Tory slept remarkably

well the balance of that night. Suggs stood the final watch, and Pat also rested comfortably. Dawn found them rested and alert.

"Any visitors?" Tory asked, yawning off a final trace of weariness.

"Just a raccoon after our bean tins," Suggs explained. "No Sioux. Our horses and mules are fine."

"That's a relief at least," Tory said, grinning. "Care to risk a fire?"

"Well, by all odds we should be dead," Suggs said, "I guess there's no harm cookin' a bit of fresh meat."

"Fresh meat?" Pat asked, grinning broadly.

"Didn't say I let that coon get away with raidin' our camp, did I?" Suggs asked. "After all, *he*'s no relative of Tall Bull."

TWENTY-ONE

It was Tory who first spied the trailers. At first he thought it was just a whiff of dust blown up by a brisk morning breeze. But when it persisted, he left Pat with the mules and rode ahead to tell Amos Suggs.

"You'd expect us to pick up company after lettin' those Sioux go," Suggs growled. "No surprise. Still, I don't suppose it would hurt to have a look."

Leaving Pat to continue, Suggs led Tory to a stand of boulders indicated on Lucius Bratton's cryptic map. The two of them waited patiently until they finally detected three riders.

"Not Sioux," Tory observed.

"No," Suggs agreed. "More trouble."

As their faces grew distinct, Tory recognized the lead rider as Isaac Pettis. How the former cavalryman had managed to track them through all the twists and turns Suggs had made through the hills was a mystery. It was also troubling.

"He knows where we're headed," Suggs said, frowning. "At least part of it. No white man could have stayed with us in this country."

"If he knows, why didn't he just go and find the gold himself?" Tory asked.

"That's the question, isn't it?" Suggs answered. "Most likely he only has a piece of what he needs. Not all of it."

"We won't shake him this time, will we?"

"Not till we find what he already knows is up ahead, son. Or unless our Sioux friends happen along those three. That could help."

Tory rarely wished anyone ill, but at that moment he was strongly inclined toward willing the Sioux horse stealers toward Pettis and his companions. Afoot, the trio would be less of a menace. As it was, they were the worst sort of trouble, made unpredictable and dangerous by their greed.

There was, of course, another alternative. It didn't take long for Suggs to suggest it, either.

"They're coming along right under these rocks," the old man pointed out. "You still got a soldier's eye with that rifle?"

"You mean ambush them?"

"It's what they mean to do to us," Suggs said sourly. "With Pat and the mules up ahead, they won't expect us behind them. We could end their troubles and ours both."

"Wouldn't the shots draw attention?" Tory asked.

"Better now than later," Suggs insisted as he pulled a Sharps buffalo rifle from its scabbard alongside his saddle. "Well, son, could you hit one of 'em? If I drop Pettis, I figure we'll have time to kill all three if you get the one on the left. Got to kill him, though. Those are likely the Karch brothers, and they got fine instincts for survivin'. We miss, they'll be on Pat and the mules quick as lightnin'."

"It's been a long time since I've even considering shooting at a man," Tory confessed. "I'd have to have a better reason than I do this minute."

"A better reason than gold? How about your life?"

"Maybe we should have brought Pettis into it from the first."

"You'd be dead by now if you had," Suggs said, returning the rifle to its sleeve. "It's not a game we're playin' here. Like it or not, people will die in this country in the next few days. What you've got to get straight in your mind is who will do the killin' and who will do the dyin'."

Tory nodded, but he really didn't want to think about it. Once Pettis and the Karches passed, Suggs led the way through the trees. Lucius Bratton had indicated a creek a mile or so ahead, and Pat would be waiting there with the mules.

It was hard going, weaving through the pines as they bypassed Pettis's little band. The three trailers seemed in no particular hurry. Tory noticed from time to time that Pettis would climb down and examine an upturned leave or point out a muddy track left by the mules. Careful as Pat was, it was impossible to conceal the path. It was a matter of whether Suggs would lead the way to the creek before Pettis got there.

You were right, Tory thought as he read Suggs's mind. *We should have settled accounts with those fellows when we had the chance.*

Tory became more concerned for Pat's safety by the minute. He wanted to push on faster, but Suggs urged caution.

"You never know for sure what's up ahead," he said, waving Tory back whenever the younger man approached. "Pettis is in no particular hurry, is he? Give *him* a chance to make a mistake."

Tory knew the old-timer was reminding him that the three riders could have been sprawled on the trail, dead. Only if Tory had been able to shoot, though, and he remained uncertain of himself. He was a Bratton, after all. What if the curse of his parentage returned? What if Tory, too, ran away?

They were only puny boys. Three of them. Tory couldn't help thinking it was odd, how everything was happening in threes that day. He, Suggs, and Pat made three. Pettis and his batch were three. And now these Sioux!

Tory slid his Winchester out of its saddle scabbard as if by instinct, but Suggs waved for him to hold fire.

"They're no danger to us," Suggs argued. "Leave 'em be."

Tory wasn't afraid of the boys, though. He was afraid *for* them. From his perch atop the ridge Tory could see Pettis and the Karches riding straight toward the youngsters' little camp. They couldn't have been there long or they would have seen Pat. Pettis wouldn't, couldn't, miss seeing them.

The shots came quickly, with a vicious rapidity that shattered the peace of the bright afternoon. Shouts and screams filled the air.

"Fool boy's shot my horse!" Pettis shouted angrily.

"Won't shoot another!" one of the Karches boasted.

There was a lot of whooping and hollering until Isaac Pettis's voice boomed out, silencing the other voices.

"Hush!" he cried. "You'll wake the dead!"

By then, despite his natural-born caution, Tory had inched his way forward. Through the mist and the powder smoke hanging in the trees he could see Pettis standing over a pair of young bodies. The Karches were inspecting two Indian ponies, trying to pick the most suitable for the mount killed by a Sioux arrow.

"Come on," Suggs whispered as he rode alongside Tory. "Best we get to Pat."

"We've got time now," Tory said, glaring at the other white men.

"No time to waste, son."

"I'm not your son," Tory said angrily. "I haven't been anybody's son in a long time."

He wasn't even paying attention to Suggs. Down below

he could see a third Sioux boy hopelessly trapped beneath
his horse. Squirming and fighting to work his way free of
the animal, he could only look up into the eyes of Isaac
Pettis. The ex-cavalryman laughed as he cocked his pistol
and fired at the boy.

"Finish him, Pettis!" one of the others yelled.

It was only then that Tory realized that Pettis was playing with the boy, just shooting close to him and not in-
tending to kill. Suggs shrugged his shoulders. The young
Sioux began chanting, and Pettis fired again. The chanting
stopped.

"We should have shot those fellows," Suggs said, motioning for Tory to turn away.

"You were right," Tory agreed. As he started to ride
away, though, he saw the young Sioux move. By then
Pettis was on his way back to his companions. *He's not
dead,* Tory realized. Without saying a word to Suggs, he
started down the slope toward the trapped Sioux. He got
to within twenty yards of Pettis before tying his horse and
approaching the wounded Sioux.

"Young fool," Suggs muttered as he joined him.
"What do you think you're doin'?"

"He's still alive," Tory explained. "I can't leave him
like that."

"Those shots'll bring the whole world down on us, boy.
Come on. We've got to get clear."

"Not yet," Tory said, approaching slowly, cautiously.
The pony boy feigned death, but Tory ignored the act. He
spotted the others up ahead, rummaging the camp for supplies. Contented that they wouldn't interfere, he turned
back to the trapped youngster. By then Suggs was already
pushing the horse away. Tory pulled the slight-shouldered
youth free, then tore strips from his own shirt to bind a
slight gash on the boy's forehead. Pettis hadn't missed by
much.

Tory next probed the boy's body until he finally gave a
low murmur. The youngster's left leg appeared to be hurt.

"Not broken," Suggs said, sitting beside the boy and whispering in *Lakota* several calming words. The boy's eyes finally opened.

"Easy," Tory said, placing two lengths of pine on either side of the battered leg. "We'll get you fixed up just fine."

The Sioux glanced up with a mixture of confusion and fear, but Suggs continued talking, and gradually the boy seemed to lose his distrust. Finally, after Tory had splinted the leg, the young Sioux managed a smile.

"Thank you," he said.

"You speak English?" Tory asked in surprise.

"Some," the boy replied. "*Sicangu. Lakota.* Why are you here?"

"Just like the rest," Tory said, helping the boy up. "Come to take gold from these hills."

The boy appeared somewhat confused and spoke with Suggs. The two carried on a rapid conversation. The young Sioux clasped Tory's wrist, nodded sadly, and tried to take a step toward the camp. He fell.

"Can't leave him like this," Tory said, pleading with Suggs.

"We've got little choice," Suggs said as the boy dragged himself forward. "We've got other worries. You've saved his life, haven't you? Isn't that enough for one day?"

"Suppose so," Tory admitted, turning toward the waiting horses.

"He won't thank you, you know," Suggs continued.

"He already did," Tory argued. "Maybe he owes us something. Maybe he'll tell his cousins, and they'll leave us alone."

"No, he said it to me straight, s—" Suggs caught himself.

"Oh?"

"White men don't belong here. Sioux won't bother pickin' out which set of white men killed their boys. They'll kill all of us. Let's catch up with Pat."

Tory nodded.

They passed Pettis and the Karches and continued onward. Indian ponies had muddied the creek crossing, and it would be difficult tracking the mules thereafter. It was nearly dusk when they located Pat almost two miles upstream from the rendezvous point. He had the mules well hidden and was hiding in a thick cover of young pines.

"What'd you do, run into the whole Sioux nation?" he called when his weary companions finally arrived.

"No," Tory said, virtually falling out of his saddle. "Pettis and his friends did that."

"You get them?" Pat asked.

"Should have," Tory confessed as Pat took charge of the horses. "Had a chance. Instead they shot three Sioux boys up the trail."

"That won't make it too comfortable hereabouts," Pat noted. "Can't you find us some good luck anywhere?"

"Not lately," Suggs added. "You know what your fool of a friend did? Splinted one of those boy's legs and bound a head wound. Sent him back to his friends."

"The Sioux know we're here, then," Pat said. He tried not to let the fear show on his face.

"It's not the Sioux that worry me," Tory said, gazing down the stream. "It's Pettis and those other two."

"Well, you save some room in your soul for worrying about Sioux," Pat suggested. "I've seen three parties of them since crossing the creek. Found something else, too."

"Yeah?" Tory asked.

Pat pulled the saddles off the weary mounts, and Tory stripped their blankets and bridles. Suggs applied hobbles and left the animals to graze. Then Pat led the way toward the water.

In the dying sunlight, the stream sparkled with shiny bits of yellow rock. Pat reached down and plucked a knuckle-size pebble of pure gold from the stream.

"We've found it," Tory said, examining the nugget.

"There's more," Pat said, waving them along. Just

ahead lay a human leg bone. There were finger bones beyond that, and a little farther the rest.

"Likely buried him in a shallow grave," Suggs said, frowning at the odd assemblage of bones. "Animals likely tore him apart. Or the Sioux did."

"We weren't the first ones here," Tory observed.

"No," Suggs agreed. "This one here would be Higgs. I don't recall his first name. He was at Washita River, though. Maybe Cheyennes found him and got a measure of revenge. Who can say?"

"So they split up," Tory said, pondering it. "Maybe Pa went after the others, hoped to bring them back. Maybe—"

"They went together," Suggs announced. "Maybe Bratton knew it was time to leave. Maybe Higgs tarried too long. Was greedy maybe. Whatever happened, he didn't get far from the creek. The soldiers didn't notice the gold here or else your pa and the others panned the surface so there wasn't anything quite so evident. Stream's turned over a few times since then. That's how it is with placer gold."

"There's a fortune here," Pat said, fingering the nugget. "A fortune!"

"According to your pa, there's even more," Suggs said, sighing. "You want to dig some here?"

"I already have," Pat said, walking over to the trees and returning with a bean tin. Inside were several nice-sized nuggets. "We could file on this land, Suggs. Have a real mining operation."

"Only one little problem," Tory said, frowning. "This is Sioux land."

"Won't be for long," Pat argued. "Sooner or later the treaty chiefs will sign it away. After killing Custer, the Sioux can't exactly hold out. And if there's no treaty, the government will just take the land."

"They've done it before," Suggs added. "Young Bratton's right, though. You can't file a claim when the country

still belongs to the Indians. Besides, I'm no miner. I say
we take what we can get, find Bratton's cache, and get
clear of here before Pettis and the Karches find us. Or the
Sioux come along.''

"Tory?" Pat asked.

"Would seem the best thing to do," Tory agreed.
"There's something about this place. I feel spooked.''

"Paha Sapa," Suggs muttered. "The Center of the
World. Nobody who ever came here felt comfortable.''

"Doesn't make you all that confident with that fellow
Higgs's bones laying over yonder," Pat added. "There's
good cover here, though. We can get something to eat,
keep a close watch, and move on after a bit.''

"Best to go tomorrow," Tory advised.

"No, not tomorrow," Suggs declared. "The horses need
a day's rest, and I want to see if Pettis is on our tail. We
can dig the creek some, at least put some nuggets in our
pockets. How much farther you figure we have to go by
your pa's map?''

"A day longer to the cache," Tory announced. "Then
we turn for home.''

"Wish I had ten mules," Pat grumbled as he opened a
tin of beans. "Twenty! We'll end up leaving gold behind,
just like Tory's pa.''

"Don't mind that," Suggs said, accepting a tin. "Not
at all. I just don't want to find my bones dryin' in the sun
like Higgs. No gold and no peace.''

"What's peace?" Tory asked.

They ate their dinner of cold beans in silence. Tory noticed that his companions were as moody as he was. He
caught Pat gazing longingly at the stream. For the first time
since leaving St. Louis, he didn't speak of Flora or the
children.

Amos Suggs kept to himself. He kept a loaded rifle at
his side even when he wasn't on watch that night.

"Best to keep yourself ready," he announced, urging
his companions to do the same.

Tory didn't trust himself to sleep with a loaded rifle that close. He had always been prone to nightmares, and that haunted place seemed to gnaw at his very soul.

"You'd do better to forget your worries and try to get some rest," Pat advised when he roused Tory to take his turn at watch. "Tomorrow may be a rest day for the ponies, but I have a feeling we won't be getting much of a furlough."

"Furlough?" Tory asked, surprised. His friend rarely spoke in military terms.

"Yeah," Pat said, chuckling to himself. "Can't help but think myself back in the army. Not that I was in it that long. Not like you."

"Strange, but it didn't seem like a long time," Tory confessed as he threw off the heavy buffalo hide. "Truth is, it was the easiest time of my life."

"Easiest?" Pat asked, examining his friend's face for traces of lunacy.

"It was," Tory said, sighing. "Everything was simple. Oh, there were hard days of marching, and the food was nothing to write home about. If you had someone to write. There was always somebody to tell you what to do, when to get up and go to bed, how far to march, that sort of thing. You didn't have to think. Back in Peoria, I was always Lucius Bratton's son. In the army I was me. So long as I did my job, held up my end, I was left alone."

"Not me," Pat said, gazing overhead. "Maybe if I'd lasted awhile longer. Things being as they were, I was just the son of a drunk and little use once I lost my arm. I don't see how you and Ax managed it, charging into those rebel rifles! I was scared to death."

"I don't know how it was for Ax," Tory said, fingering his father's watch. "I don't think he had enough sense to be scared of anything."

"Maybe not," Pat noted. "He always could run faster and jump higher than any boy in town."

"I don't suppose it occurred to him that a rebel musket ball could kill him."

"It would've crossed your mind, Tory. You would have sat down and figured it up like a column in one of my account books. Why'd you do it, charge up that fool ridge, waving the flag?"

"I'm not altogether sure," Tory confessed.

"You've had time to think on it."

"Yes, but that hasn't made it any clearer. It isn't easily understood, Pat. You, drunk pa and all, never once dreamed you wouldn't find something better down the road. I knew you would manage. Somehow I knew you would be the one to find a Flora, to father a house full of kids."

"You're evading the question," Pat reminded him.

"All right. I'll try to explain. Pat, there's different kinds of dying."

"What?"

"Deep inside, I was always afraid of hurting. Of losing an arm or leg, something like that. Like what happened to you. But dying? That never worried me."

"That's crazy, Tory."

"No, it's not. Once Victoria turned away, I knew there was no chance of redeeming myself. I could win medals and stripes and glory, but it would make no difference to anyone that truly counted. Oh, you and a few others like Will might mark my passing. Em would. But the rest would just continue on their way without so much as a whimper."

"So? A man doesn't live his life or give it up so others will note it."

"*You* don't, Pat. It's why you'll always be a brother of sorts. But me? I think when Pa ran away, he left his shame painted on my face like a shadow. They might as well have branded me. I didn't pick up the flag in hopes of winning glory or with the notion of restoring family honor. I picked it up knowing the other fellows who carried the flag got shot.''

"Nonsense."

"Think so? I raced up that hill, howling like a madman, praying the bullets would find my heart and end the pain once and for all. I just wanted it over. I watched that Sioux boy today. He closed his eyes and started singing, waiting for the end. He wasn't scared, Pat. He welcomed it. I sit here, in this place, and I'm not afraid. It's like I'm calm as at Chattanooga, waiting for death to find me."

"It's why you won't take a wife," Pat said, resting a hand on Tory's shoulder. "You're wrong, Tory. You're cheating yourself of all the good that's out there to be had. Gold nuggets are only the key that opens a door to happiness. Flora's the happiness, her and the little ones. Lord, don't you know that a man has enough of a burden to carry in this life, with one arm or two? Best he doesn't try to carry his pa, his whole family!''

"It's an easy thing to say, Pat," Tory said, rising from his bed and taking up his rifle. "But the truth of it is that no matter how crazy it seems, I can't seem to leave Pa behind. His shadow's still here. I haven't rid myself of it yet."

TWENTY-TWO

Dawn found Tory weary but restless. The three partners sat around a small fire made of dry willow and cottonwood branches. It scarcely gave off any smoke at all. The fire provided a comforting warmth and served to heat the tins of beans. They were all of them a little cross, and Tory judged that days of tinned beans and dry meat could last a man only so long.

"We could mix some flour into dough, bake some bread," Tory suggested. "We used to strip bark from a green limb, wrap dough around it, and bake it over the coals out in Georgia. I confess you wouldn't mistake it for your ma's cooking, but it would be a change from what we've had."

"You're welcome to try," Suggs said, staring at the coffeepot. The small fire seemed to take forever to bring the liquid to a boil, but they dared not build it up and risk betraying their location.

"Won't be long before we're home again," Pat said, grinning as he carried a bag of flour from the packs. "We'll treat ourselves to a big juicy beef steak and whole

plates of potatoes. Flora can cook up one of her special
County Cork stews, too.''

"Best we get back before you make too many plans,"
Suggs grumbled.

"What's wrong?" Tory asked. "We've done well,
haven't we? We've concealed our camp well enough, and
after we pan the stream here for a time, we'll move on to
the cache.''

"Sounds just fine," Suggs admitted, "but things have
a way of turnin' sour. I'm sure old Custer thought everything was fine and dandy till he topped a rise and found
the whole Sioux nation waitin' for him. We take turns
watchin' like at night. One man's always got his gun
ready, and the others have their weapons close by. If Pettis
misses us, then there's still the Sioux. Remember?''

"Be hard to forget," Tory said, mixing a bit of flour
and water with baking powder. It had been a while since
he'd cooked biscuits from scratch. Most times he took his
meals with Flora or Emiline. He had been a fair enough
cook during the war, though, and he expected he could
make biscuit dough. It turned out the old knack came back
easily, and they enjoyed the fresh bread.

"Wish we could add an elk steak," Suggs said, gazing
across the creek at a pair of giant elk having their morning
drink.

"Before long," Pat said, grinning as the coffee finally
began to boil. "Before long."

Tory and Pat followed Suggs's instructions all that day
and most of the following morning. They didn't work the
streambed hard. Instead they plucked nuggets from the surface and did their best to erase the most visible signs of
gold from the bed. A day and a half of panning filled
several tins of nuggets and one flour sack. Each of them
took their own gold, although Pat offered to share his takings of the first day.

"We could make a straight split at the end of the trail,"
Tory offered.

"Better we keep our own," Suggs argued. "That way a man works his hardest, and there are no hard feelings in the end. What's more, if we have to split up and go our own way, no one's the worse for it."

That last comment rattled Tory some. Suggs appeared to be changing each hour. While Pat grew more satisfied with every nugget, Suggs seemed determined to find even more. As for Tory, he had more than he needed after the first day's work. He was mostly concerned with returning in one piece.

There was plenty of color left in the creek when Suggs finally announced it was time to move on.

"If we don't go on to the cache, we won't have any way of carryin' off what's there," Suggs told his young companions. "Three mules can only carry so much."

Tory was a trifle confused. He judged Suggs had found a good deal more gold than he was letting on. The old-timer had emptied two sacks of flour on the hillside in order to use the bags to carry gold. One of the mules seemed overburdened, and Suggs's horse sometimes struggled to get up steeper portions of the trail. Tory said nothing, but he could feel Pat's eyes burning holes in those sacks.

"I don't think he's been standing watch," Pat said when they took an afternoon break from riding. "He's been working the stream instead."

"I don't see it really matters," Tory replied. "He could leave us out here on our own anytime if that's what he wanted. He knows the country, doesn't he?"

"He doesn't yet have your pa's cache," Pat pointed out.

"Maybe not, but I judge he could find it. All along he claimed he was entitled to a half share, Pat. After all that's happened, I suppose he was right. We couldn't manage on our own."

Tory believed that, but it wasn't entirely true. Suggs treated with another band of Cheyennes, trading tobacco for elk and buffalo hides, but when a small band of Sioux appeared, it was Tory that secured safe passage

"*Hau!*" the boy with the splinted leg called, riding
ahead of his companions. The young man grinned and
pointed to the healing scar on his forehead. He then presented Tory with a fine buckskin shirt to replace the rag
torn into binding strips. "I'm *Pispiza*," the boy added.
"You ride in peace."

"Tory Bratton," Tory said, offering his hand. The
Sioux ignored the gesture, made a faint wave instead, and
rejoined his party. They then rode away.

"What's it mean?" Pat asked Suggs.

"He's payin' his debt," Suggs explained. "Did you no-
tice the blue coats those two at the end were wearin'?
Seventh Cavalry issue. Those boys helped kill Custer, and
I don't figure they have much love for us. Let's hurry on."

A new urgency seemed to fill their movements
thereafter. Suggs abandoned his earlier caution and even
threw up dust from time to time. Whenever they reached
a stream, he took the time to conceal the trail, but more
than once Tory spied a bit of blue cloth on the opposite
hillside.

"They're following us," Pat observed.

"Don't know that I mind that bunch following," Tory
said, wiping the sweat from his brow. "There are others I
wouldn't care to have along, though."

As they began to wind their way along a narrow trail
between a rocky notch, Tory suddenly grinned. The last
of his father's passages, the one that had so long confused
him, came into play.

"Hold up!" he called. "Stop!"

Suggs pulled his horse up short and glared back at Tory,
who had already convinced Pat to halt the mules. The grin
on the young man's face soon erased the older man's
doubts.

"I understand," Tory explained, recalling the passage.
"We're here."

"Where?" Suggs asked.

"At the cache," Tory explained. "It's Pa's note exactly. Book of Matthew, chapter 2, verse 22. 'He was afraid to go thither: notwithstanding, being warned of God in a dream, he turned aside into the parts of Galilee.' "

"I think you're as crazed as your old man," Suggs declared.

"You don't understand," Tory said, laughing. "It's the part of the Bible where Jesus is fleeing for his life from Herod. Oh, I don't know that it would make sense to you, but don't you see? For Pa it was everything. It was what he told Pettis. He was trying to make up for what he'd done to Em and me. It was like Mary and Joseph trying to protect their child. They turned away from the path. There's got to be a way through here somewhere. Let's look."

To the naked eye there wasn't a spare inch of room in that notch, but Suggs found the place. It opened into a small valley, and on the near slope was a low cave.

"That'll be the place," Tory said, pointing to it. "Perfect place to stash half the world."

"Good hiding place, all right," Pat agreed. "Why didn't they stay there?"

"With Ree scouts after them?" Suggs asked. "With Sioux all over the place? No, they had to get clear of this country and wait for things to settle down."

"It's the right place," Tory said, more certain than ever when he noticed three cryptic scratches near the side of the cave. The valley was close to invisible from its approach, and the cave wasn't that different from dozens of others in those hills.

"Best thing to do is take the animals on inside," Suggs declared. "We'll make ourselves a torch and have a good look. Agreed?"

"Sure," Tory replied. "Only makes sense to be cautious from here on out."

"You think there's as much gold in here as we think?" Pat whispered.

"Seems like a lot of trouble to go to if there's not,"
Tory said, dismounting. "Only trouble we may have is
finding a way to haul it all off."

"Don't go banking your gold yet, boys," Suggs warned.
But even the old-timer had a glint in his eye. By the time
they had the animals tended and a torch made from strips
of blanket cloth soaked in coal oil, they were all three of
them eager to see a fortune.

At first they were disappointed. The cave quickly
shrank, and it was a considerable effort for them to get
through to a larger room inside the hillside. It was there
that Pat noticed something glinting on the cave floor.

"Nugget," he announced, holding it to the light. The
twisted bit of golden metal was the size of a man's finger.
Up ahead more bits and pieces met their eyes.

"Were in a hurry, the fools," Suggs said as he finally
located several displaced rocks. Behind them were sacks
of nuggets and leather pouches of gold dust. It didn't rep-
resent the hundreds or even thousands of dollars that Tory
had expected to find. No, here were tens, maybe hundreds
of thousands.

"This isn't all," Tory said, examining the haul. "If it
was just Pa's gold, there wouldn't be any need of hiding
it."

"He's right," Suggs agreed. "Likely this was the
younger fellow, Rodman. He would have been in a hurry,
careless. Old Bratton would have taken his time."

"Yes," Tory agreed. "He would have found a less obvious place, too."

They continued to work their way through the cave until
they arrived at two forks. Suggs was searching for sign on
the cave floor, but Tory was imagining his father. He recalled watching Lucius Bratton and Abner Drury playing
chess. Bratton's father-in-law was always falling for the
traps. Bratton left an obvious opening, and when the older
man tried to avoid it, the real trap fell.

"Stop," Tory commanded. "The gold's not in there. It's out here somewhere."

"Why hide it here when you've got two narrow passages ahead?" Pat asked.

"Because there are traps there to snag you," Tory declared. "Don't ask me why I know, but I do. Raise the torch. There!"

Tory turned and marched toward a narrow crack in the cave wall. He reached his arm through until he felt something damp. A woolen sock! Gold!

"Find anything?" Suggs asked hungrily.

"Pa's gold," Tory explained. "It's here all right."

"How?" Pat asked. "How did you know?"

"It's the way Pa was," Tory explained. "Chose the obvious but covered it with tricks and traps. He didn't want anybody else to find it."

"Just him, eh?" Suggs asked, accepting the first sock Tory freed from its hiding place.

"No, remember the passage," Tory muttered. "A dream? I think he knew he wouldn't get out of here alive. He didn't care in the end. He let Pettis go to bring me the watch. Nothing mattered but getting that watch to me."

"He was trying to make it up to you, Tory," Pat observed.

"Only way he knew how," Tory added. "Odd thing was that it wasn't the gold any of us wanted."

"Well, it's what brought *me* here," Suggs reminded Tory.

"Won't hurt," Pat added.

"Maybe not, but it seems odd just the same," Tory said, lifting the final sack from the cleft. "I understood him so well. I followed his trail, didn't I? I knew where the gold would be. But he never understood anything about me. All he ever needed to do so far as I was concerned was own up to his mistake and come back."

"Maybe," Pat said, staring at a sock full of nuggets. "My own pa never figured out anything, either. If he

would have put a bottle aside long enough to look me once
in the face, he would have realized I didn't expect him to
make a fortune. Instead he ranted and raved and drank and
beat my ma till she just walked out into the river and
drowned herself.''

''I never knew that, Pat.''

''Pa said she went to Chicago,'' Pat added, ''but I knew.
And when he started on me, I left. You told me you
weren't brave, Tory. That you just didn't care. Well, I
wasn't all that different. Just not as lucky, I suppose. I
only lost an arm, and I didn't get any medal.''

''You ended up with Flora, though,'' Tory told his old
friend. ''A fresh start. A house full of youngsters, and now
you're rich.''

''You're right, though,'' he whispered. ''The gold's
nothing if I don't get back home. Promise me again you'll
get me home to Flora?''

''I promise, Pat.''

''And when we're back there, we'll find you a cousin
to give you sons, Tory. You can tell them about *Paha Sapa*
and Sioux Indians and Mission Ridge. They won't ever
have to hang their heads in shame, Tory. They'll have a
pa to be proud of.''

''Maybe,'' Tory said, grinning sadly. ''But we've got
to get out of here first.''

''Come on!'' Suggs called impatiently from the mouth
of the cave. ''Hurry along, boys. We've got gold to collect.''

''Guess it's time to get back to work,'' Tory said, lifting
a sack. ''Work rarely waits, does it?''

''Not that I've noticed,'' Pat admitted. ''Come on.''

From the first instant they gathered the entire cache together, it was clear they lacked enough mules to get all of
it out of the hills. Tory guessed the animals might transport
a third of it. Suggs insisted they could haul all of Bratton's
gold and more besides.

''I had me a look in that cave,'' Suggs told his partners.

"There's a vein cut through there as rich as any I've heard of. A man can scratch his whole life out and not come to the end of it."

"You do that," Pat replied. "Me, I've got enough. I'm ready to head home."

"Nobody's leavin' yet," Suggs insisted. "I've got two kegs of powder packed for this very purpose. I know the use of it, too. Before my army days I helped build railroad tunnels. I can rip a hole through the core of that vein and expose enough of it to make us rich a thousand times over."

"You're not listening," Pat added. "I've got enough. Tory?"

"Me, too," Tory agreed. "There's time to come back later if you want."

"No, I aim to do it now," Suggs insisted.

"And if we choose not to stay?" Pat asked.

"Wouldn't be wise," Suggs warned. "We've been partners a time now, and I've grown accustomed to your company. Still, gold is gold."

"You'd stop us?"

"I need your horses," Suggs explained. "A pack mule can carry only so much, but with a travois tied behind, he can haul three times the load."

"So that way we can get all the cache clear," Tory noted. "Why blast the cave? All you'll do is bring down the Sioux on us, not to mention Pettis and his friends. It's crazy."

"I could drop you boys anytime I want," Suggs growled.

"I guess you've known that right along," Tory replied. "I sure never made any secret of it. Thing is, though, why bother? How much money can a man spend? It won't bring your Cheyenne wife or boy back. I'd hope by now you know I'm not afraid of dying. Only thing that ever troubled me was my pa, and I figure maybe we've come to terms of sorts. Tell you what. You ride out with Pat and me, and

I'll come back and help you blast the whole Black Hills
to perdition. By then maybe the Sioux will have settled
down, too.''

"That's a young man talking,'' Suggs declared, raising
his rifle. "You think you've got forever, but you don't.
No, we do it now or never. If the Sioux have in mind to
kill us, they'll do it for an ounce or a ton of gold. The
blast'll likely scare the fire out of them, and we'll have a
good chance to clear this place before Pettis and his boys
arrive. I need help, but I can do it alone if I have to. Well,
boys?''

The rifle swung from Pat to Tory, and the two old
friends sighed. There was no arguing with a buffalo gun.

They made the first pony drag that same afternoon. The
other two followed. Suggs walked the hillside and tra-
versed the cave six times before deciding where to plant
his charges. As he prepared the powder, Tory and Pat
moved the animals a quarter mile away and repacked the
gold.

"You know he's turned crazy,'' Pat observed as Suggs
clambered over the mountainside.

"No, just a bit touched,'' Tory declared. "My eyes got
a little big when I saw that first nugget, didn't yours? Then
I realized it was a trap, just like those tunnels of Pa's. I
shouldn't have talked you into this, Pat.''

"You what?''

"Shouldn't have—''

"Tory, I'm a grown man. Truth is, we didn't have a lot
of choice. Old Suggs knew that. We don't have much better choices now.''

"We could cut loose and ride,'' Tory suggested.

"Two young fools who don't know the country?'' Pat
asked. "Fine chance that'd be. I'd rather take a try at the
Sioux.''

"Sorry I got you into this.''

"Tory, you can keep saying it, but it won't make it true.
Anyhow, we're not dead yet.''

Tory managed half a grin.

That afternoon, their third at the cave, Suggs finally ignited his first charge. Tory expected the whole mountain to erupt, but actually the well-placed charges only blasted fresh fissures in the cave walls. The noise was enough to wake the dead, though, and it flattened trees a half mile away.

The horses did their best to rear up and bolt, but Tory had secured them firmly. They remained in place, although he and Pat had to secure the packs again. The mules proved particularly adept at shaking their loads loose.

Suggs was less than delighted with his results. Although a fair amount of gold was dislodged from the cave walls, the vein he expected to stretch a mile into the mountain ended abruptly seven or eight inches into the hillside. The ore on the opposite side was mostly quartz. For all his trouble, he had gained very little.

"There's no way to carry raw rock all the way back to Custer City," Suggs lamented. "You boys were right. It was a wasted effort."

"Well, you might have been right," Tory said. "You're ready to leave now?"

"We could still pack a few more pounds on that third travois," Suggs argued.

"You're growing awfully greedy," Pat pointed out.

"Well, maybe you're right," Suggs admitted. "There's a lot here to keep three men content."

"But not six," a familiar voice announced from the nearby trees.

Isaac Pettis stepped out, a new Winchester rifle in his hands. The Karch brothers appeared nearby, blocking the path to Suggs's big buffalo rifle.

"No need to make yourself a corpse, Amos," Pettis warned as Suggs inched toward his knife. "Remember, I've seen your work before. I won't hesitate. So, you found Bratton's stash, did you? I knew it was around here somewhere. Yonder in that cave, huh?"

"That's right," Suggs said, glaring at Pettis. "Biggest strike since Sutter's Mill."

"You would have done better to wait and do your blasting later," Pettis added. "We might never've found this place but for the dust cloud you raised."

"Well, sometimes you're lucky," Suggs said, frowning. "Sometimes you're not."

"Was time I had a stroke of good fortune," Pettis declared. "Ben and Charlie here were due, too. Your bad fortune's our good luck. We'd cut you in, Amos, but I know it would only bother you, sharing your take. These boys here would probably be a bother, too. Best we cut our losses and finish with the whole batch of you."

"Seems best," Suggs said, narrowing his gaze. "Care to see the cave?"

"Wouldn't mind," Pettis said, waving Suggs forward. The Karches paused long enough to tie Pat and Tory to a pair of pines. They then followed Pettis into the cave.

TWENTY-THREE

It was the darkest day Tory could recall since his grandfather had passed on the news of Achilles' death and their father's disgrace. It seemed as if all the suffering and toil had been for naught. Worse, Tory had managed to drag his best friend into the same peril.

To give Pettis and the Karches credit, they were nothing if not thorough. They had managed to locate the mules and the carefully loaded travois tied behind each. Pettis had walked through the mine with Suggs and spied what remained to the casual observer a great vein of gold. Only a man who had actually seen gold pounded out of ore using a stamp mill could guess at what great work remained. Suggs had convinced Pettis that it was simply a matter of more blasting.

Tory had known from first sight that there would be no treating with the Karch brothers. Their steel-cold eyes and heartless glances told of a past of hired killing and wholesale larceny. Ben, the eldest, boasted openly of killing three Kansas families who had blocked the passage of a railroad spur. Charlie, the younger, claimed to have peeled

the skin off a sixteen-year-old girl in order to convince her
father to betray a miners' plot.

"Turned out it was a waste of time." Charlie cackled.
"I had the wrong man. Fool was a clerk at a mercantile,
and he knew nothing. Killed the girl for nothing."

"Oh, you enjoyed it, Charlie," Ben said, laughing.
"Confess."

"I did," Charlie added.

Later, when Pettis and Suggs argued over the proper
way to blast the rest of the gold from the cave, the Karches
untied Tory. Leading him to the mouth of the cave, they
stripped him bare, searching for hidden nuggets.

"Figure I put one in my ear?" Tory asked when Ben
poked a finger there.

"You watch your tongue," Ben warned. "Charlie's still
fond of that knife. Might just decide to peel you."

They spared Pat such close examination. The stump of
an arm unsettled the killers, and they seemed put off. Tory
didn't suspect they would hesitate shooting, but examining
that fold of skin seemed to be more than they could stomach.

The Karches left Suggs to Pettis. The two older men
appeared to be reaching a sort of agreement. Suggs finally
agreed to oversee the blasting provided Pettis agree to a
quarter share for him.

"One more thing," Suggs added. "You have to let the
boys go."

"Got kindhearted in your old age, Amos?" Pettis asked.

"They brought us here, didn't they?" Suggs asked.
"They won't share in the good fortune, and that's bad luck
enough. Killin' them wouldn't accomplish much. They
can't go complain to the law. What would they say, that
they were stealin' gold off treaty land? We can keep their
rifles. Even if they had the sand to stir up trouble, they'd
be toothless without guns."

"I don't like loose ends," Ben Karch complained.

"Those two don't matter," Pettis replied. "We need Suggs to do the blastin', though."

Tory doubted any of them would escape alive. He caught sight of a glimmer in Suggs's eye, though.

"He's got a plan," Tory whispered to Pat.

"Hope it's a good one," Pat replied.

Whatever Suggs was planning, it appeared odd from the first. Tory knew there was no rich vein hidden in the mountainside. The best of the gold was already exposed. Pettis and the Karch brothers had no extra horses to carry ore. No, they would be counting on Tory and Pat's saddle ponies, and perhaps Suggs's mount as well. Could three men manage so many animals in hostile country? Probably not. They certainly wouldn't have time to fiddle with prisoners.

Suggs did have a surprise in store for Pettis and the others. He primed the charge and raced out of the cave to take cover behind a wall of boulders.

"Wait and see," he told Tory as a low rumble roared through the cave.

"That it?" Pettis asked.

"The very thing," Suggs answered.

Pettis, eager to see for himself, raced inside the cave. The Karches were only steps behind.

"Duck again," Suggs warned, and the three of them hid in the rocks. A second explosion three times the size of the first tore a hole in the side of the mountain. The cave simply collapsed on itself. Amid a great whirl of dust and powder smoke, two distinct shrieks pierced the stillness.

"You set a second charge," Tory noted as the dust began to clear.

"A second and a third, just in case," Suggs explained. "We won't have to worry over those fellows, not ever again. Guess they're content enough, trapped in there with the gold. Me, I figure you two were right. We've got enough."

A third blast seemed to punctuate that statement. There were no shouts this time.

Tory matched the tired old man's weary grin. Suggs had seemed to regain his senses at the critical moment.

"We can stand around congratulating ourselves or get clear of here," Pat remarked. "Might be a Sioux or two will notice half a mountain blown away."

Tory stared at the towering swirl of gray dust rising skyward. It could likely be seen twenty miles away, maybe farther.

"Best we hurry, boys," Suggs agreed. "Bring along the extra ponies. Won't hurt to have spare mounts."

"I don't guess there's any way to make sure they're dead," Tory said, studying the collapsed cave mouth.

"I don't believe it would be wise to try and find out," Suggs replied. "Let's get ourselves clear of this place."

They did their best to settle the nervous animals and tie on the pony drags. It would be hard going, but Tory couldn't find cause to complain. He hadn't expected to be alive after the blasting. Now he was sitting atop a horse, leading a world of wealth and power, with his best friend behind and a famous scout leading the way.

It wasn't the easiest journey Tory had ever set out upon. Pettis and the Karches had uprooted most of the cover concealing the cave from the outside world. The pony drags finished the job. No Sioux Indian would have trouble locating the cause of their morning excitement.

"What's the best way to go?" Tory asked when a perplexed Amos Suggs suddenly halted their little caravan.

"Not that way," Suggs said, pointing to a long line of bare-chested horsemen.

"Didn't take 'em long, did it?" Pat asked.

"No, and they look none too friendly," Tory noted.

"How would you feel if somebody came in and blasted your cathedral into pieces?" Suggs asked. "I told you. This place is sacred to them."

"We're not the ones that blasted it," Tory reminded the old man. "Remember?"

"I do," Suggs said, sighing. "Lost my head for a time, boys. I confess it. I tried to make it up to you. You heard the deal I struck with Pettis."

"They would never have honored it," Tory said, searching for a way around the approaching riders. "Pettis? Well, he might've agreed, but those other two were preparing to kill us the moment they set eyes on us."

"He's right," Pat added.

"I know," Suggs confessed. "It's why I set the extra charges. And it's why we've got trouble."

Suggs then turned them west, away from Custer City and safety. It was an odd direction, but then Tory guessed the old scout might have a bit of the chess player in his blood, too.

"Sometimes you have to be where they suspect you're not," Suggs explained later. "Leaving a trail like we are, it will only be a matter of time before they catch up."

Even so, they were more fortunate than some. Two miles from where a gray pallor of dust and death continued to hang over the mountainside, Suggs led the way past a raided mine camp. There were two men stripped and mutilated beside a shallow stream. A woman lay a bit farther off. Tory said a prayer for her. He was inwardly grateful not have had to look at her tortured body.

A hundred yards downstream, they splashed onward in an attempt to conceal their trail. Tory guessed at worst they wouldn't throw up dust from the travois trailing each mule. He wished they had chosen a different route. Two dead white boys lay in the shallows.

"The younger one's not much older'n my Tim," Pat said, dismounting. The older one might have been thirteen. Their upper arms and shoulders were hacked with knives.

"Likely they were swimming," Suggs said as Pat gently closed the youngsters' eyes. "Sioux came on 'em quick. They didn't even have a chance to grab their clothes."

Tory glanced at the far bank, where discarded trousers and shirts rested in branches. Except for the defensive wounds, the only marks made were killing wounds. Only a bit of each forelock had been taken as a trophy.

"Don't!" Suggs warned as Pat started to drag the corpses clear of the stream. "Move 'em and they'll know we've been this way."

"They'll know anyway," Tory argued. "You had boys. Can't you understand what Pat's feeling?"

"I know that their sufferin's over," Suggs declared. "We have to worry about ourselves just now. Get mounted, Pat. We have miles to cover before night falls."

Pat glanced up with a mixture of regret and pain. Tory knew he was feeling more than he could express.

"Lord, I hope I'll never see my boys like that," Pat said as he climbed atop his pony.

"Remember, I promised to get you home to them," Tory said, forcing a smile onto his face.

"I know, and you mean it, too," Pat replied. "The thing is, you can no more carry my burdens than you could your pa's, Tory. It's enough for a man to put one foot ahead of the other. That's what Flora always says. If I don't get back, Tim and Patrick will have a man's load to carry at a younger age than they should, but didn't we, old friend? It doesn't always make you a weakling, accepting responsibility."

"Not weak," Tory agreed. "Just sorrowful."

They did their best to put distance between themselves and the cave that afternoon. Tory judged that they passed better than five or six miles down the stream before turning back south and east. Suggs didn't know the land there so well as the territory farther north. From time to time he rode atop a ridge to look over the next valley.

"A man could settle himself in a place like this," Pat remarked as they wove their way through the rugged pine forest to yet another pass. "It's as pretty a place as I've ever seen."

"Pretty, but haunted," Tory said, feeling a chill brought on by more than the late-afternoon breeze.

"You see something?" Suggs asked, turning to glance back for a moment.

"I don't really see anything," Tory admitted. "Not with my eyes anyway. It's more of an itch, the kind of sensation you get on the eve of battle."

"I know the feelin'," Suggs agreed. "Where are they?"

"I can't say for certain," Tory said, swallowing hard. "Maybe ahead along that ridge, though."

"Good place to wait," Suggs said, nodding. "They could make a rush at us and use the settin' sun to blind us. Good plan. They must have an experienced hand with 'em."

"So what do we do?" Pat asked.

"Well, we don't ride along like before, waitin' for them to pounce," Suggs said, grinning. "No, we swing up this ridge here and get to high ground. By then it'll be too dark for them to organize to hit us. They come at us hard, by darkness, they're as apt to shoot each other as us."

"And in the morning?" Tory asked.

"Don't suppose you recall that Sioux death chant, do you?" Suggs asked. "It'd be appropriate, I'd guess."

Tory hung his head and waited for Suggs to turn the little column up the ridge. The heavily laden pony drags found the going particularly difficult, and they reached the crest only with the aid of the spare ponies. As Tory and Pat began freeing the animals of their burdens, Suggs took his rifle and headed into the woods. A few moments later a shot rang out. The scout returned, dragging along a small deer.

"I'll get a fire started," Suggs announced.

"But I thought—" Tory objected.

"They even gave the Lord himself a last supper, didn't they?" Suggs asked. "It seems to me we're entitled to equal consideration."

"Feeling Christ-like, are you?" Pat asked.

"More sinner than saint," Suggs confessed. "Just now I want meat in my belly, though. We'll let Tory bake himself some of that stick bread. Have ourselves a feast. I've got two tins of peaches hidden away, too."

"A feast," Tory declared.

"Wouldn't do not to appear fit for our final fight," the old man said, forcing a grin onto his face. "To think of it, though, I've never had close to this much gold in my entire lifetime. Now, to die when it's all so close. Lord, you've proven a trickster."

"We're not dead yet," Tory insisted.

"Look out there, boy," Suggs said, pointing to the flickering lights that marked the fires of eight different Sioux encampments. "Fool that I am, I've brought you right into the heart of the hostiles. I've gotten us all killed."

"I told you before," Tory said, freeing the first of the mules from the travois. "We're not dead yet."

"Near enough," Suggs muttered as he kindled a fire. "Near enough."

It was an oddly quiet night. The skies overhead were clear, and millions of stars sparkled overhead. The air had a sharp edge to it, and Tory was glad Suggs had allowed them to build up the fire.

"Don't know that it matters now," he grumbled. "They know where we're at."

Tory couldn't help welcoming the fire and the filling meal, even it was only to prepare them for a hard day tomorrow. He chewed the roast venison and dipped strips of biscuit twists into fat. He felt as if he'd been hungry a month, and it was difficult to describe the joy at being stuffed.

"I don't see how you manage it," Pat told him later as they spread out their hides beside the dying embers of the fire. "You seem so calm. All I can think about are my little ones, how Flora will never even know what's happened to me."

"I told you before how it is with me, the night before a battle," Tory explained. "It's all so clear. You forget everything. There's no tomorrow, no yesterday. There's just the here and now. When they come, I'll just stand there and fire my bullets until I've got no more. Then they'll kill me."

"No regrets?"

"Maybe that I won't get to meet that cousin you have planned for me," Tory said, grinning. "All my life I've been fighting alone, though. I've been a pariah, ashamed of my own father. Now, finally, I know that just once in his life I mattered more than life did. Pettis was telling the truth when he said Pa told him to go. Lucius Bratton couldn't save himself, but he tried to give the fortune to me. It's a shame really. It wasn't important."

"You wouldn't turn away from it, though."

"Pat, if I thought we could leave the gold and make our way out of here tonight afoot, I'd do it in an instant. Wouldn't work, though. We're no different than Pettis or those Karch brothers. Our own greed was the trap, and now it's about to blow up on us."

The three partners kept watch in shifts as before. Tory had the final watch. As he sat against a crooked spruce, listening as much as watching, he couldn't help noticing an eerie refrain carried by the Dakota wind.

"So, has it all come to nothing?" Tory whispered.

For a moment he saw the face of his dead brother appear on the moon overhead.

"Tor, I never could understand you," Achilles told him. "You spent your whole life hiding in shadows, but whenever you ran out ahead of the others, you won yourself glory."

Later his father's face appeared.

"Hector, how could I have known it would lead to this?" the man's sorrowful voice asked. "Forgive me?"

"I do forgive you, Pa," Tory answered. "Not so much for running away or for leaving me at Grandpa's, but for being a man. We're all of us too weak by half, I guess. Some more than others, but all are found wanting in some way, shape, or fashion.''

Two hours shy of dawn, Tory detected movement on the slope below. He hurried over to rouse his companions, and they were all alert and ready when the first arrow flew high into the sky and arched its way downward. It struck a pine branch and knocked a bit of dew onto the ground beside Pat.

"So this is how it will be," Pat grumbled as he shook off the moisture. "No head-to-head fight. They'll just shoot their arrows into us until everything atop this ridge is dead.''

"No, that won't get the job done," Suggs said, throwing a buffalo hide over his back. "A hard hide is as good as a shield. These are boys most likely or old folks. See the stone points? They won't provide the killing wound.''

"Why shoot then?" Tory asked.

"Shake our nerves," Suggs answered. "Might hit a horse or two, maybe even one of us. They'll still have to come in, though, and we'll not be easy to kill.''

"Nobody's all that easy to kill," Pat said as he loaded a spare revolver. It wasn't easily done with just one hand, and he liked to have a spare handy.

"You're still thinking of those boys," Tory said, helping his friend with the loading. "It's all chance, isn't it? Who lives. Who dies.''

"I believe in more than chance," Pat said, pulling a simple wooden cross from under his shirt and kissing it. "I have to, Tory. It's faith that keeps me sane. I know if my time's up, then Flora will have help raising our family. I know—''

"Pat, I've told you before," Tory said, flinching as a new avalanche of arrows came crashing down onto the camp. One knocked the empty coffeepot askew. Two others found one of the flour sacks full of gold and made odd clinking sounds against its side.

"You can't still believe we'll escape!" Pat exclaimed.

"I do," Tory said, firing a shot toward a creeping Sioux. The bullet passed two yards ahead of the man's forehead, and he instantly retreated.

"Almost had him," Suggs announced.

"You didn't mean to," Pat observed, giving his friend an odd gaze. "What are you thinking, eh?"

"Not much," Tory admitted. "Just that as long as no blood's shed, we can come to an agreement. Once the killing begins, there's no chance."

"There's no chance anyway," Suggs said, joining them. "Boys, listen to 'em. They figure we're the ones killed those youngsters on the creek. That's why they're out, don't you see? This is revenge, and they won't be turnin' away."

"Then it's my fault," Tory said, sighing. "I let the third one go. He's the one brought them word. It's why those miners died, too."

"That boy gave you a shirt," Suggs said, shaking his head. "Put it on, boy. Show 'em who's up here. Maybe they'll remember. Saved us once already."

Tory nodded. He crawled to his pack as another shower of arrows smothered the camp. This time Pat's horse went down, shrieking in pain. One of the mules also died. Tory got himself dressed and made a point of showing the shirt on the hillside. He barely returned to cover before a pair of rifle shots greeted his appearance.

"Almost got that shirt ventilated for you," Suggs said, laughing as Tory scrambled under his buffalo hide.

"Well, it wasn't my idea," Tory reminded the old-timer.

The Sioux kept their distance for better than an hour, but they continued to send their arrows into the camp. Another mule collapsed.

"We'll be afoot in another hour," Pat complained as he stared at the lifeless form of his horse. "I really liked that pony. She seemed to know just what to do just when I wanted it done. That's more than a little thing when you're a one-armed man.''

"Pat, we've got the extras, the three Pettis's batch brought in.''

"That paint's already down,'' Pat said, pointing to the unshod mount Pettis had ridden. "And how do we move the gold?''

"Amos?'' Tory asked, sidling over beside the older man. "We can't just sit here and wait while they kill our horses.''

"This is as good a place as any to die,'' Suggs muttered. "We'll never get all the gold out now anyway.''

"Gold?'' Tory asked. "It's me I'm worried about.''

"Then go,'' Suggs growled. "Why don't you charge through the whole Sioux nation?''

"There are worse notions,'' Pat said, joining them. "You can see 'em now, creeping between the trees, nearly all of them on the western slope. There are just the bowmen on the east slope. We couldn't move a pony drag down that side, but we might could lead some horses.''

"Pack up all that gold on a few ponies?'' Suggs asked.

"We can take what we can and leave the rest here, where it came from,'' Pat explained. "I know we'll not be buying any railroads next week, but we could get back maybe. There's no Pettis to worry us once we're clear of these people, and we aren't near as apt to stir up a fuss in Custer City, either.''

"There's merit to it,'' Tory agreed. "Amos?''

"No need to panic just yet,'' Suggs argued. "This is just their way of wearin' us down.''

"With all those camps around us?'' Tory asked. "They've already whittled down our horses, and they can't miss hitting one of us much longer. Then what? You don't mean to leave a wounded man to his fate?''

"I won't leave the gold,'' Suggs insisted.

"Can you tell us how to get clear of Sioux country and

find Custer City?'' Tory asked. ''So Pat and I can have a try at least?''

''You're that set on it?'' Suggs asked.

''I don't see another way,'' Pat said, pointing to the morning cook fires appearing in the other camps. ''In another hour we'll lose the slight chance that's left to us.''

''I'll start readyin' the animals then,'' Suggs said, suddenly rejuvenated. ''Help me, Pat. Tory, you keep an eye out for trouble, won't you?''

''Yes, sir,'' Tory agreed.

TWENTY-FOUR

It was a hard thing, packing up to leave. Tory stole a glance from time to time at his companions. It tore at their souls, leaving so much of the gold behind. There were only three saddle mounts left, though. They would be able to take only what could be packed on the remaining mule and the extra pony.

Is that how it was for you, Pa? Tory silently asked the morning mists. *Did it haunt you, leaving the fortune you'd spent your whole life looking for stashed in that cave?*

Tory didn't like to think what Amos Suggs might be thinking. When Suggs called for him to join them, he discovered part of it. Every particle of supplies, their camp gear, even the buffalo hides were tossed aside. The mules and the spare pony were packed heavily with sacks of nuggets. The tins had been buried beneath a distinctive speckled rock.

"Whoever gets clear can come back and claim the rest," Suggs explained.

"I've done my adventuring," Pat said, speaking soberly. "Tory and I'll split what's on that horse, God willing. It's more than enough to get us back on our feet."

"The rest is yours," Tory agreed. "Provided we get out alive, that is. Ready?"

"No, but one time's good as another," Suggs said, grinning. "I heard a general say once that the most surprisin' tactic a man could try was a sudden charge. Stupid thing to do, I suppose, but it will surprise anybody with the sense to see it."

"A little luck wouldn't hurt, either," Tory declared. "Who leads?"

"You do," Pat said, tying the pony's rope to his saddle horn. Suggs took charge of the mule. "Scatter those boys with the bows, and we'll have a half day's start on the others."

"We won't be able to do much, leading the pack animals," Suggs added. "You remember that medal of yours, boy. Remember how you charged those rebs. That's sure to put you in good stead for what's needed now."

Tory nodded, took a deep breath, and charged down the eastern slope. With the sun's reflection dancing off his pistol, spurs, and every other piece of metal on his person, Tory was more apparition than human as he swung wildly through the boys' camp, firing here and there, scaring more than frightening. Tory was half-blinded himself by the morning son, but he led the youngsters, some of them in their early teens, along a meandering creek while Pat and Suggs coaxed the pack animals down the ridge and on eastward. Tory wasn't trying to hit anybody. He didn't have time to take aim. Instead he distracted and diverted the young Sioux from closing the escape route.

It was only afterward, when the older boys began to shout commands, that the first arrows flew toward Tory. He ducked one and dodged a second. A third missed his horse's flank by less than two inches. As he turned and raced away from the ridge toward the safety of his companions, three young Sioux jumped out to block the trail.

Tory cocked his pistol, but he held his fire. Before him stood *Pispiza*, the young man who had been trapped beneath his pony. They recognized each other in the same instant, and the boy also held his fire. He also motioned for his companions to lower their bows.

"You didn't kill my cousins," *Pispiza* said, staring hard into Tory's eyes. "No?"

"The ones who did were in the cave," Tory explained, pointing toward the explosion and making gestures to emulate the uproar."

"They're now dead?" the boy asked.

"I believe they are," Tory said truthfully. "If not, they're trapped under a wall of rock."

"Better," *Pispiza* said, waving for Tory to continue. "You wear my shirt?"

"Thought you might remember me better in it," Tory said, smiling faintly.

"Don't come here again," the boy said in parting.

"You watch out for yourself, too," Tory replied. "Not all white men have soft hearts."

When *Pispiza* shared the words, his companions found little to laugh about. Neither did Tory. Instead he raced on to join Pat and Amos Suggs.

If fortune had smiled on them as brightly as that morning sun, the three partners would have hurried their way to Custer City with no further ado. Rarely could Tory recall a time when he had set foot on a gentle path. Instead, not a half mile after rejoining the others, he spotted dust to the east. Suggs pointed to another party closing in from the north.

"We know what's behind us," Suggs said, frowning. "How do you want to try it, boys?"

"How else?" Tory asked. "Meet 'em head-on, and God save us all."

"Amen," Pat added.

"Guess we find out if we drew the lucky straw this time," Suggs said, waving his companions along.

They weren't long in finding the Sioux, either. There were thirty of them this time, and none were small boys come along to hold ponies. Mostly they were from Tall Bull's band, and the Bull himself rode at the head of their column. They were riding hard, and Tory guessed they had a particular purpose in mind. He hoped they weren't looking for miners, but the fresh scalps hanging on one tall man's lance were red and yellow hair.

"Didn't pick those up chasin' Pawnees and Crows," Suggs pointed out.

There would be no easy escape from this band. Tory knew that. No one would stop a brother from killing him here. This time it would be fighting and dying. Only that.

Tory's instinctive move was to charge the approaching riders, to startle and confuse them. But Pat couldn't run alongside, not hauling a poor overpacked horse. As for Suggs, well, a mule just didn't always go where you wanted it to. In the end Suggs led them into a thick stand of pines, hoping to escape notice. It didn't work, though. Three voices called out together, *"Wasicum!"* Moments later the Sioux attacked.

Tory wasn't sure when the first blow landed. Three or four of the Sioux came racing toward the trees, and he went out to meet them. He fended off a lance with his pistol and shot one of the riders through the shoulder, dropping him onto the rocky ground. An arrow deflected off Tory's rifle scabbard. Then he felt the fiery touch of a flint-tipped arrow tear the flesh of his neck.

"Tory!" Pat called as a new group reached the trees. Tory tried to fight his way back to his old friend, but a pair of rifle balls tore through his pony's chest, and the animal collapsed.

Tory managed to jump clear, but he remained on the ground, temporarily stunned. He couldn't seem to make sense of what was going on all around him. When a broad-chested Sioux raced toward him, screaming and notching an arrow, Tory recovered long enough to shoot the man through the face. He rolled off his horse, landing a few feet away. Tory stumbled over, drew out his Winchester and two boxes of ammunition, and used the dead animal as cover.

It worked for a minute or two. Three arrows and a pair of rifle bulls tore the poor creature's flesh. Except for spatters of blood, though, Tory remained mostly unhurt. Then a giant of a man wearing the horns of a buffalo jumped down and approached on foot. Tory hadn't been ready for such a bold assault, and he had no weapon to parry a lance blow. The Sioux had a thick bullhide shield that he used with uncommon skill to protect his exposed side.

"Time to see whose magic is strongest, eh?" Tory asked, holstering his pistol. As the Indian prepared to thrust his lance, Tory fired his Winchester. The great shield seemed to swallow the small lead projectile, and a shout even deeper and more ferocious than before bellowed out of the angry Sioux. Tory worked the lever down and back. He then fired a second time. The shot nicked the shield and deflected upward into the Sioux's left eye.

Tory stood transfixed as the big man tottered and then fell. It was only when the shield rolled away that Tory saw a great gaping wound in his attacker's chest.

"I had to kill you twice," Tory said as he stepped past the giant and grabbed the mane of the man's war pony. The lathered horse was tired but unhurt. Once mounted, Tory tried to seek out his companions.

He spotted Suggs first. The old-timer was standing beside a dead horse, fending off two attackers. Tory shot one through the side, and Suggs then clubbed the other with his rifle.

"Come on, Amos!" Tory called, reaching out his arm. "Climb behind me."

"Got to catch the mule," Suggs said, hopping off to where the frantic animal sought an avenue of escape.

"Tory!" Pat shouted.

"Go on, boy!" Suggs yelled. "I aim to be rich or dead!"

Tory caught a final glance at the old scout as a circle of riders closed in on him. One moment Suggs was fuming and cussing ill fortune. The next he vanished in a surge of demon lances.

Tory got to Pat's side at the critical moment. Pat's left leg was trapped by his dead pony, and he was defenseless. Two onrushing riders fired arrows, but both missed the mark. Tory's sudden arrival scattered them both.

"Can you get loose?" Tory asked.

"Bet your life on it," Pat said, freeing himself.

"More likely we're betting yours," Tory said, lifting his old friend up behind him.

"What's happened to Suggs?" Pat asked. "The mule? I saw my packhorse fall fifty yards back."

"Suggs's finished," Tory explained. "We are, too, if we hang around here."

"Tory, the gold!"

"What do you have in mind, leaving one of us?" Tory asked. "We're riding double as it is!"

Pat glanced back as if to discover some solution, but there was none. Tory turned that way and saw it, too. Another fifty Sioux were riding down on them. They might be a quarter mile away now, but they wouldn't be if Tory turned his horse toward the gold packs.

"Tory, there's thousands, maybe millions of dollars back there," Pat argued.

"Won't a one of them listen to your children's prayers," Tory replied as he nudged the weary worse eastward. "What was it Suggs said? Be rich or die?"

"Not much as far as choices are concerned, I guess," Pat admitted. "Get us out of here, Hector Bratton. It'll have to be somebody else's fate to find that gold."

Tory urged the Indian pony onward, but it made only

slow progress. Then Tory spied a spotted pony grazing beside a dying warrior.

"Take this one," he said, leaping onto the ground. He made a slow approach toward the skittish animal, whispered a soft song, and climbed atop. The two friends then rode on eastward, leaving the Sioux to celebrate their solitary victory.

They made more than ten more miles before nightfall. From the top of a low ridge they could see the distant lights of a mining camp. The wind carried the notes of a player piano, and Tory couldn't help gazing back at what might have been his own fortune.

"Ever thought about it, Tory?" Pat whispered from his place on the bare ground across the way.

"About what?" Tory asked.

"Gold. Death. I wonder how many men have died because of those shiny yellow rocks?"

"More than a few," Tory supposed. "Victoria's pa once told me whole nations were sold into slavery over gold. Wars were fought because of it."

"Makes no sense," Pat declared. "What's it all matter anyway? A thousand deaths? A million?"

"Too many died just today," Tory said, sinking his hands into his face. "Amos Suggs. I killed two or three myself. I don't want to think how many widows and orphans I caused. We came near enough to dying ourselves."

"I was as good as dead myself, Tory," Pat said, creeping closer so that he could study his friend's tired eyes. "I would've gone back for the gold. You know that, don't you?"

"Oh, it was just a thought, Pat."

"But you had it, too, didn't you? Fame and fortune! Riches!"

"No," Tory said, shaking his head. "I'm not my pa, Pat. I'm not even sure why I came along. Sure wasn't because of any dream of being rich."

"You promised you would get me back safe."

"We're close, Pat," Tory said, signing. "Close."

Distances were deceptive in the mountains, though. What appeared so close was still a hard day's ride east of them. Weary and hungry and near played out, the two old friends fell asleep in the rocks.

Tory awoke to the crackling of a morning cook fire. He managed to pry open an eye and was preparing to scold Pat about building a fire when he caught sight of his friend's frightened eyes.

"Pat?" Tory asked.

"We've got company," Pat answered, motioning toward three young Sioux. They had already collected the fire-arms, but they seemed in no great rush to complete the killing. Perhaps they had some torture in store for the young white men.

"Do you speak English?" Tory asked. "Understand?"

"Speak enough," the tallest of the three said. "Sit. Soon you eat."

"Eat?" Pat asked.

The Sioux chuckled among themselves, and Tory felt an icy-cold sensation creeping up his spine. Not far from where the horses lay grazing rested a long lance. A freshly cut scalp lay hanging in a nearby tree. The gray flakes matched Amos Sugg's hair exactly.

"We're next," Tory whispered.

"No," a new voice told them from behind. They turned and saw the same teenager Tory had freed from the dead horse. How many times could one boy rescue a fool of a man?

"*Pispiza?*" Tory asked.

"You remember," the boy said, grinning.

"I didn't fire over somebody's head this time," Tory said, staring hard into the boy's eyes. "I killed one, maybe more, of your people."

"I, too, have killed," the youngster explained. "When

my people fought Yellow Hair and before. It's how it is
with us, our peoples.''

"Then I don't understand why you won't kill us," Tory
said, gazing at the others beside the fire. "If you release
us, they'll think you're—"

"White?" *Pispiza* asked. "No one will ever mistake
who I am. My father walks with the peace chiefs, but I
have gone with my cousins to fight. I understand there can
be no peace between our peoples.''

"But you saved us?"

"One man can always save another," he added. "A
white man taught me that.''

Tory nodded, although it was difficult to imagine that
slight-shouldered sort of a Sioux boy passing as a man.

"I thank you for the life you're giving me," Tory said.
"And for my friend. More for him than for me, if the truth
be known.''

"I saw how you went back for him," *Pispiza* explained.
"Now, I must explain what you must promise. You will
come no more into *Paha Sapa* to dig the yellow metal
from our heart. And you will not return with horses or
weapons.''

"Agreed," Tory replied.

"I would spare a horse, but I have already given my
own to pay for your lives. It's all I could do.''

"It's enough," Tory said. "Maybe one day you and Pat
here's boys can put this war behind you and become
friends.''

"No, the fighting is only beginning for me," the boy
explained. "For them, too. There's only dying waiting for
us.''

"It's not much of a way to end a life," Tory argued.

"You're not *Sicangu Lakota*," *Pispiza* said, nodding
somberly. "My father sent me to learn from your people.
I know your words. I also know your hearts. No *Lakota*
can walk your world. You should eat and drink. Then you
must go.''

The Sioux boys brought them fried brook trout and bread fried from their own flour. Then *Pispiza* pointed toward the nearest mining camps. The two old friends then began the longest walk of their life.

"Ease up," Tory said as they cleared rifle range of their own camp. "They won't follow us anymore, Pat,"

"How do you know?" Pat asked. "Because that boy speaks English?"

"I don't know for sure, I guess. Certainly not because he speaks English. Plenty of men speak that same English who kill and murder anybody in their way."

"Got that point to make, I agree," Pat said, easing his pace. "You figure that boy will see us safely through because he's got a debt to pay. Because of what happened at the creek when Pettis and the Karches shot those other two."

"Yeah, I do, Pat."

"You know, I guess in a way it's what your pa was trying to do, too. Give you something he took away."

"I hadn't thought that way about it, Pat, but in a way, maybe he did just that."

"How so?"

"Old Suggs told me there'd come a day when he met his wife and kids again. All the world's a circle, he told me. When we lose our way, we just have to travel a little longer before we find it again."

"Hope old Suggs found some peace in the end."

"I hope we all do, Pat," Tory said.

They walked more than fifteen miles before stumbling into the outlying tents of what called itself Russian Camp. It was only then that Pat produced a pair of tins full of gold nuggets. It was a considerable mystery to the miners how two young men, one with a single arm, could walk out of Sioux country with as close to twists of pure gold as anybody had seen.

The two strangers never so much as whispered their

names, though, and neither was seen there again. After a while it was just another ghost story told in the shadow of a canvas and poles that had once been a mining camp.

EPILOGUE

That winter Patrick Harper's cousin Sarah Kilkenny arrived in New York. Within the month she was stepping off a westbound train at St. Louis. Pat and Flora invited her to accompany them to dinner with a distinguished young merchant and gunsmith. Following a generous dinner of steak and potatoes, they strolled down the street to have a drink at the Riverfront Saloon.

It was a wild, smoke-filled den of iniquity and perfectly to the liking of a youngish Irish girl too long confined to a third-class berth aboard ship and passenger car. They were listening to a lovely soprano filling the room with bittersweet ballads from Cork when a waiter refreshed the drinks.

"You must be rich to afford such a feast," Sarah exclaimed when she caught sight of the bill.

"Hector's founder of the feast," Pat explained.

"Mr. Bratton, well, I can only thank you for it."

"It's only right you be welcomed properly to St. Louis," Tory replied. "Can't have you thinking we're the wilderness here."

"Oh, you're all too grand by half again," Sarah told them. "And rich to boot!"

"Oh, he's not rich," Pat said, laughing. "Not anymore."

"Did you lose your money then, sir?" Sarah asked.

"In a way," Tory confessed.

"Don't let him squirm off the hook, cousin," Pat urged. "Get him to tell the rest, how he had a million dollars on the back of a mule. All he had to do was get it safely to Custer City."

"Well, you were along, weren't you?" Flora asked. "Don't make it appear as if Tory gave the whole lot away like feed for chickens."

"What *did* happen, Mr. Bratton?" Sarah asked.

"The strangest thing," Tory told her. "I found my way."

"Found your way?" the young woman asked. "However do you mean?"

"I found what was important," Tory told them. "Raise your glasses with mine. To life. To friends. To family."

"Here," Pat added, touching his friend's glass. The women added there own as well, and the party continued. It was only when the singing stopped that Flora announced it was time to close the evening.

"She's here to learn from Flora," Pat explained as they waited for the women to collect their shawls. "A week with my brood, and she'll be eager to start her own."

"Pat—"

"You can't hide in St. Louis any easier than in those hills," Pat argued. "Now you've found yourself, it's time you shared with someone else."

"Could be," Tory admitted.

"Ever consider going back, digging up Suggs's treasure?"

"That's an adventure for boys, Pat. Maybe Tim and Patrick. By then maybe even Deadwood will calm down some."

"Wouldn't do, sending the boys on a errand, Tory. An adventure needs a trace of danger."

"Maybe it does," Tory said, scratching his chin. "But I don't think we could have dealt with any more excitement ourselves."

"No, we had all we needed."

The women returned then, and Tory escorted the Harpers and their cousin down the street to their new three-story home on Brook Street. Sarah gave a good-night wave, and Tory bowed.

"You won't let this one get away now, will you?" Flora asked. "Pat's running out of cousins."

"I'll keep it in mind," he said, grinning.

PENGUIN PUTNAM

online

Your Internet gateway to a virtual
environment with hundreds of entertaining
and enlightening books from
Penguin Putnam Inc.

While you're there, get the latest buzz on
the best authors and books around—
Tom Clancy, Patricia Cornwell, W.E.B. Griffin,
Nora Roberts, William Gibson, Robin Cook,
Brian Jacques, Catherine Coulter,
Stephen King, Jacquelyn Mitchard,
and many more!

Penguin Putnam Online is located at
http://www.penguinputnam.com

PENGUIN PUTNAM NEWS

Every month you'll get an inside look at our
upcoming books and new features on our site.
This is an ongoing effort to provide you
with the most interesting and up-to-date
information about our books and authors.

Subscribe to Penguin Putnam News at
http://www.penguinputnam.com/ClubPPI